Readers love The Wheel Mysteries
by SUSAN LAINE

Sparks & Drops

"I can't wait to see what happens next to Gus and Niall. I absolutely recommend this to romance and mystery lovers alike."
—Scattered Thoughts and Rogue Words

"All in all, *Sparks & Drops* is both a good mystery and a sweet romance, two of my favorite genres rolled into one."
—Gay Book Reviews

Devil's Own

"She… wonderfully depicts the growing love between her two main characters and prompts the reader once again to fall for Gus and Niall and their witty and endearing relationship."
—Joyfully Jay

Fireworks & Wild Cards

"As with the other books in the series, this is a fascinating fast-paced murder mystery with lots of characters and subplots to follow all at once."
—Rainbow Book Reviews

By SUSAN LAINE

Falling for Rain
Flushed
Haunted Heart
Sage Advice
Sauna Lover
The Sensualist & the Untouched
Two Tickets to Paradise (Dreamspinner Anthology)
The Witching Hour

HEROES AT HEART
Yellowbelly Hero
Yellow Streak
Code Yellow
Good as Gold

ISLESHIRE CHRONICLES
Lofty Dreams of Earthbound Men
Wishing Wings

LIFTING THE VEIL
The Wolfing Way
Genie's Wish
Hunter's Moon
Monsters Under the Bed
Love of the Wild
Stealing Dragon's Heart

SECOND CHANCES
Accidental Chemistry
Twice by Chance

Published by DREAMSPINNER PRESS
www.dreamspinnerpress.com

By SUSAN LAINE (CONT.)

SENSES AND SENSATIONS
Love in Plain Sight
A Luminous Touch
Sensible Commitments
Sounds of Love
The Sweetest Scent

THE WHEEL MYSTERIES
Sparks & Drops
Devil's Own
Fireworks & Wild Cards
The Disciple
The Wheel Mysteries: Books 1 & 2 (Author Anthology)

Published by DREAMSPINNER PRESS
www.dreamspinnerpress.com

SUSAN LAINE
THE DISCIPLE

DREAMSPINNER
PRESS

Published by
DREAMSPINNER PRESS

5032 Capital Circle SW, Suite 2, PMB# 279, Tallahassee, FL 32305-7886 USA
www.dreamspinnerpress.com

The Disciple
© 2016 Susan Laine.

Cover Art
© 2016 Brooke Albrecht.
http://brookealbrechtstudio.com
Cover content is for illustrative purposes only and any person depicted on the cover is a model.

ISBN: 978-1-63477-661-5
Digital ISBN: 978-1-63477-662-2
Library of Congress Control Number: 2016909825
Published October 2016
v. 1.0

Printed in the United States of America
∞
This paper meets the requirements of
ANSI/NISO Z39.48-1992 (Permanence of Paper).

Chapter 1

WHAT THE heck is that guy doing?

Gus Goodwin, the owner of The Four Corners neo-pagan shop, watched the stranger out of the corner of his eye. He'd never seen the young man before. Most of those who frequented his shop were regulars, and he knew their names, faces, and faiths like the back of his hand.

But this person? Nothing rang a bell. Gus had never seen him before.

His recognition skills might have failed him. But his involvement in three murder cases in the past year had given Gus a nose for trouble. And this guest at his shop raised all kinds of alarms.

For one thing, the man wandering about stopped every few steps, hid behind an item, and gave Gus furtive glances, as if checking him out or assessing him. And Gus knew better than to expect the behavior to hint at mere shy flirtation.

No. This was déjà vu all over again.

In the spring, this was how he'd met Niall Valentine, the private investigator who was now Gus's fiancé. They hadn't set a date yet, but they were living together, had been for a month. Despite Niall's unfortunate habit of watching sports when Gus's documentaries were on and the frequent fights and scuffles for domination of the remote control that got ugly at times, they were doing okay.

Right from the start, from the first glance, first words, and first smile, the attraction and chemistry had been there. Love had followed swiftly on their heels.

Gus couldn't say what quality or aspect he'd initially been charmed by, as Niall's style was unkempt and shaggy despite his tight, lean muscles, short black hair, and steely blue eyes. His perpetual stubble, raggedy jeans, button-down with a dark tie, and leather jacket would have given a fashionista a heart attack. Then again, Gus was no better, since he wouldn't be caught dead in a suit and tie—or any type of formal wear. So although Gus and Niall were dissimilar in most respects, they matched in intelligence, attitude, and personality. They were like birds of a feather.

This guy perusing his store without actually looking long at anything except for Gus, however, was nothing like Niall, who had a way of fitting in wherever he went and with whomever he met. Gus decided to test the waters.

"Can I help you, sir?" he asked politely, raising his voice to be heard over the whirring din of the ceiling fan and the low ambient music playing in the background, a soft acoustic guitar mixed with a flute.

The guy started, swallowing and visibly paling like a kid caught doing something he ought not to be doing. "Uh, n-no, thanks. I-I'm just, uh, looking around, if that's okay?"

Gus smiled, hoping to relax his jumpy would-be client. "Yes, of course. If you need any assistance, don't hesitate to ask. There's a lot of stuff here, so I can give you any details on the treasures you find."

Blinking and biting into his lower lip, the guy nodded, looking a bit frantic, and returned to the shelves. Gus couldn't figure him out. Typically his customers wore talismans, symbols, clothes, or tattoos that helped Gus identify what faith they followed, enabling him to offer them the appropriate help.

This guy was a mystery. But he did have the cutest little lisp when he spoke.

A beep sounded on his cell phone on the counter, indicating he'd gotten a text. So Gus ignored the secretive stranger and read the message. It was from Niall. *Indian takeout tonight?*

Gus smiled as he typed in a response. *No. Made dinner for us. ETA?* Spicy food was one thing they had in common. Unfortunately the café around the corner, Bailey's, which they often frequented around lunchtime, didn't serve any spicy food. But it didn't matter since Gus had a dish prepared for tonight.

1 hour. C U. If there was one thing to be said for Niall, it was his uncanny ability to be succinct and direct. Gus was pleased Niall was on his way because that meant he would spend the night. For the last two nights, Niall had been on a stakeout and thus unable to sleep in his own bed with Gus in their apartment above Gus's shop in Tacoma.

"Excuse me?" A timid voice startled Gus. It was the stranger, standing at the counter, a small necklace in his hand. He was kind of little—in height, weight, and voice—with auburn hair, hazel eyes, and tanned skin. Oddly, he seemed scared out of his mind. Gus stiffened, prepared for anything. "I-I w-would like this, please." It sounded like a question, though it probably wasn't.

Gus smiled enthusiastically. "Cool." He noted the price tag of the steel-and-silver necklace, which featured an X with a circle between the two upper rungs. The symbol represented a deadly bane. "That'll be $12.99. Cash or credit? And do you want a bag with that?"

The guy shook his head so hard it was a miracle it didn't fall clean off. He retrieved his wallet, fumbled through it, and held out a credit card. Before Gus could take it, the man pulled it back, his cheeks flaming.

"S-sorry. I-I'll pay with cash." He dug around in his pockets until he produced a couple of bills and some loose change. "Th-thank you." He snatched the necklace and ran out the door before Gus could give him his receipt or a bag.

Gus rolled his eyes. "That wasn't weird at all, no sirree." Then he shook his head once and went back to work.

"HEY, BABE." Niall came in through the side door so he wouldn't have to go through the shop, which was already closed. The climb up the stairs annoyed him after a hard day. But he wasn't about to complain to his boyfriend, who greeted him with a hearty kiss. Plus, it was the second floor, not the twentieth.

Gus giggled into the kiss, making it impossible for Niall to get past his lips. "We're not doing it in the vestibule. Besides, dinner's ready. So hustle." He pushed Niall off but slapped his butt, dancing away with fairy-like adroitness, laughing as he went.

Niall growled. Then his stomach grumbled. Hunger won over indignation.

"What's for dinner?" Niall asked as he stomped into the kitchen—after ditching his coat and shoes—and plopped onto a seat, rubbing a tired hand across his face. "Man, it's been one of those days." Then he shoved a small package onto the table, next to his plate. "This was in your mailbox. It's for you."

Gus laid a steaming hot casserole pan on the table. Niall's nostrils flared as he inhaled the delicious odors. "Yes, my hungry Tigger," Gus said. "It's beef and cheese lasagna. Your Italian favorite."

Niall murmured his appreciation, but riveted his gaze on the hot food instead of his hotter boyfriend. "Ah, you're the best, baby. Gimme."

Gus chuckled as he scooped a huge portion onto Niall's plate. "Eat up, my starving hero. It's all for you." When Niall cocked a questioning eyebrow, Gus smiled. "I cooked a portion of veggie lasagna for myself." Indeed, next to his plate rested a small earthenware bowl with lasagna. If it hadn't been for the green things sticking out, the meal would have appeared pretty identical with Niall's.

"Great." Niall dug into his scrumptious casserole, savoring each salty, creamy, meaty bite. Secretly he admitted to himself, with a modest amount of shame, that he loved the fact that he had an awesome cook for a boyfriend. The spectacular sex wasn't a negative either.

"How'd the stakeout go today?" Gus asked, then took a mouthful of his casserole.

"Caught the cheating bastard in the arms of a drunken stripper in the back of a crappy Ford Pinto," Niall answered between bites. "The dick tried to bribe me first, and with a lousy fifty bucks no less. When that didn't work, he tried to slug me. I used restraint, babe, believe me. I didn't break his jaw like I envisioned. Yeah, he's got a black eye and perhaps a loose tooth or two. But he's also in lockup now, so I don't gotta care. Since the cops also arrested the stripper, he's got no leg to stand on with his wife. Gave her a copy of the arrest record and the pictures I took and got paid a bit extra. Case closed, with pockets full of cash."

Gus chuckled. "You beast." He winked at Niall, who grinned back. After chewing awhile in silence, Gus went on, "Something odd happened to me today. This strange guy came to the shop, wandered about aimlessly, and kept staring at me less than surreptitiously. It was so weird. And the thing is, I don't think he was interested in me."

"Huh." Niall pondered that carefully while sinking his teeth into a chunky piece of meat. He chewed and swallowed before asking, "You get the stalker vibe from him? Was he intimidating or threatening?"

Gus frowned, shaking his head. "No. To be honest, he looked scared out of his mind." He cocked his head, and his curly blond bangs fell over his tropical-green eyes. Niall recognized the look as Gus being pensive. "You know, I just remembered one thing. He bought this little necklace and offered me a credit card—but then yanked it back like his hand was on fire. I don't think he wanted me to see his name."

Now Niall had cause for concern. He had honed his intuition in the military, and right now his instincts screamed at him. "But you didn't recognize him? Never seen him before?"

"No. Never. I know all my regulars by name, and Tacoma isn't exactly a tourist hot spot." Gus munched on a mouthful, appearing contemplative again, his gaze wandering around the room. "But I'm certain he knew who I was. Everything in his behavior suggested it."

Niall frowned, worried. Gus had been plagued before by all kinds of crazies, from the murdering kind to the right-wing religious sort occasionally protesting in front of his shop. But most of those incidents had taken place before Niall had come into the picture. Since then it had been quiet. Did Gus have a stalker now? That didn't bode well. For the prowler, to be exact. That much Niall could swear.

"Maybe it's high time for you invest in some security systems," Niall offered.

Though he'd made the same suggestion many times, Gus shot him down each time. For him the world was a bright place, where people smiled at strangers and it rained pure sunshine.

Niall was far less optimistic. In his world murderers, rapists, pedophiles, and madmen wandered the streets, ready to devour innocents for fun without a shred of remorse. And in his stark universe, the rain was mostly acid.

Gus sighed deeply, rolling his eyes. "I have an alarm on the front door and a security camera—"

"That camera hasn't worked reliably in all the time I've known you," Niall cut in with a brutally honest reminder. "It's in color, sure, but it keeps shorting out every few days."

"Okay, I admit that much. I'll get it fixed." In Gus-speak that meant a time so far into the future it needed an infinity symbol to describe it. Niall was onto him by now, and he let his true opinion show with a stark glare. Gus avoided eye contact and cleared his throat. Then, with another sigh, he relented. "Okay, fine. I'll see a man about a horse this week."

Niall scoffed. "It's Friday tomorrow. Making an appointment for a house call is gonna take too fucking long. No. I'll arrange for it. If we have to wait for you to do it, we'll be sitting, old and gray, in rocking chairs on the front porch."

Gus laughed. "We don't have a front porch. Just a backyard." Despite the scolding, he beamed, his smile wide and true. "Nonetheless, I like how you see us growing old together."

Niall didn't answer immediately. He watched Gus blush and duck his head. Honestly, Niall had stopped thinking about the expiration date on their relationship ages ago. The words had come out so easily because his heart knew what and who it wanted. Niall had loved Gus probably since the day they met, since the moment he'd laid his eyes on the beautiful green-eyed blond who lived his life like a California surfer: carefree and laid-back.

Falling in love didn't feel half as frightening as Niall had expected it would since coming home from his last tour overseas the year before. Loving Gus was easy. Even if the man needed a swift kick in the backside at times.

But sometimes Gus could be *too* carefree and reckless. Niall swore to himself to watch out for Gus and keep an eye on this mysterious stranger who reeked of fear and trouble.

To deflect the current topic, Niall nodded toward the postal package. "You forgot to open your parcel." He took another bite as Gus pulled the packet closer. "Who's it from? Were you expecting something? I thought your shop stuff comes to your downstairs mailbox."

"Typically it does." Gus shrugged, so Niall wasn't overly concerned. Gus frowned, his head cocked. "Weird. There's just my home address. No postage. Huh. Must've been hand-delivered. Hmm…. Maybe it's from a friend."

A curious smile on his lips, Gus ripped open the brown packing tape and parted the top flaps. A shocked gasp preceded his bolting up and staggering backward, horror in his expression. His chair clattered to the floor, falling hard.

"What?" Niall jumped up too, in full alert mode.

Gus pointed at the package with a shaky hand. His mouth moved, but no sounds came out. Niall rounded the table and peeked into the box, where brown packing paper enveloped a small dark wooden strongbox with a glass lid.

Inside the miniature chest, on a bed of black faux velvet, rested a silver necklace—covered in blood.

Chapter 2

"WHAT THE hell is it with you two? Were you both cursed at birth, or were you just born under unlucky stars?"

Virgil Hughes was a homicide detective with the Seattle Police Department, in his late forties and wishing for early retirement. He was a curmudgeon. Cynical and curt were also good words to describe the man, who was bald as a cue ball, pudgy around the midsection, and had remarkably bushy eyebrows. He'd quit smoking at the behest of his wife, but during troubled times he often slipped, as evidenced by the chewed cigar currently between his lips.

Niall had known Hughes since childhood, as the cop had been Niall's father Owain's partner on the force. He trusted Hughes with his life and considered him a friend. Because of that Niall felt confident making light jest at Hughes's expense.

"Wow, I didn't know you believed in astrology."

Hughes gave Niall the stink eye over the dining table at Gus and Niall's place. "Watch it, boy. I can still whip your backside raw." Niall chuckled but said nothing, so Hughes continued, "That was how you found the package? You didn't touch anything, I trust?"

Pale and wan, Gus shook his head briskly and hugged himself. Niall held his waist and pulled him closer for comfort. "Gus opened the flaps, but neither of us touched anything else." Niall suspected it would be unlikely for any prints to be found, but he could always hope.

Hughes grunted, clearly displeased. "You two aren't short on enemies."

"Most of the bad guys we've faced are dead," Niall reminded him. "The Domville brothers, Florian Talbot, John Abrams. All dead. One murdered, two shot by cops, and one killed by lethal injection. So yeah, all dead."

Hughes sighed. "Not everyone." His gaze shifted between Niall and Gus, and his look warned Niall to expect the worst. "The reason I got here to Tacoma so quick after you called was that I was already in the neighborhood. I was coming to tell you that… that Gil van Es escaped from prison. He hypnotized a guard into giving him his clothes, gun, and ID. Basically van Es just walked right out through the front door. We've got a BOLO out on him, but… basically, he's in the wind."

Niall was right. Worst news possible.

"GREAT," NIALL muttered under his breath.

Gus shivered and leaned into Niall, who immediately straightened up and tightened his hold on Gus. "Thanks," Gus whispered, and Niall offered him a strained smile, probably meant to encourage and reassure. In Gus's current state of mind, both intentions fell short. "Hughes? Do you think van Es might come after me and Niall?"

"I won't let him touch a hair on your head," Niall said in a low, dangerous voice that shouldn't have turned Gus on, but did. Niall tousled Gus's blond curls, and much to Gus's surprise, the intimate gesture strengthened Gus's faith in Niall to thwart any threats.

Still, the masculine side of his psyche bristled. "That's nice of you, my brave knight. But I don't think it's my hair he's gonna want to slice and dice."

Hughes harrumphed before Niall could comment. "I'm gonna post a squad car—"

"No," Gus protested. "Pagans have been persecuted enough throughout history. If and when they see a cop car standing watch, that's gonna make a lot of people curious and nervous. It's bad for my business."

"Gus, be reasonable," Niall interjected, frowning and looking vexed. "You just said you're worried van Es might try to kill one or both of us. We need protection."

Peeved, Gus narrowed his eyes. "You mean *I* need protection."

Niall's eyes narrowed as well, and on him the look appeared a thousand times scarier than on Gus. "I would never call you a dude in distress. But van Es has killed before, and I have no doubt he'll kill again if he so wishes. And we're probably at the top of his hit list."

Gus shook his head, ready to argue. But he'd known Niall for many months now and was well aware getting Niall to back down on protecting those he cared about was tantamount to hitting your head on a boulder. Nothing good would come of it.

Besides, there were more important things to consider. "We can discuss that later." He shifted attention to the parcel with the necklace, both now in the hands of police forensics teams at the police station. "I'm pretty sure that necklace is the same I sold to a customer earlier today. I already told you that. What's been done to find him? For all we know, that could be his blood."

"You gave us the surveillance tapes from the shop and the money he touched," Hughes replied, surly as usual. "We're gonna try to identify him. But if he's got no criminal record and no file in any of the criminal databases, tracking him down is gonna be like trying to find a needle in a haystack."

Gus nodded, understanding the limitations of the police department. "I'm gonna ask around if anyone recognizes him. Neo-pagan customs and faiths are varied, but our circles are still relatively small. Chances are someone knows who he is."

"Unless he bought that necklace on a whim or as an excuse to spy on you," Niall said in his stark style.

Gus snorted. "Well, that's too pessimistic for me. I'm not ready to admit defeat."

Niall smiled, one corner of his lips lifting in dry humor. "Neither am I, babe. But I'm not gonna hold my breath until we find him either. That's just common sense."

Gus pursed his lips in dismay. "Why does your common sense have to be so cynical?"

"I'm being realistic." Niall turned his attention to Hughes. "There may or may not have been a crime involving the owner of that necklace, but it's definitely a threat of some kind."

Hughes nodded gravely. "Agreed. What's on your mind, Junior?"

Gus watched with mild amusement as Niall's face darkened. He hated that nickname, which was why Hughes used it so often.

Niall scoffed and said, "I've got a few favors owed to me. I'll let you know once I'm sure what to do. In the meantime, I hope you can find the owner of that necklace—alive and well."

"Yeah, me too. Call me if anything else comes up, and stay safe. I'll keep you in the loop on whatever the lab guys find." Hughes nodded his good-byes and left.

Gus hated that their lives had been intruded upon again by an ominous warning of blood and death. Last time around he had lost friends. And now a murderous fiend had escaped and was skulking around in the shadows, ready to destroy at will.

"Van Es would be an idiot to strike against us," Niall said quietly, his low voice that of a consummate professional, unwavering. Gus appreciated that his man was like a steady rock who would keep them both out of harm's way. "If he's smart—and I think he is—he's out of the country by now. Besides, it wasn't us who brought him down, remember? His own group, the Cabal, sent him to us, gift-wrapped I might add. If there's anyone he's got a beef with, it's them, not us."

Gus considered Niall's words carefully. It was a rational conclusion. If van Es sought vengeance, his best bet for getting it came from the direction of the Cabal, not Gus and Niall. A reassuring thought, Gus decided, and slight relief washed over him, smoothing the rough edges of his fears and doubts.

"You're right," Gus admitted, only a bit grudgingly. "Van Es would be a fool to attack us, for several reasons." He searched Niall's blue-gray eyes for comfort and answers. "So… now what?"

"We go on with our lives." Niall pulled Gus into his arms and kissed him softly. He even did that sweet swaying thing that soothed Gus's nerves perfectly. "We'll wait and see. I for one believe that bloody necklace doesn't mean someone's dead but that someone's trying to frighten us, or you specifically. Little do they know threats don't work on either of us."

Gus hugged Niall, saying nothing. They had encountered dangers before. It was hard for Gus to admit, even to himself, that he worried now because he had so much to lose. At long last Gus had found a great guy, true love, like-minded friends, a thriving business, and a community of acceptance and caring. Yes, there was a lot to lose.

NEXT MORNING Gus slept in. His night had been fraught with problems, his sleep fitful, full of nightmares and interruptions that startled him awake, sweaty and trembling. As a result he was grouchy and exhausted by the time he finally managed to pull himself out of bed and into the bathroom. In truth, the motivation to rise hadn't come from any inner strength of character, but from a need to piss.

Yawning and scratching his bare belly, Gus stumbled barefoot into the kitchen, wearing only his worn-thin pajama bottoms. He needed coffee, and he needed it now. If he could shoot a dose directly in his veins, he would have.

In his groggy state, Gus almost walked into the ladder in front of him. Blinking and staggering backward, Gus took in the metal ladder first— and then the man standing on it. Or, to be precise, Gus saw tight jeans showcasing a perfect plump ass and a T-shirt that had ridden up to reveal the delectable indentation at the small of a rather muscular back.

"Huh?" Gus wasn't used to seeing strange hot guys in his apartment at first light. At least not since he'd started seeing Niall. Not that Niall wasn't hot. Which he totally was.

"Oh. Hey, babe. Didn't see you there." Niall stood by the coffee machine, sipping from a cup. Already dressed in jeans and a sleeveless undershirt, he placed the cup down on the counter and walked up to Gus, grinning. "Good morning." He kissed Gus on the lips.

Gus didn't respond. His brain was too muddled before an injection of coffee. But he did point at the other man, still standing on the ladder. "Who. Is. That?"

Niall frowned as though he had no idea what Gus was talking about. Then he glanced over his shoulder, seemed to remember they had a guest, and smiled. "Oh, right. Gus, meet Logan Matthews. Logan, this is Gus Goodwin, my guy. Logan's an old Army buddy of mine."

Logan jumped down from the ladder. Only then did Gus fully realize how imposing the man was. He had to be at least six five and obviously athletic with big, bulging muscles. Add to that the fact that he was gorgeous and Gus wasn't sure if he liked the guy. Logan had short blond hair, a trimmed blond beard, tanned and hairy skin, a slightly crooked nose, full lips, and hazel eyes. Yes, he was all man—and Gus felt an irrational surge of jealousy.

"Hi, Gus. Nice to meet you." Logan extended a hand to Gus.

Gus accepted the welcoming gesture on autopilot. "Hey." He spoke to Niall out of the corner of his mouth. "Coffee. Then explain."

Niall chuckled, fetched a cup of steaming coffee, and gave it to Gus, who inhaled half the liquid contents in a few seconds. His confused expression must have smoothed as the coffee relaxed him because Niall asked, "Better?"

"Uh-huh." Gus even managed to offer a flicker of a smile. Then his gaze moved from Niall to Logan and back again. His raised eyebrows formed their own question.

"Well, you said yesterday you didn't want police protection," Niall explained, using his professional voice, the somewhat know-it-all tone mildly aggravating Gus. "Logan here was in town, so I asked him to recommend me some state-of-the-art home surveillance systems. He came in to install them out of the goodness of his heart."

Gus heard the edge in Niall's tone, the warning that said Logan was a good guy whose presence was an act of kindness, so Gus shouldn't do or say anything that would drive the nice man away. In truth, Gus felt a bit insulted by Niall's assumption that Gus would behave like an asshole to a total stranger, let alone to one of Niall's friends.

But Gus kept his mouth shut on those issues, which he would deal with later once he and his boyfriend were alone.

"That's awfully kind of you, Mr. Matthews," Gus said and meant every word. These days everyone seemed to have an angle, and it was great to meet someone who wasn't so selfish or shallow.

"Please, call me Logan." The blond giant smiled, flashing perfect pearly whites. Gus had no doubt the man got all the action he could ever want, and more.

Gus smiled back politely, despite his sleep-fuddled brain still trying hard to catch up. "Logan." Then he gave Niall a warning glare. "Exactly what kind of private security systems are being installed in my home?"

Niall at least had the good grace to blush slightly, and he rubbed the back of his neck. "Nothing too invasive, babe, I promise. Just a few precautions, that's all. The kitchen hallway leads to the front door by the side of the building, so there's gonna be a camera inside and outside so we can monitor anyone coming in or going out."

Logan nodded, seemingly in agreement with Niall's statement. "I've added some of the current basic home security systems," he explained in a low, sexy voice that reverberated inside Gus's rib cage. God, to hear that man in bed? Gus shivered in spite of himself. After all, he wasn't dead below the waist.

"There are motion sensors wired into the window frames," Logan went on, "and the front and back doors, both in the apartment and the shop below."

"My shop?" Gus heard the rising pitch in his own voice and decided to take things down a notch. "So… simple environmental sensors that trigger if an intruder tries to break in."

Logan smiled. "That's one of their functions, yeah. They can also monitor other factors, like a rise in temperature in case of a fire or flooding on the floors in case there's a leak."

Gus was surprised to hear that. "Wow. I didn't know these sensors could do all that."

Logan chuckled, an amiable sound Gus liked. "Multifunctionality is a key concept in today's security systems."

"You're an expert?" Gus asked, curious to learn of the man's background.

"I'm in private security at the moment. Military background helps." He pointed at the camera he'd just installed into a shadowy corner of the hallway. "All the systems are integrated into one so they're easier to control and keep track of with a single device. They can be hooked into a cell phone or a tablet, or you can have a special remote controller. You can access the system remotely, and even lock the doors and windows from a distance. You can also switch the lights inside and outside on and off, and with a couple of additional sensors, detect if any object in the house is being moved when no one's supposed to be there."

"Cool." Despite being impressed, Gus still had concerns. Perhaps he'd just read too many Orwell books. "Still, I don't want anything too intrusive, especially in the shop."

Logan nodded again in obvious agreement. "Valentine here told me you'd feel that way, and it makes perfect sense. People want safety, but they also want transparency and subtlety. Your request isn't weird at all, and it's perfectly feasible. No worries. You won't spot the cameras or the sensors. Only the three of us will know they're there."

Gus admitted he was relieved to hear Logan's response. In fact, he was quite in awe of the man's amiable manner and skillful knowledge. "That's good to hear. Thank you."

Niall nudged Gus with his shoulder, smiling. "I'm glad you're on board, babe. You can watch the camera feed live on your cell or tablet, so you can see what's happening even if you're not there. This time no one's gonna break into the store and light it up again."

Gus was grateful Niall reminded him of what had transpired mere months ago when a murderer had broken into the shop, killed a man there, and then set the place on fire. Gus had to concede to the reality of their situation. Someone sinister had the two of them on his or her radar, and it didn't look like they were going to stop anytime soon. The bloodied necklace proved as much. In short, Niall had done the right thing.

"Thanks, Niall." Gus hugged his boyfriend briefly. When he pulled back, he saw the warmth in Niall's eyes and knew he'd done good. "I'm gonna jump in the shower and open the shop. Lughnasadh is coming soon, so I've got to get the place ready for the festival."

Niall grinned at him. "Have fun. Later." He resumed discussing something technical with Logan, their voices lowered but their gestures animated.

Gus watched them for a moment. Though a part of him detested this intrusion into his private life and sacred space, another part warned him of dangers ahead. The bloody necklace was an ill omen of things to come, and Gus had to accept this was his life now. The best thing he could do was come to terms with Niall and Logan's expertise in such matters and simply go on with his life in the hopes that nothing bad would happen.

As Gus swiveled around on his heels and headed toward the bathroom, coffee mug still in hand, he had a sneaking suspicion his future with Niall would be anything but a bed of roses.

Chapter 3

"HOW LONG have you known Logan?" Gus asked. He sat in a booth with Niall at Bailey's, their usual lunchtime venue.

Niall suppressed a chuckle. He'd anticipated the seemingly innocent question. Gus's casual-sounding tone merely confirmed Niall's suspicions. "Years. We met during basic training. He's a good guy."

Gus nodded, shifting the greens of his broccoli and ramen noodle salad around on his plate, his mind clearly a mile away. "He seems nice."

Niall shook his head, amused. Gus's evasions and simplistic comments told Niall that his boyfriend had insecurity issues, clearly coupled with a dose of jealousy. "If you want to know if Logan and I slept together…."

Gus's head whipped up, his spring-green eyes wide in shock. His mouth opened, but nothing came out. Red slashes appeared on his cheeks. *Busted.*

Niall took Gus's hand over the table. "Yes, I've slept with Logan." Niall saw Gus's expression harden, and he felt Gus trying to pull his hand back, but he gripped tighter. "That was years ago, in the war zone. Neither of us had boyfriends at the time, and we were alone in a strange country, surrounded by people who wanted to kill us. It was mostly stress relief. Certainly not love. We never dated. We never had the kind of a relationship I have with you. So trust me, babe. There's nothing for you to worry about."

Niall released his hold on Gus, expecting him to pull his hand back and perhaps retreat within. But Gus kept his hand in place, though he worried his bottom lip. Niall couldn't even imagine what his boyfriend was thinking. He could only hope his thoughts were good ones.

Finally Gus nodded slowly, and his features softened. "I… I can understand that. Your reasons, they make sense, especially given the situation you were both in. And… he's kinda hot." A small smile ghosted across his lips, and Niall knew they would continue to be okay as a couple. After all, neither of them were virgins when they met; they each had a sexual past with several partners.

"He is at that," Niall admitted but quickly added, "But I'm involved with this other guy now, and he's way hotter."

Gus's cheeks grew crimson, and his lips shook from pent-up laughter. "He sounds like a sexy dude."

Niall chuckled. "He sure is. Sometimes so much so that I almost embarrass myself in public and get arrested for indecency." He rubbed his foot along Gus's leg under the table, ensuring they were on the same page.

When Gus flinched and blushed even more deeply, Niall knew he'd succeeded. They continued to dine in silence, but this time the mood and spirits were both raised. Niall enjoyed his pineapple chicken teriyaki, a dish Gus had brought to his attention. Apparently pineapple juice improved the taste of a man's juices, and since Niall wanted Gus to enjoy giving him head, he had incorporated sweet fruit into his daily diet.

Aside from the delicious foods, Niall and Gus kept giving each other furtive, heated glances, promises of things to come.

"WHAT'S UP?" Niall asked once he'd clicked open the call from Hughes. He knew he shouldn't drive while talking on a cell phone, but he needed to find out if a course change was necessary.

"Hey, Junior," Hughes grunted in his typical gruff fashion. "The lab tests indicate the blood is definitely human." Niall cursed out loud, and Hughes agreed with a harrumph. "According to DNA profiling, the sample comes from a healthy redheaded male with hazel eyes. We were given top priority since there could be a missing but still living victim of attempted murder out there. Still, as I'm sure you know, the conclusions of FDP aren't 100 percent accurate. More prediction than fact."

Niall was well aware that genetic probabilities from blood tests were approximations, not holy words written in stone. Red hair genes couldn't help in tracking down a suspect or a victim since hair color could be dyed, and hazel eyes could be changed with colored contact lenses. Fair skin, however, could be deduced from the genetic markers for red hair. So it was highly likely that the owner of the blood was Caucasian. Not that it narrowed down either the suspect or the victim pool.

"Okay. Anything else?" Niall asked, hoping Hughes had learned more than that from other evidence.

"We got loads of fingerprints from the coins and the counter at Gus's shop," Hughes replied. "Most are only partials. So far, nothing's shown up on AFIS. I suppose that means the shop is mostly frequented by law-abiding citizens. Great for Gus, but no help to us."

Niall informed Hughes of the security measures now in place in Gus's shop and home, thanks to Logan. "Did the surveillance tapes from the shop show the guy buying the necklace?" The original camera at the shop was too old and unreliable for good intel. But Niall dared to hope.

"Yeah." Hughes snorted, which Niall knew was the detective's pleased sound. "We got a good look at him. Coincidentally, he's got reddish-brown hair and hazel eyes, so…."

Niall swallowed. The man had been hurt or killed? The blood suggested an injury of some sort. Certainly that possibility lessened the likelihood that he was a potential stalker.

"When the guy was at the shop," Niall told Hughes, "according to Gus he behaved skittishly. Like he was afraid of something."

"Or someone." Hughes sighed. Though he was a cop, he didn't appreciate mysteries, only clear-cut solutions and bad guys behind bars. "I sent the best picture of him the tech guys were able to make out to your cell phone. The magnification's still grainy and unclear, but it should give you a rough idea of who to look out for."

"You think he might not be dead?" Niall asked. That eventuality was his wish too for the best possible outcome. There hadn't been *that* much blood in the box after all. This whole thing could still turn out to be nothing more than a sinister prank.

"He ain't dead until I see the whites of his eyes staring back at me." Hughes's cynical tone was not without a certain dry humor. The electric static of the police radio rattled briefly in the background. "I got a call," Hughes said. "Later, Junior." The call disconnected.

Niall didn't get the chance to say good-bye. Hughes was a homicide detective, so he was often busy. Niall was grateful the man had even bothered to help out with this small matter of a bloodied necklace, since it wasn't a crime per se. The package didn't qualify as more than a vague threat or minor harassment. Niall had convinced Gus to make an official report since without one Hughes wouldn't have been able to assist them.

At least now if something happened, they had a police report to show a previous threat.

Or, more to the point, a threat aimed at Gus. Why a peaceful Wiccan shopkeeper like Gus was a better target than a private investigator like Niall, with a military background, was anyone's guess at this stage. All they could hope for was that nothing escalated or exacerbated the already inflamed situation.

As he drove home, back to Gus from yet another day of meaningless pursuit of home-wreckers and adulterers, Niall prayed for Gus's safety. Though Niall didn't believe in any kind of god or goddess, spirit or entity, he had to let the universe know somehow that whatever came their way, Niall would stand in defense of everything he held dear.

"YOU OKAY, babe?" Niall asked Gus as he rubbed his shoulders under the warm shower spray. Gus only hummed happily in response. Niall considered that a win.

Being naked with Gus was one of the best things about their relationship as far as Niall was concerned. Though they rarely had time or energy for long bouts of lovemaking, they found the time to be close and intimate at least once or twice a week, sometimes more.

Hot water sluiced over their bodies, thick rivulets running down their flexible wet skin. Niall gently massaged Gus's shoulders and neck and then slid his hands down the lean back where strong athletic muscles rippled under soft skin. Niall dipped down and kissed Gus under the ear, where he felt the quickening beat of Gus's pulse.

Gus moaned. "Mmm, yes. How I've waited for this. All day in fact." He raised his arm and wrapped it backward around Niall's neck to bring him closer.

Niall chuckled. "I aim to please." He wound his arms around Gus's waist and chest to pull him flush against him. After a day of worrying, finally getting his hands on his boyfriend had Niall more than half-hard. And the snug crevice between Gus's buttocks proved a perfect spot for his dick to slip and slide.

Gus rocked back into Niall. He placed his hand over Niall's hip and dug his nails into the skin. "I want you so bad, Tigger."

Niall laughed. "Gus, babe, maybe you shouldn't call me that when we're trying to get it on, okay? It sounds so… *not* hot."

Gus glanced over his shoulder to playfully flick his tongue at Niall. "You have such odd hang-ups with words sometimes." He planted a kiss on Niall's lips. "Does hon work for you?"

Niall suppressed a grimace. He'd never been into terms of endearment with previous guys he'd been with. Then again, none of them had been anything like Gus, who might not have been feminine exactly, but who had a more open relationship with his feminine side than most men Niall knew.

Besides, Niall himself called Gus *babe* all the time.

"Sure." Niall flipped Gus around in his embrace, pressed them together, and kissed him with gusto. Gus wound around Niall like a crushing vine, and he parted his lips to allow Niall to plunge his tongue deep into Gus's mouth. Their tongues touched and glided against each other until they grew breathless and had to pull apart.

Gus giggled, panting as well, and dropped down on his knees on the tiled floor of the shower. He gripped Niall's hips and took the tip of Niall's cock into his mouth. Niall's legs shook as he fought against the need to fuck Gus's mouth with his dick and take his senseless pleasure. But he loved Gus and refused to do anything that might hurt him.

But, *hot dayum*, Gus was good at sucking cock. Niall could have sworn the man had a dozen tongues, all wrapped around his shaft, or that Gus could create a total vacuum with his mouth and surround Niall's prick with sublime suction. And that teasing hot breath and that tiny humming that vibrated inside and out, sending Niall's brain flying so high he couldn't reach his reason even if he tried.

Niall would have been perfectly content to climax inside Gus's mouth and down his throat. But that would have made him a bad, selfish lover. He wanted Gus to come first, with Niall buried within him to the hilt.

Niall caressed Gus's cheek, making Gus look up at him with a question. "Can I fuck you, babe?" Niall asked roughly, his control waning, his voice hoarse from passion.

Gus stood and smiled, a spark of love and desire in his eyes. "You needn't even ask."

Reducing the flow of the shower spray to a trickle to conserve water (because Niall knew Gus would appreciate his consideration), Niall turned Gus around again and knelt on the floor. He parted Gus's firm buttcheeks and licked across his hole, tasting only clean skin.

"Oh, by the Goddess, so good," Gus whimpered, shaking against the wall, his cheek pressed against the wet tiles, his eyes closed and his lips parted. Niall never closed his own eyes, so he saw Gus's rapturous expression clearly. He'd never seen anything as beautiful.

Niall ate Gus out to his heart's desire. Giving pleasure to Gus always felt amazing and perfect, as though he couldn't be a worthwhile lover if Gus didn't moan sinfully and tremble like a leaf. Niall wiggled the tip of his tongue inside, causing Gus to jerk and groan louder. He suckled on the tender opening, planting kisses there and on his asscheeks, even biting gently.

"Oh fuck, yeah," Gus murmured. To Niall that signaled Gus's submission to pleasure and how close to climax he was.

Niall reached for the shower rack, fumbling around blindly among the bottles for the tube of lube he knew would be there. At least it had been the last time he'd checked. When finally his fingertips hit the right tube, Niall concluded the damn thing was almost empty. They had to restock or stop having sex in the shower. Since the latter was unlikely, a shopping trip lay ahead.

With swift adeptness, some of it born from need, Niall coated Gus's hole and channel with lubricant. Then he smeared his cock with lube too, stood, pulled Gus's lower body closer, and steadily pushed his cock in. Gus moaned and quivered, his head thrown back. His hands shook and his fingers crooked as he seemed to seek leverage against the wall.

Niall wrapped his arms around Gus's waist as soon as he was fully seated inside him. "Ready, babe?" he whispered, unable to find his voice. Being inside Gus was tantamount to pure bliss, and it never ceased to take Niall by surprise. His hips jerked forward, making Gus howl, and Niall's self-control was slipping fast.

"Slow, hon, slow." Gus breathed out the words, so Niall almost felt them instead of hearing them. Niall thought about waves slowly ebbing and flowing, trying to calm his mind. After several years he'd learned it was serenity, not tension, that allowed him to better stave off orgasm.

Of course, sometimes Niall felt foolish, as though he were doing Lamaze breathing.

And there, a brief flickering image of a woman giving birth, and Niall was back in full control of himself.

Gus relaxed and unwound around Niall. He felt the tight pressure along the length of his dick easing. "Now, Niall," Gus whispered, lust again evident in his raspy tone.

Niall pumped in and out in small, slow increments at first. Soon he picked up the pace as Gus's body surrounded him and rendered all conscious movements things of the past. Niall's body and need took over, and instinct propelled him to plunge deeper and faster inside Gus. The wet heat of Gus's channel equaled heaven to Niall, who had lost all semblance of self-control.

"Fuck, I need you so fucking bad, all the time, no matter where I am," Niall muttered in heat, his hold on Gus tightening. "Can't even think straight when I catch a glimpse of you. I know your body, what you need, what you want. It's me, and that drives me so fucking crazy I think I'd lose my mind if I couldn't have you."

"I'm yours, Niall," Gus murmured. "Love you so much."

Gus craned his head back in search of Niall's lips. The position was awkward, but they managed to get a few luscious licks and lip-locks between breaths.

Gus started to push back in sync with each thrust Niall made. Their rhythms matched for a good long while, until need overrode their harmonious coupling and forced them to wildly and passionately jerk for their climb toward the peak of pleasure. Niall reamed Gus till he couldn't even fathom what he was doing, his movements a blur and his eyesight hazy.

"God, Niall, I'm gonna come," Gus cried out. Niall hadn't even seen when Gus started pumping his dick, his hand flying on his cock.

The sight alone caused a spark shower inside Niall's mind and body, and waves of orgasm crashed over him. He spilled his seed deep inside Gus since nothing separated them. The pleasure was so intense Niall felt his cock might literally rocket right off his body. Gus's channel rippled and constricted around him as he climaxed, and his spunk spilled out in ropes against the wet wall and floor.

Both of them worn out and out of breath, Niall gently pulled out of Gus and gathered his lover close. On unsteady feet, they swayed together back to front for a while, savoring the sweet radiance of afterglow.

Gus turned his head on Niall's shoulder and planted a tired kiss on his cheek. "I love the way you talk during sex. It's such hot praise it isn't even dirty. I think my brain's melted." He chuckled quietly.

Niall smiled, happy that his partner was happy. "It's all true. Every time I have you, I know I'm gonna want you more next time. Can't help it. Love you too much to ever be satisfied with anything less than you."

Gus beamed, turned around in Niall's embrace, and kissed Niall lazily, as though they had all the time in the world. Eventually, of course, they washed away the evidence of their mutual ardor, dried off inside a huge terry towel, and went to sleep together in their shared bed, in the nude, side by side, limbs entangled—and more in love than ever.

Chapter 4

GUS WAS reading the newspaper and sipping his morning cup of cappuccino while Niall whistled in the shower, when there was a knock at the door. Still tired from yesterday, Gus slouched to the front door (which was actually on the side of the building) and opened it.

Hughes stood in the faint drizzle of late-summer rain, his grouchy mood evident in his grim expression. "Morning, Goodwin. Invite me in before I melt."

Gus waved him inside, and Hughes shook his coat and stomped his booted feet to get some of the rain off. Gus beckoned the detective into the kitchen and offered him a steaming cup of coffee, which Hughes practically inhaled in an instant, his hardened features softening.

"Thanks, Goodwin," Hughes said appreciatively. "That's good coffee."

Gus basked in the glory of the praise, so unusual for the surly cop. "I bought a special coffeemaker that produces dozens of different varieties. Niall likes his coffee black and bitter, while I prefer sweeter and creamier. So… what's up?"

Hughes placed his cup on the table, his hands around the hot mug and his expression serious and solemn. "We found the guy you met at the shop." Gus was pleasantly surprised, but the second he saw Hughes's lack of a returned smile, he figured something was wrong. Hughes said, "Yesterday I got called away to the southernmost part of King County. There's a small privately owned settlement east of Palmer, north of the Green River, practically in the wilderness. The local sheriff called us in when they found a body there."

Gus gulped in shock. "A-a body…?"

Hughes nodded, his features bleak, reached into his inside coat pocket, and pulled out a small manila envelope. He spread it open on the table and offered Gus a picture of a young man smiling at the camera, alive and seemingly happy. "That the guy?" Hughes asked.

Gus swallowed hard. The familiar features, the auburn hair, the hazel eyes, the twink-like look about him, were all there. He nodded sadly. "Yes." He couldn't believe this was happening again. Death kept a constant vigil over Gus, and violence had become a part of his everyday life. "You found his... him dead?" His voice squeaked at the end.

"Who's dead?" Niall asked, a rough steely edge to his voice even as he stepped into the kitchen in nothing but a towel around his waist.

"The scared guy from the shop," Gus replied glumly and gave the picture of the dead man to Niall.

Hughes grunted an affirmative. "Yeah. But there's more to this case. I didn't come here just to tell you that."

Niall snorted in obvious dismay. "I bet." He tossed the picture on the table. "Now that *he's* involved, I guess so are we."

Gus looked at Niall over his shoulder, confused. "What are you talking about?"

Niall frowned, appearing baffled. "Didn't you look at that picture?" Gus nodded, still in the dark, so Niall added, "Didn't you notice the guy on the left?"

Gus picked up the picture again. Before looking at it, he asked Hughes, "Where'd you get this picture? I mean it's clearly not of the, uh, corpse."

"The owner of the property gave it to me after he identified the body at the scene."

Gus gasped as recognition set in. He'd stared at the photo and only seen the scared guy at his shop. He'd paid no attention to the other young man standing next to the deceased, his arm over his shoulder in an intimate fashion.

"Oh. My. God. It's... it's Autumnsong!"

"So that's the infamous Autumnsong?" Hughes raised his eyebrows and whistled low. "Not quite how I imagined him, to be honest."

"He usually wears more makeup and flashier clothes." Gus sighed heavily, not knowing what to think of the situation now. If it hadn't been for Niall, he wouldn't even have recognized the average-appearing Autumnsong in the photo. "He's been more than this flamboyant every time I've seen him, with heavy black makeup around his eyes, feather boas around his neck, and skintight pants no normal person would be able to walk in."

"Yeah, he's some kind of dark queen of satanic twinks," Niall provided, arms crossed over his chest, an intimidating scowl on his face. He had to be angry at the latest development in the case, Gus surmised. Every time Autumnsong surfaced, trouble was brewing.

In that, Niall's emotions mirrored Gus's. "Autumnsong knows— uh, I mean, he knew the victim. What's his name?"

Hughes flipped open his notebook. "Rowan Tuff, age twenty-two, last known address on Mercer Island, but that was from two years ago. No criminal record."

"And he was found where, exactly?" Niall asked, taking a seat at the table, pouring a cup of coffee for himself, and sipping slowly. But the normally cool Niall radiated anxiety and concern, to which Gus could relate.

Hughes shifted on his seat, discomfort evident in his body language. "That's kind of the reason why I came to see you face-to-face. We still have to confirm identity from DNA, of course, but the property owner was pretty sure it was him from some clothing and where the body was found. We couldn't have identified the deceased without the estate owner's help, since…."

As Hughes's voice faded, Gus and Niall exchanged glances. Niall asked, "Since what? I've known you too many years, Virg, for you to be shy about a suspicious death."

Hughes barked out a laugh. "Suspicious death? We couldn't ID the body at first because his face and body were beaten to a pulp and then partially incinerated for good measure. There wasn't much left to identify him with. Not enough intact teeth or facial features, and fingerprints burned off. He was more a bag of loose bones and filthy, singed rags than an intact body."

Gus leaned back, grimacing, disgust roiling in his stomach. "That's horrible."

Niall nodded and rested a hand over Gus's, gently squeezing for comfort. Gus smiled a little by way of thanks. Niall might have been used to the horrors and violence the human race was capable of, but Gus had always tried to see the positive and the good in people. Lately, he'd been forced to revise his views on the world, and that saddened Gus.

Had he irrevocably lost his innocence?

Hughes cleared his throat, giving Gus a wary glance. Perhaps he worried over Gus's sensibilities, which Gus knew the detective thought were delicate to say the least. Gus didn't think Hughes was a racist or a sexist, just old-school in his views about not causing distress to damsels—or their male equivalents—in distress.

"This whole thing was weird from first glance," Hughes stated, his gaze aimed at his coffee mug rather than his companions. "You see, there were a lot of oddities. First, the condition of the body, tortured and practically mutilated. Second, the location where he was found, well, it was a kind of… a shrine."

Gus leaned closer, now more curious than concerned. "What kind of a shrine?"

Hughes fidgeted again, so Gus knew to expect something the good detective was less than familiar with. "The whole private property is full of shrines and altars, temples and places of worship. It's a sort of spiritual sanctuary, apparently. The owner was quick to remind us of their freedom to practice their religion in peace without any interference from the law."

"What faith do they follow?" Gus asked again.

Hughes harrumphed in displeasure, but then he sighed in defeat and replied, "They're Radical Faeries."

"THEY'RE… WHAT?" Niall asked, his utter confusion clear to Gus.

"The Radical Faeries are hard to describe with any degree of certainty," Gus said, but he tried anyway. "They're a countercultural movement of mostly gay and queer men who want to bring spirituality into the gay lifestyle. They usually follow contemporary neo-paganism, environmentalism, and forms of anarchism, as well as have a strong social conscience and moral values related to the gay rights movement and the genderqueer lifestyle."

Gus watched with mild amusement as Niall and Hughes looked at each other, wide-eyed and obviously stumped. He understood their mental plight. Had Gus not studied new religious movements in college, he might not have known any of these spiritual groups even existed.

"Okay, let's try this," Gus said, making a second go of it. "They think queers and gays can do more than just hook up with strangers and spend all night at clubs. They care about spiritual matters, nature, human rights, personal liberties, and so forth. But they also don't want to conform to the heteronormative society—"

Gus sighed when he saw the blank expressions on Niall's and Hughes's faces. Dammit, what was he supposed to do if he couldn't use civilized language? Finger-puppets?

"Okay, okay." Niall waved at Gus to be quiet before he could go further. "Religious folks at a farm, basically, is that what you're saying?"

Gus rolled his eyes and pursed his lips. "That's a pretty broad generalization and not quite accurate."

"But… close?" Niall's hopeful look had Gus let out a breath and nod. There was no point in arguing further. Niall and Hughes were big boys, so they could form their own opinions. Niall faced Hughes again. "So, this dead dude, Tuff, he was found at an altar?"

"Yeah." Hughes checked his notes again. "It's an outdoor site, situated on top of a tiny mound, with a campfire under this wooden construct and with a torch on top."

Gus gasped. He snatched Hughes's notebook and doodled on it for a second. Then he handed it back and asked, "Like this?" The rough image resembled an hourglass-shaped bonfire made of four tall intersecting branches with a circular sun image on top. Hughes nodded, frowning. Gus smiled, addressing Niall. "Remind you of something?"

Niall snapped his fingers. "The bloodied necklace. The deadly bane symbol." Cocking his head, he appeared pensive. "Coincidence or by design?"

"You mean, by the killer or by the victim?" Gus added a twist to the speculations and got an intrigued quirk of an eyebrow in response from Niall.

"Anyway," Hughes cut in with a voice louder than that of his companions. "The place is called… wait a sec. Ah, yes, Mount Paradise Sanctuary."

Gus contemplated what he knew, which wasn't much. "I think I've heard of it. But I've never been there. And I'm not an expert on the Radical Faeries. To be honest, we don't move in the same circles."

"I thought they were pagans like you," Hughes commented.

"Ah, well…." Gus reddened. "I'm not really into their countercultural ideas. I mean, I think marriage should be for everyone, gays and straights. RF members, most of them at least, view marriage as something for straight people only, viewing it as an antiquated institution that they have no desire for. They're all about freedom of expression and free love, though."

Niall and Hughes regarded each other with shared sarcasm and mumbled in unison, "Hippies."

Gus slapped his forehead. "Oh, for the love of—for two examples of educated males, you sure can show a lot of prejudice and preconceptions. I'm somewhat insulted."

Niall looked away, coughed a bit, and then turned back, his cheeks crimson. "It's not like we said free love is a bad thing." Then he took on a professional tone, as though he had slipped into his business suit to talk to a client. A remarkable feat considering he wore nothing but a low-hanging towel. "You going up there for further inquiries?"

"Yup." Hughes straightened on his seat, his inquisitive gaze flicking between Niall and Gus. "Care to join me? It's a long drive, and I wouldn't mind some company. You especially, Goodwin. I hadn't even heard of the Radical Faeries until last night."

Gus hesitated. "Well, I'm honored, but, uh, I'm not really an expert on that particular group. Not everyone even classifies them as neo-pagans."

"Every little bit helps." Hughes quirked an eyebrow.

Gus felt like he was being challenged, or studied like a bug under a microscope, so he nodded. "Sure, why not? I have to call Izzy to have him mind the store while I'm gone." Niall gave him a baffled look, and Gus laughed, shaking his head. "I've told you a million times, hon. Isidore Norwood, or Izzy as he prefers to be called, is that college student and practicing witch who's been helping me around the shop for the past month. I can't believe you forgot. Again. You met him two weeks ago, you numbnuts."

Niall's cheeks reddened again, and he rubbed the back of his neck in a self-conscious way. "Right, yeah, that guy." Clearly he had no idea who Gus was referring to. Niall stood, gripped his towel before it could fall, and ambled toward the bedroom. "Two minutes," he called out behind him.

"Me too," Gus affirmed. Then he got up and followed Niall to the bedroom, cell phone glued to his ear to call Izzy as he simultaneously tried to yank out clean clothes from the drawer and plan on which thermos to put his fresh coffee in (he had, like, six of them).

Unsurprisingly it took them twelve minutes, not two, to get on the road.

Chapter 5

THE DRIVE took them the better part of two hours, with two pit stops—one for gas and another for a piss break. While Gus loved the views of the forests and mountains along the way, Niall was in a bad mood. He despised long car trips, feeling edgy and stir-crazy in less than an hour. They had to change seats midway so Niall could spread out awkwardly on the backseat and Gus could chat with Hughes in the passenger seat. That situation suited Niall fine.

"Who's the landowner?" Gus asked Hughes, scribbling his own notes while surfing the net on his iPhone.

Hughes grunted and dug out his notebook from his front inside jacket pocket. "Hold your horses, Goodwin. Right, here were go. Jacob Marlowe, fifty-nine, retired. He's owned the land for over thirty years, apparently." He flipped the notebook cover flap closed and shoved the whole thing back in his pocket.

Gus nodded. Niall watched his movements from the backseat, waiting patiently to hear what Gus had uncovered from his own online research. "Ah. Jake Marlowe, former heavyweight champion of the world, circa 1979. Wow."

Hughes harrumphed dryly. "Huh. Who'd a thunk it?" His rhetorical statement dripped cynicism. Niall could relate.

"He was just a kid back in the sixties," Gus went on, his hand moving over the iPhone screen. "Guess witnessing some of the wild, emergent freedoms of that era but not being part of it in any real capacity made him want to recreate some of it. The same was true with the original Radical Faeries, as their group was established in 1979 but was influenced by the countercultural movements of the 1960s."

"Far out." Hughes could be succinct with his dry humor, and Gus's giggle revealed his appreciation of that. Niall noticed, with no small amount of glee, that Hughes's upper lip twitched as though he could barely contain his amusement. That was a victory for Gus. Hughes wasn't typically the type to start bellowing with laughter.

"Here's a picture of him. Old one, it seems. But back in the day, the man was hot."

Niall grimaced in secret. He didn't like Gus checking out other guys, not in theory and certainly not in practice. But he kept the jealousy to himself and said nothing.

He pushed himself up long enough to get a glimpse of the picture on Gus's phone. In the old photo, Marlowe couldn't have been much more than twenty or thirty, so the time of the shot must have been in the 1980s. Tall and beefy, with short-cropped, not quite crewcut but close, black hair and eyes like blue ice, Jacob Marlowe epitomized a wrestler in his prime, fit and muscular and quite scary. His mass alone would make him a tough enforcer in a fight.

Niall fell on his back against the seat. Sure, the guy had been attractive, in a back-alley bruiser sort of way. Niall hadn't thought that might be Gus's type. Or perhaps Gus just noted a hot guy without any real feeling. Niall definitely hoped so.

"You're awfully quiet back there." Niall started at Gus's voice and saw his boyfriend staring at him from the passenger seat. And he was smirking too, as though he assumed Niall would have naughty thoughts. *Yeah, right.* "What's on your mind?"

Niall harrumphed, crossed his arms over his chest, and closed his eyes, saying, "Are we fucking there yet?"

MOUNT PARADISE Sanctuary was located on a forest-covered mountainside between the Howard A. Hanson Reservoir and Eagle Lake. The area was filled with lush wildflower meadows in between woodland copses, a small lake sunk in a natural basin, and a clear-blue brook bubbling and streaming downhill to Piling Creek and to the reservoir. Mount Rainier National Park was situated to the east and south, and the Okanogan-Wenatchee National Forest expanded to the northeast.

The air was hot and sunny, typical late-summer weather, with the temperature peaking in the midseventies. Mountain breezes cooled the air, but the view waved and wobbled in the heat coming off the road, and all three men had to shade their eyes from the afternoon glint. An ever-present buzz of insects came from all around, and birds sang in the trees. The mountain meadows bloomed with wildflowers, and alongside the

Douglas firs and red cedars grew whitebark pines, noble firs, and spruces. Splashes of colors were everywhere in this the season of abundance.

Gus was in paradise. He sighed with longing. He had the privilege to live in one of the most beautiful regions in the world, so he should really make time to appreciate it more. Perhaps he could entice Niall to a bike ride in the national parks or going kayaking or hiking….

A sharp slap on skin startled him. Niall stood beside the car next to him, cringing at having killed a bug against his neck. A few specks of blood attested to a partially successful attack.

"Fuck, I hate the outdoors," Niall mumbled, waving his hands about, apparently trying to dissuade any other insects from approaching him. "Give me a big city any day of the week."

Gus turned away to hide his disappointment with Niall. Gus was a Wiccan. He loved nature. That was why he lived and worked near Point Defiance Park, to be close to the earth from which they all came. How come he hadn't noticed Niall's aversion to nature before now? Had they never discussed these things? Surely the subject must have come up at least once or twice….

"The road doesn't go farther than this." Hughes pointed to a rugged footpath uphill, his disgruntled look matching Niall's. Gus felt even more depressed. "This is the best way to the grounds. The body's been taken to the ME's office. C'mon."

They hiked uphill for a couple of minutes. The rocky ground soon turned into a decent dirt road, though not wide enough to accommodate a vehicle. Unless it was a motorcycle or a bike.

Gus inhaled the smells of summer, occasionally closing his eyes and simply savoring the moment. The leaves of alders, maples, and dogwoods rustled pleasantly in the wind, and every flower they came across perfumed the air with sweet scents. Gus spotted cascade blueberries here and there but knew to avoid the shrubs because of hidden sumac bushes.

"Want a blueberry?" Gus asked Niall, smiling happily. Just because his companions were in a sour mood, that didn't mean he had to be.

Niall grimaced. "With my luck a red fox or a bear has pissed on them. No thanks."

Gus frowned. Niall's dissatisfied attitude annoyed him. But Gus had lived long enough to know that people didn't fundamentally change.

Leopards didn't change their spots. If Niall didn't like nature now, maybe he never would. That thought brought Gus's mood down even more.

A simple wooden gate appeared ahead, flanked by lush white oaks, tall green grass—and a weather-beaten No Trespassing sign written in bright red block letters. No structures on the compound were visible from their vantage point.

"They've got a small office close to this here entrance," Hughes supplied as he opened the creaking gate, his voice terse. Gus tried to overlook the obvious disdain the other men felt toward their surroundings and probably toward the practitioners living there. But he didn't like it. "They've got a couple of stewards and several caretakers."

"What do these people do here anyway? Dance around in circles and pray during gay sex?" Niall chuckled at his own jest, and Hughes barked out a laugh.

"Hey!" Gus had had enough. He punched Niall on the arm. With a grunt of pain, Niall stumbled sideways, glaring at Gus half in irritation, half in confusion.

"The hell?" Niall grumbled, rubbing his arm that had to hurt.

"That's enough," Gus said, extremely vexed. "Everyone is still presumed innocent and not guilty by default, or am I wrong? And no one is persecuted because of their faith, right? These people deserve better than your snotty remarks."

Niall stepped forward, appearing sheepish and contrite, his cheeks reddened and his gaze bashful. "Yeah, you're right." Niall brought his hands up in an I-give-up gesture. "But I'm not your enemy, Gus. I mean… you know better than anyone that I absolutely *adore* dancing in circles around a maypole and hopping over bonfires in my birthday suit and—"

"Okay, okay," Gus cut in, fires of embarrassment flaming on his face. The coven he'd belonged to in his early days as a Wiccan had affectionately called him Grasshopper due to an incident of leaping over a bonfire buck naked. "You learned your lesson. Check." He understood Niall was trying to bring levity into the situation. Guess neither of them wanted to fight, Gus concluded. They smiled briefly at each other, and the tension in the air began to fade.

"You're my favorite person in the world," Niall continued softly, placing his hands over Gus's shoulders, his palms warm and heavy, his touch familiar and soothing. "And I don't want to do anything to upset you."

"Then stop acting dumb," Gus said with a playful pout, his lower lip sticking out. He loved Niall with every cell in his body and every beat of his heart. Gus hated being angry with Niall for any reason, for in his mind they were a great match.

Niall conceded to Gus's statement with a minor bow. "Yeah. When you're right, you're right." His grin told Gus the tiny tiff wasn't the end of the world, or the end of their relationship.

"Damn right," Gus mumbled, smiling again. Niall chuckled, and then he bussed Gus's cheek softly. The weirdness now defused, they both turned their attention to the wooden gate and the estate beyond it.

Hughes rolled his eyes, shaking his head. "Okay there now, boys? Need more time for hand-holding or hearts and flowers or—"

"Shut up, you old codger," Niall interjected, warmth in his chiding tone.

Gus suppressed a giggle and a snort. He was grateful Hughes did his best to see the world as a positively changed place, a safe and good place for gay people too. That kind of transformation of thought wasn't easy for everyone, so Gus appreciated Hughes's attempt at open-mindedness.

Hughes opened the gate, and the three men walked through and headed up the path, which veered to the left toward the single structure they could now easily see. The tiny log cabin ahead was painted dark red. The door had two windows side by side at eye level. A large maple tree extended its leafy branches over the roof, and wind chimes rang a melodious jingle from somewhere unseen but nearby. Gus's troubles dissipated.

"It's beautiful here," Gus murmured. He didn't wait for Niall to respond, for it seemed his mind was elsewhere.

As they walked up to the cabin, Gus took note of their surroundings. The darkened soil of a fire pit was visible uphill, even through the tall meadow grass, with an unlit bonfire standing tall in the center. To the right of the gate they'd entered, the grounds rose toward two greenhouses, both with shadows of people working inside visible through the frosted glass. Beyond them a conical sweat lodge had been erected, but no smoke plumes appeared from the top. Several fire-safety stations with extinguishers and red water barrels with long green hoses hanging on the sides dotted the otherwise green landscape, and here and there amid the verdant edges of the forest, Gus spotted small cabins and huts.

"How many people live here at any given time?" Gus asked Hughes, expecting the detective to have done his research.

Hughes checked his notes, confirming Gus's suspicion that Hughes had his ear to the ground every second he was on the clock—and probably off of it too. "Two caretakers live here year-round. In the summertime, there's an additional two caretakers, two stewards, and a bunch of guests numbering from half a dozen to several dozen. Currently... twenty-two in all."

"And all their whereabouts have been confirmed during the time of the murder?" Niall asked.

"Most of the guests and caretakers participated in an all-night sing-along around the fire pit from sundown to sunrise." Hughes shook his head. Gus assumed Hughes had a problem with the activity itself, but was soon proven wrong. "Unfortunately, the event wasn't mandatory, and the fire made it impossible to tell how many were actually present. There was a barbecue about thirty feet away, so people were coming and going from one light source to another."

"The blaze would have blinded people from making accurate assessments of who was there," Niall said, hitting the nail on the head with his theory. "So basically everyone has and doesn't have an alibi."

"Yeah, that about sums it up," Hughes grunted, flipping the notebook closed and shoving it back in his pocket.

In front of the office stood two people. The one facing them was a tall, lean surfer type with waist-length brown dreadlocks and swirling black tribal tattoos all around his tanned, trim body. He wore a white tank top, knee-length dark red shorts, and black flip-flops. Young and gorgeous, whether gay or straight, Gus figured the guy could get anyone he wanted.

Of the other person, Gus saw only the back, and that man wore simple blue jeans, a gray T-shirt, and had short brown hair.

But one thing was for sure: neither of them was Autumnsong. Where the hell was he?

The dreadlock dude glared as Gus, Niall, and Hughes approached. They heard him say to his companion, "You talk to them if you wish. I want nothing to do with their harassment." Then he stormed off uphill, his gestures animated and angry as he rushed away, grumbling under his breath.

After a long sigh, the other man turned around.

Gus stopped dead in his tracks, gasping out loud in shock. How could *he* be here?

The average-height, brown-haired man had *the* most symmetrical features Gus had ever known in a man. He wore a blue tie loose around his neck, seemingly for no purpose. A light stubble covered his strong jaw, and sleek, gray, rectangular-shaped glasses showcased his forest-green eyes.

He was so symmetrical that he appeared almost... bland. But Gus knew the man to be a charming, seductive, and usually successful gentlemen's man. A classic portrait of a player.

The man's perfect, trimmed eyebrows rose in surprise. "August?"

Shit.

Chapter 6

NIALL DID his best to remain calm. But that was difficult when a complete stranger first used familiarities with Niall's boyfriend and then proceeded to hug him like a long-lost friend—with benefits. It didn't help matters that the man, appearing to be in his mid- to late forties, seemed to be a perfect specimen of the human race, handsome and agreeable.

"August, my goodness. Amazing. I had no idea you'd be here. What on earth are you doing here? This is a really bad time." The man kept touching Gus, holding on to his shoulders and embracing him, again and again.

Niall was two seconds from beating the man to a pulp.

But it was Gus who gently pushed the man away. That was also when Niall observed how strained and forced Gus's smile actually was. Clearly whatever amiable feelings had existed between them, Gus didn't share them in exact proportion to this hugging stranger.

Niall decided to step up to the plate, and he extended a hand in greeting. "Hi. I'm Niall Valentine, and this is Detective Hughes of the SPD. And you are…?"

"Um, Niall, this is—" Gus swallowed, having gone pale. "—Dr. Alex Kittridge, my former college professor in religious studies and an expert in neo-pagan movements, among them the Radical Faeries."

If Niall applied a bit too much pressure than was comfortable during a handshake, he didn't feel too bad about it. "Nice to meet you. Are you a guest here?"

Dr. Kittridge smiled, a perfect expression of pleasant amusement, neither corner of the mouth higher or lower, his teeth pearly white. He really had a natural grace. "Oh, no. I'm one of the caretakers here."

"You are?" Gus sounded surprised to hear that. Niall puzzled over the reason.

Dr. Kittridge laughed, a harmonious sound that annoyed Niall to no end. Probably due to the fact that he could understand the magic of such a voice, its ability to seduce.

And *that* sudden thought brought an extremely dangerous and unpleasant idea into the forefront of his already troubled mind: Had there once been more than a professional relationship between Gus and Kittridge?

Niall felt nauseated.

"I haven't gone native, if that's what you're suggesting." Kittridge winked at Gus as if they shared some special bond Niall wasn't privy to. Niall gritted his teeth to prevent himself from claiming Gus in front of this guy. He knew Gus wouldn't appreciate such a show of ownership.

"So… you're studying this group of people, Professor?" Gus asked slowly, frowning. Niall wished, and not for the first time, that he could read minds. He would have given anything to be able to get the lowdown on this Dr. Alex Kittridge.

"Well, I suppose it started out that way," Kittridge said, shrugging, the very picture of nonchalance. "As you know, even among neo-pagan circles, the Radical Faeries are considered something of an oddity, a curious mix of spirituality, social rebellion, and drag. My goal is to show conclusively that they are, in fact, no different from any other neo-pagan groups. Surely the social dimension alone describes that homology of—"

"Dr. Kittridge?" Hughes cut in and stepped closer, his expression stern. Niall could have hugged his friend for interrupting the doctor's tirade. "Has your steward prepared what I asked for last night, namely the list of everyone present?"

Kittridge glanced over his shoulder in the direction the dreadlock guy had gone off to and then cleared his throat, looking humble. "You'll have to excuse Caretaker Bodhi's bad manners. He has had poor experiences with law enforcement. But yes, sir, he did give me that list of names."

While Kittridge fumbled in his back pocket, eventually retrieving a folded and scrunched piece of paper, Gus asked him, "Alex, how long have you been a caretaker here?"

Niall watched with no small amount of aggravation as Gus's cheeks flamed red and he gave Niall a furtive glance, worrying his bottom lip. So…. Niall's boyfriend and Gus's ex-professor were on a first-name basis. *Swell.*

Rationally, Niall knew he was a fool to get upset over the possibility Gus had slept with his professor. The man seemed virile, smart, and charismatic. And even if something had happened between them, that was in the past. Especially since, judging from Gus's reaction, this reunion wasn't on the top of his list of favorite things.

"Oh, a couple of years." Kittridge handed the list to Hughes. "I was doing fieldwork with another neo-pagan group, and I chanced a meeting with one of the founders of this sanctuary, Jacob Marlowe. He had a profound, undeniable presence, reminding me of cult leaders, remember, August?"

Gus blinked, and his fading blush turned beet red again. "It's, uh, just Gus now."

Kittridge smiled apologetically. "Yes, of course. Sorry. I always found your true given name appealing." Then he coughed again, as though returning to his professional mode. "Anyway, Marlowe owns the property here, about a hundred and twenty acres in total. The sanctuary, on the other hand, comprises of roughly eighty or ninety acres."

"Dr. Kittridge?" Hughes interjected once more, his impatience coming through clearly in his fidgety body language. "Take us to the crime scene."

Kittridge nodded. "Of course. This way."

Following a path through the clearing, Kittridge took the lead in the procession uphill. Gus, however, seemed to fall deliberately behind, so Niall matched step with him. For a while neither spoke. Niall waited as patiently as he could. The ball was in Gus's court. Niall recalled they had not really talked about their exes until Logan came along. Perhaps it was high time they cleared the air.

"Yes, I slept with Alex." Gus's small voice was barely audible.

Niall swallowed hard, his throat and tongue dry. An irrational surge of jealousy damn near knocked him off his feet. He managed to breathe out, "Okay."

"I wasn't in love with him," Gus said, releasing a long sigh. "We had an affair. It was totally inappropriate. But we did it anyway. I think I was… a bit starstruck. Alex is a big name in the field of new religious movements, and add to that our mutual interests, and…. You know, same old, same old. The familiar tale of the older mentor and the younger novice."

"Who left who?" Niall hoped he didn't sound as gruff as he did to his own ears. After all, he loved Gus, and he didn't want to alienate or hurt him.

Gus gulped. Out of the corner of his eye, Niall saw his Adam's apple bopping. That did not bode well. "He…. Alex broke things off. Not with words or anything. One day he just packed his bags and told me he'd be gone for twelve-to-eighteen months in some distant corner of the world for fieldwork and research. He didn't ask me to wait, and I wasn't inclined to do so either. If ever there was a sign that two people were all wrong for each other and that a relationship wasn't working, that was it."

Another absurd thought crossed Niall's mind. He really would have preferred that Gus had done the leaving. Because that way there wouldn't have been any unresolved issues. Now? Who knew.

"I see" was all Niall said.

Niall stopped when Gus caught his arm, the grip featherlight, as though he wasn't sure if his touch was welcome. "That was seven years ago, Niall. I was nineteen, a boy who knew next to nothing about the world."

Niall shook his head. "It's fine, Gus. I promise. You don't have to defend yourself to me. I didn't come into this relationship with blinkers on. I knew right from the get-go we both had our own sexual histories and relationship baggage. You don't have to explain."

Gus sighed again, this one so long his whole posture actually drooped, his shoulders slumping and his gaze dropping to the ground. "But that's just it. Alex is here now, so it's not just in the past. This is the present, and he… he's here."

Niall placed his fingers under Gus's chin and lifted until their gazes met. Niall smiled to encourage his boyfriend to see he wasn't mad. "Yeah, he is. Then again, so is Logan, *my* ex."

Gus frowned. "Okay, that's true. But you two didn't really have a relationship. You just fucked." It was unusual for Gus to curse so blatantly; Niall interpreted that as nerves.

Niall shook his head. "Logan was and is a comrade in arms. That kind of bond takes a lot of trust and loyalty. A friendship. No, it's not like what you apparently had with Kittridge. But not entirely dissimilar either." He nudged Gus with his elbow. "C'mon. We can have the full ex talk once we get home. For now, we have a crime to investigate. You with me… partner?"

Gus smiled, this time sunny and relaxed, and he nodded. "Absolutely. Partner."

Together, side by side, they hurried after Hughes and Kittridge.

THE SUN altar didn't impress Niall. It was a simple raised wooden platform with a few stairs going up and with four tall wooden beams in a bonfire-shaped position, holding aloft a brass bowl with dry sticks and shreds of newspapers inside for lighting fires. Nothing in particular screamed that the site was devoted to the worship of the sun.

A uniformed police officer guarded the site from cross-contamination, interference by locals, and other criminal acts to sabotage the crime scene. Hughes talked to him, their voices too low to be overheard as they exchanged notes, probably to gain information about everything that had transpired here since last night.

"Who found the body?" Niall asked, staring at the blackened stain in front of the rack. The body wasn't there anymore, but it was easy to see where it had rested. Soot and dried blood lay mixed around the vague human shape.

"Marlowe, Bodhi, and myself," Kittridge answered. "We saw a faint glow up here, so we rushed over to see if someone had forgotten to smother the fire in the bowl after a worship session."

"These fires aren't continuously lit?" Niall asked for clarification. It would have made sense for a sun altar to have permanent bonfires.

"No, absolutely not." Kittridge shook his head vigorously. "The danger of forest fires is too great. One uncontrolled spark, and the whole wilderness might just go up in flames. There's also a sign in front of the stairs that clearly states anyone worshiping here will have to take care to light and extinguish any fires. Plus, there are water stations nearby for any emergencies."

"What did you see when you arrived at the scene?" Niall continued. Hughes must have asked the same questions already, but Niall hadn't because he hadn't been there. Also, the possibility of catching Gus's ex in a lie was too good an opportunity to miss.

Kittridge paled, swallowing and blinking. If he was guilty, he was a good actor. "I… I saw right away he… he was dead." He closed his eyes and seemed to fight to control either nausea or tears. Niall hated that he felt sympathy for the guy, but he did.

"Were any of the fires lit?" Gus asked. Niall glanced at his boyfriend, surprised that he had commented at all since he'd been silent thus far. Maybe Gus had gotten over the shock of seeing his ex near a murder scene.

Kittridge frowned, appearing pensive. "No…? No, I'm pretty sure they weren't."

"But you claimed you and Mr. Marlowe and Bodhi all saw a fire burning here," Niall said, wondering if Kittridge had a poor memory or if he was a liar.

"We did." His own statement seemed to give Kittridge food for thought. "We all saw it, an orange glow uphill here, through the woods. But if the fire bowl wasn't lit…." His features tensed when he seemed to understand what they had seen. "Then it must have been… Rowan… on fire, dying. Oh my God." He held on to his stomach, going green. He was a hairsbreadth away from throwing up, Niall concluded.

"Did you hear anything, Alex?" Gus asked, interrupting Kittridge's potential vomiting spell. "Did he scream in pain?"

Kittridge appeared lost and confused. Then he shook his head. "I… I don't think so. I mean, there was a great deal of noise coming from the fire pit area. Lots of people were dancing and singing, shouting, and playing games and instruments." He looked around, but Niall saw his gaze had gone glassy, as though he were reminiscing. "But… in spite of all that commotion, I'm fairly certain we would have heard a man screaming in agony from being… burned to death." He gulped as though bile had risen to his throat.

"How well did you know him?" Gus asked. Niall stared at his companion, surprised again at how blasé and casual Gus seemed. It was as though Kittridge's emotional display had zero impact on Gus. Since Niall knew Gus to be one of the most empathetic people he'd ever known, this unresponsive act puzzled him.

"Who, Rowan?" Kittridge sighed, still holding on to his stomach, looking queasy. "Not well at all. I'd seen him and even spoken to him on several occasions, but we didn't spend any time together. He was just one of the many faces hanging around here."

Niall watched Gus step forward, dig out a photo from his jeans pocket, and show it to Kittridge. "Do you recognize one or both of these men?"

This was it, Niall suspected. *Autumnsong.*

Chapter 7

ALEX KITTRIDGE took the photo of Rowan Tuff and Autumnsong, both smiling at the camera, young and carefree, their arms around one another. He frowned, tilting his head left and right, his expression thoughtful.

Niall waited with bated breath. If Kittridge knew Autumnsong, they might get a lead on the elusive young man who professed to being a practicing Satanist. Niall doubted the veracity of that claim, even though Autumnsong did know a lot about satanic rituals. One thing didn't lead necessarily to the other.

"That's Rowan, on the right," Kittridge replied. "I think this was taken… last summer. I can't be sure, you understand. But those colorful paper ribbons in the background, on the branches of the trees, they were used last year in our Litha celebration."

"Okay." Gus pointed at the picture, and Niall knew who he was pointing at. "And this person? Do you know him?"

Kittridge chewed on his bottom lip, again appearing reflective. "I think… yes, he used to come here, but quite irregularly. Haven't seen him in a long time, though. Oh, what was his name? Ken… maybe?"

Niall nodded inwardly. He and Gus didn't know much about Autumnsong, but he had revealed to Gus his first name: Kin, an Asian name. They had no idea what his surname was. Two murder cases, both involving Autumnsong to an extent, and they had virtually nothing to go on. Perhaps this time they would gain more information.

Although to be fair, Autumnsong hadn't been the killer in either case.

Kittridge regarded Gus with curiosity. "Is he a person of interest?"

"Which of you three identified the body as that of Rowan Tuff?" Hughes cut in with perfect timing. Niall could have kissed him. None of them had any answers about Autumnsong, so the less said, the better.

"I didn't," Kittridge replied, looking away from the blackened crime scene. "I think it was Jacob who told us it had to be Rowan. I seem to recall he recognized the clothes on the… uh, on the body. What Rowan wore, that is."

"And Bodhi?" Niall asked.

Kittridge sounded chagrined as he shook his head. "I honestly don't remember much of the details. The sight of his…. Shock, I think, has done an excellent job at erasing those gruesome images. I'm sorry I can't be more helpful." He shuddered visibly and hugged himself, his gaze still wandering everywhere except to the stained platform.

Niall could relate. When one saw a dead body for the first time, especially someone they knew, it could be a traumatic experience. It wasn't like watching a movie, where the act of seeing through a TV or a silver screen created distance, turning even the most gruesome scene clinical and senseless.

"I'm sorry. Please excuse me." Kittridge started to walk away. Whether he intended to remain close-by or vanish to the nearest bar was anybody's guess.

Niall inched closer to Gus, who watched Kittridge's retreat with a frown on his brow. "You okay, babe?"

Gus started and then nodded quickly, flashing a smile that did little to convince Niall of Gus's state of mind. "Yes, sure. Just… a lot, you know." Gus shook his head, and his gaze veered back to the platform. "Don't you think it's odd that the platform, which is constructed with planks, didn't burn to a cinder along with the body?"

"Good catch, kid," Hughes said, a faint smile briefly gracing his lips. "We noticed that too. It seems the platform had been doused with water. Plus, the body didn't have time to burn for very long. Marlowe and Bodhi smothered the flames with a fire blanket from a nearby station."

Niall rubbed his jaw, a scratching sound from his stubble loud in his ears. "Does that mean that the murderer didn't want to start a wildfire? How considerate of him or her. So, not your garden variety pyromaniac, then."

"No. I think… what if the killer didn't want to destroy the sun altar?" Gus suggested, a casual shrug following his words. "That would suggest this place holds special significance to him. He could be a believer who didn't want to destroy a place of worship."

"One of the faeries, then." Niall gave both Gus and Hughes a questioning look to see if they agreed. Neither of them showed any signs of dissent, so he turned back to Gus. "Do all these faeries worship the sun?"

Again Gus shrugged. "I don't know. I'm not an expert on this group. But… if they are anything like typical neo-pagans, their beliefs are highly individualized. Each person has their own personal faith that could differ vastly from the beliefs of others."

Hughes let out a long breath. "Great. I'd hoped your expertise might help me eliminate suspects, not increase their numbers."

Gus looked crestfallen, so Niall took his hand and squeezed. His action was rewarded by a soft smile. "Virg, you saying all these twenty-two people are still suspects? You weren't able to narrow the suspect pool even a little bit?"

"No, that's not what I'm saying… Junior." Hughes's glare could have started a few fires on its own. Niall merely chuckled, as much as he detested the nickname. "There were several we could confidently rule out. Half-a-dozen musicians by the fire pit, a couple of performance artists dancing in full view, and five other people in the, uh…." Hughes's cheeks turned bright scarlet as he blushed, and he coughed in discomfort, like he had a bad taste in his mouth. "Five people were in the, uh… uh, in the love shack, engaged in, um… extracurricular activities. With digital recording devices, no less."

Niall had a hard time containing his laughter. He had to bite down hard. Love shack? Five men orgies? He could get down with this kind of spirituality. Wisely he left that unsaid.

Gus, however, was a different story. "They have a love shack here also? It seems they have reconstructed much of the Wolf Creek Sanctuary down south, with disparate altars and shrines placed throughout the grounds, greenhouses, and love shacks and offices all present. The owner of the land, Jacob Marlowe, must have visited that site and recreated it here."

"Fascinating," Hughes grunted, clearly not meaning it. "In any case, we could rule out seventeen people who were pretty much constantly in plain sight or not gone long enough to make it to the sun altar, let alone beat Tuff to death and then torch him."

Niall did the math. "That leaves five unaccounted for. Who are they?"

Hughes checked his notes. "Hang on a bit. Jacob Marlowe, Bodhi Jha, Alex Kittridge, Ethan Sadler, and Quentin Cross. Of these five,

Sadler is another caretaker, and Cross is an event organizer. According to the deputy here—" Hughes thumbed at the officer standing beside him, who puffed his chest in pride, beaming. "—none of them have solid alibis. According to their statements, Marlowe was meditating at the Gaia altar. It's located at the other end of the grounds from the sun altar, so basically farthest away. Bodhi was tending the greenhouse, Kittridge was reading and doing research in the office, Sadler was changing sheets in the barn—apparently that's their communal dormitory—and Cross was arranging the stage area for a midnight theatrical performance of… wait, I got it.… *Bathhouse: The Musical.* Don't ask me what the heck that is, I only know it was supposed to be done in drag." He shrugged, closing the notebook.

"At what time was the body found?" Niall asked.

"Just before 11:00 p.m.," Hughes replied. "By then it'd been dark for about two hours. Sunset was around nine last night. And Tuff was last seen just before nine."

Niall pondered all that he'd heard. "So of the twenty-two people on the grounds that night—sorry, twenty-three if we include the deceased—six were alone. One ended up dead, and the rest have no verifiable alibis and no witnesses to their whereabouts."

"All that is important, of course," Gus interjected softly. "But I'm more interested in the oddities plaguing this case. The bloodied necklace, for one. Is it coincidence that the symbol of the necklace matches the sun altar where Tuff was murdered? Did Tuff foresee his own death? And if so, why did he buy the necklace? A hint or a warning, maybe? And most importantly, if he knew he was in danger, why didn't he run?"

"I take it you don't believe in coincidences?" Niall commented, giving Gus an amused glance. Gus had an uncanny way of combining disparate elements to form a cohesive whole. Niall could do that too, but to a lesser extent.

Gus shook his head. "No. Too farfetched. Even though… accidents do happen. I just think it's unlikely in this instance. What do you think?"

Niall shrugged. "I'll reserve judgment till we get lab results on the blood."

Hughes checked the screen of his cell phone. "No news yet. But I expect I'll hear from them soon about the blood tests to see if the blood on the necklace and the blood from the body do in fact match."

"Even if they do, that just raises more questions instead of answering them," Gus said. "Why would Rowan's blood be on the necklace? Did he put it there himself, or did someone else do it for him? Either way, why do that at all? And why send the damn thing to *me*? I didn't even know Rowan."

"Whoa, babe." Niall stopped Gus's flood of questions with a gentle chuckle. "We'll get to the bottom of things. No need to go off the deep end just yet, okay?" He glanced at Hughes. "So what's next?"

"Interviewing the suspects." Hughes's steadfast voice gave Niall a much-needed boost in confidence. They would figure out the truth, find the killer, and make it home for dinner.

Although that was mostly wishful thinking.

"So Detective Hughes doesn't think it's possible that an outsider could have come into the grounds and killed Rowan?" Gus asked, his concerned gaze landing squarely on Niall as they walked downhill toward the office.

Niall frowned. "Sure, it's within the realm of possibilities. But also improbable. We're far away from any major thoroughfares or towns, so it's unlikely for a murderer to just happen to find this place, stop by long enough to commit murder, and then disappear without a trace."

"But according to the news and statistics and whatnot, there are literally thousands of serial killers in this country alone, prowling for unsuspecting victims."

Gus's insistent voice and his one-sided reasoning suggested he would have preferred the killer to be an outsider or, more to the point, a nonfaerie. Niall understood Gus's need. It was hard to imagine someone you knew or someone who shared your values and faith had committed such an atrocity as murder.

"The actual number of currently active serial killers is closer to fifty, according to the FBI," Niall countered. "With that in mind, how probable is it that one happened to come to the sanctuary on the day a man bought a necklace with the same symbol on it as the place where he was killed?" Niall hoped Gus would see that the odds of that happening were slim indeed.

Gus's smooth brow furrowed as he seemed to ponder the reply. He worried his lower lip, and Niall knew it wouldn't be long now. Then Gus sighed. "Not very. Oh, I guess you're right." He sounded positively depressed, and Niall hated raining on his parade.

"Hughes isn't ruling out anything at this stage, though," he said to cheer Gus up.

Gus smiled shortly back at him, gratitude shining in his green eyes. "Thanks, honey." Niall knew he would come to like and even appreciate the endearment.

They arrived at the footpath leading to the office, garden, and the dormitory, and Niall heard a commotion ahead. He hurried his steps, followed quickly by Gus and Hughes.

In front of the office stood a crowd, all speaking at once. On the cabin's porch, trying in vain to calm down the roaring mob, stood a man unlike any Niall had ever seen (he didn't attend Pride parades, which probably accounted for his cluelessness). Immediately upon laying eyes on the man, Niall knew he could be no other than Jacob Marlowe.

Incredibly tall, at least six foot six, and quite broad and bulging, the big bear of a man must have been in his late fifties or early sixties. His silvery hair had to be long or a wig because it was gathered on top of his head in a complex, Geisha-style coiffure. He had heavy eye makeup and painted lips, but Niall was distracted from the female impression by the presence of a trimmed gray beard and gray chest hairs. Completing the Japanese fashion statement was a simple and subdued, plain, dark blue silk men's kimono, tied with an obi sash, and he wore wooden flip-flops.

As he got closer, Niall observed Marlowe's tanned, craggy skin, hinting an outdoorsy and healthy lifestyle. Due to the hue of his skin, his big, ice-blue eyes flashed arrestingly, catching everyone's attention.

"Calm down, people." Marlowe had a deep voice, so hoarse it reverberated in Niall's rib cage like a powerful bass. Niall actually stopped dead in his tracks to hear better and not miss a single word. "I have been informed by the police that this sanctuary might not be safe for us anymore. To that effect, I humbly request you all return to your homes for the duration of this time of crisis."

An uproar of disagreement followed. Clearly the twenty-one men in the crowd didn't share Marlowe's concern for their continued safety. Out of the corner of his eye, Niall observed Gus give the people a sympathetic look. Gus obviously empathized with their plight. But unlike Gus, Niall tended to listen to the voice of logic over sentiment. The police couldn't guarantee the safety and well-being of this group, so those no longer viewed as persons of interest had to see reason and leave the area.

Marlowe brought his arms up, without a word, and the crowd quieted again. An awe-inspiring feat, Niall thought. "I know how you feel, believe me. I hate the idea of leaving our home and haven as much as you. But… I will *not* jeopardize any of you. I refuse to do so under the guise of preserving our faith, integrity, or freedom of choice. Losing any of you to this vile murderer…. I could not bear that. Please, do not ask that of me."

The group had gone eerily quiet, their gestures sedate and their gazes lowered. Clearly Marlowe's words had sunk in. Niall's disposition toward the leader of the Radical Faeries had risen up several notches.

"Thank you all for your friendship, love, and loyalty," Marlowe said, his booming tone reaching everyone with ease, and he rested his hand over his heart. "Go safely."

"Hold on, folks." Hughes stepped up, and everyone turned to him. "You are all indeed advised to vacate the premises—except for the following individuals: Jacob Marlowe, Bodhi Jha, Alex Kittridge, Ethan Sadler, and Quentin Cross. Thank you."

Muted murmurs spread as the group slowly embraced one another and dispersed toward the dormitory. A few with backpacks already to hand headed toward the entrance to the estate. No public dissent or resistance appeared. Niall attributed the new mellow ambience and full obedience to Marlowe's gift as a speaker.

A heavy silence, tense with anticipation, descended upon the remaining few until only Niall, Gus, Hughes, and the five suspects were left.

Chapter 8

THOSE LEFT by the office were a motley crew indeed, Gus thought, not knowing whether to laugh, cry, or stand still. Marlowe's Japanese style, mixing male and female, was impeccable, but the others present weren't short on innovative dressing either.

Bodhi Jha had changed from his previous tank top and shorts to brown leather pants and nothing more. He now resembled a Native American. He even had white-and-red war paint all over his bare upper torso, the patterns matching the lines and curves of his tattoos. With his waist-length dreadlocks and exotic features, he was truly a sight to see.

Ethan Sadler was the cutest little twink Gus had ever seen. Probably thanks to the big gossamer rainbow-colored butterfly wings on his back and garland of flowers over his fair hair. Like a perfect little fairy prince, Ethan had glitter all over his face, body, and wings in addition to the soft pastel-hued makeup. Whatever he did for a living, it clearly didn't include a lot of time outdoors, because he was quite pale. He wore a skimpy, glittering thong, and nothing else. At least he had no prosthetics on his ears to complete the elvish impression.

As for Quentin Cross, the best word to describe him was definitely *flaming*. And not just because he was gay, but because of his drag costume. The mass of hair, bright fire-engine red, that framed the sides of his face and cascaded down to his waist in gentle waves had to be a wig, Gus thought—partly in envy as he liked the color. Cross's skintight dress was an equally burning red, bedecked with sequins and jewelry that sparkled under the sunlight. The dress must have had padding since his bosom and hips appeared rounder than was normal for men. On his cheeks he had red, heart-shaped skin decorations. He was a drag queen of the highest caliber: stunning.

Only Alex stood apart from the others in his regular, even boring, attire. Perhaps he'd been honest when he'd claimed he'd not gone native, Gus pondered, not yet convinced one way or another.

Hughes made no move to separate the members of the group for individual grilling. He clearly intended to question them together here rather than back at the station. Maybe he thought they might have less time to work on a unified front or an outright fabrication if he didn't give them time to match up their stories. It was possible they might unintentionally give something away or trip each other up if Hughes questioned them now while they were still shocked by the realization that they were the only suspects. Or at least that was what Gus assumed, not being an expert on police procedures.

"Mr. Marlowe?" Hughes asked, and the tall, muscular man in the kimono nodded in a regal manner. "At the time of the murder, between 9:00 and 11:00 p.m., you were meditating at a Gaia altar."

Marlowe nodded again, his hands tucked into his sleeves and settled over his stomach. "That's correct. The altar is situated at the southwesternmost corner of the sanctuary grounds, by the sweat lodge and sun deck. The path passes the barn and forks in two, one leading to the office and gate out of the grounds, the other heading to the lake and the northern altars and shrines."

Alex stepped forward and extended papers to Gus, Niall, and Hughes. "Jacob asked me to print out maps of the area for you so you can get more familiar with the full estate."

Alex smiled sweetly at Gus as he handed him the map. But Gus found it hard to return the gesture. Too much water under that bridge. Gus had said his good-byes to Alex in absentia, and he saw no reason to get back on friendly terms with an ex. Alex hadn't been a bad lover, but his first and only love had been his career. That wouldn't have changed even if Gus had waited for him. So becoming a friend with an old flame, not to mention someone whose priorities were never going to veer away from the me-myself-and-I path, didn't seem like a good idea.

Instead, Gus focused on the map. The entrance gate was to the south. To the west were the office, the outside garden area, the stage, barn, communal composting toilets, chicken coup and geese corrals, crop circle, sweat lodge, sun deck, solar shower, the lake, and numerous shrines and altars beyond the tree line. To the east were the greenhouse, several individual guest log cabins, tent camping area, the pump house, and even more altars and shrines in the woods. In the center of the grounds was the fire pit, dominating the area of collective activities.

Gus was pleased to see that the Radical Faeries of the Mount Paradise Sanctuary employed a multitude of green technologies and ecological methods of sustainable living. That was one of the characteristics of their lifestyle, and Gus applauded each and every one them.

"Did anyone see you at the shrine?" Hughes asked.

Marlowe frowned, seemingly concentrating on recollections. Then he slowly shook his head. "No.... At least I don't think so. I was busy meditating. My method includes chanting with my eyes closed, so I had no way of detecting if anyone was present."

"And how long were you, um… meditating?" Hughes continued dryly, scribbling in his notebook.

"I opened the night's festivities by lighting the bonfire," Marlowe replied. "That must have been around, say… eight, eight thirty? Thereabouts. I sang a song or two with the musicians and then headed directly to the Gaia altar." He gestured toward Ethan. "As I went, I saw Ethan here entering the barn with an armful of fresh linens. I think we waved at each other but then went on our separate ways."

Ethan nodded, a sleek little gesture, his slender frame shivering as he hugged himself. "Yes, I saw Jacob heading down the path, past the sun deck we use for sunbathing. We don't have a lot of clocks here on the premises, except for the office, but I'm pretty sure it was around 9:00 p.m., or close to." He shrugged casually.

Gus was inclined to believe both men. Nothing in their words stuck out, and their body language suggested they had nothing to hide. Of course, Gus was experienced enough to know that everyone had secrets. But that didn't mean those same concealed issues had anything to do with the murder. More often than not, they didn't.

Then again, secrets were not acceptable in an active murder case. Not for those investigating, anyway. Niall and Hughes would prod and poke till they got their answers.

"And you, Mr. Sadler, you were at the barn?" Hughes commented, his eyes narrowed in suspicion. "For two hours?"

Ethan blushed fiercely, and Gus knew to expect a revelation. "I, uh… I…." He let out a deep sigh, slumping. "I didn't spend the whole time in the barn, no."

"Where were you, then?" Niall asked, his tone cool and composed. Gus suddenly wanted him in the worst way possible. They should have fucked in the shower before Hughes came to collect them for the car trip. Gus itched to get his hands on a naked Niall. Soon, he promised himself.

Ethan fidgeted in place. The wings on his back fluttered. "I was... I went out the backdoor of the barn and then sneaked into the... the love shack," he confessed, so utterly embarrassed by it that Gus had to suppress a chuckle at the cute, endearing sight. "I didn't do anything. I just... I just watched. That's all."

Gus saw Niall and Hughes exchange glances. None of them needed reminding that at the love shack, during the time of the murder, there had been a five-man orgy going on.

Marlowe placed a big, callused hand over Ethan's lean shoulder. "Oh, Ethan, if you'd wanted to, you could have joined in. Anytime you wish. I'm sure none of them would've minded."

Ethan seemed ready to be swallowed by the earth. "I... I'm not ready to... to do that. Not yet. Maybe... one day?"

Marlowe nodded and smiled encouragingly, even quite paternally. "There's always a place for you here, Ethan. In any activity you wish to participate in—be it planting seeds at the greenhouse or getting your cock sucked at the love shack." He patted Ethan's shoulder, and the young man seemed much appeased and comforted.

Gus glanced surreptitiously at Hughes, who looked about ready to pass out, his cheeks ruddy and his gaze aimed anywhere but at the young novice and his mentor.

"Can anyone, uh... corroborate your story?" Hughes asked, clearing his throat several times for good measure.

Ethan shook his head at first. Then he worried his bottom lip. "At first I looked from the outside, through a crack in the planks. But then I... I snuck in. And they were filming the, uh... the whole scene, so... I might show up on camera?" He shrugged again, his eyes big and wide, like those of a child wondering at the beauties of the world, innocent and pure as the driven snow.

Hughes harrumphed. But Gus guessed the detective wrote down and remembered every little detail and would verify their accuracy at his earliest convenience. "Okay. What about you, Dr. Kittridge?"

Alex thumbed back over his shoulder. "I was inside, in the office. But I did attend the opening ceremony when the bonfire was lit. So I must have gotten to the office some time after nine o'clock. There is a clock on the wall there, but I'm afraid I didn't really look." He pointed at Bodhi. "Just as I went in, however, I saw Bodhi head up the path toward the greenhouse."

"But the same path goes past the greenhouse and up to the hills where the sun altar is," Niall commented, quirking an eyebrow. Gus heard the hard edge in his boyfriend's voice and had a hunch Niall wasn't taken with Alex the same way Gus had once been. Then again, Gus himself had gotten past that stage in his life. He couldn't blame Niall for his cool approach. Gus had to show Niall that he had no reason for jealousy.

Bodhi growled and spoke through gritted teeth. "Yeah, the path goes to lots of places. But I went nowhere except for the greenhouse. Tomatoes are in season."

"You mean it took you two hours to harvest them?" Hughes asked incredulously.

Bodhi growled. "Yes. I dug around in the dirt for the better part of two hours, planting seeds and harvesting ripe vegetables for the Lughnasadh festival to come in a few days' time. And in between I said several prayers to Mother Earth in thanks for her abundant bounty. I can show you the calluses and blisters on my hands, the soil and dirt on my clothes, and the baskets and buckets full of fresh produce. All proof of my hard work."

His antagonistic tone made Gus cringe inwardly. Nothing aroused a policeman's doubt and ire like a hostile demeanor. The trouble was, Gus understood why Bodhi felt the way he did. Bodhi had plenty of reasons to have experienced prejudice and hatred: the caramel color of his skin, the Goddess faith he followed, and the gay sexual orientation he was born with. Undoubtedly Bodhi Jha had known persecution by haters many times over.

Being suspected of murder was just another slight in a long line of insults for him.

Gus saw Hughes grimacing and knew the situation would go rapidly downhill if the detective spoke.

So he rushed to speak himself. "Working with the earth is a noble pursuit." Gus smiled a little, and Bodhi did indeed stop scowling, his attention veering from Hughes to Gus. "Not a single accusation is being made. Not even the gods and goddesses are omnipotent and all-seeing. Mortals are no better. These police officers' only goal is to find a brutal murderer who took the life of one of your friends. They intend no insult. All of us here seek the truth, in one form or another. That is what matters."

Bodhi stared at Gus for a long time, wearing a frown. His expression turned stony and then relaxed. He inclined his head with a curt nod. "I understand. We all serve the Goddess and the greater good." His calmer gaze returned to Hughes. "I have no witnesses to the time I spent alone in the greenhouse. But I was there. And… I had no reason to wish Rowan dead." Bodhi lifted his chin, seemingly in an act of defiance. But Gus saw unshed tears glistening in his eyes. "Rowan… he was my brother."

Frowning, Niall drew in a breath. "You two look nothing alike."

Bodhi's eyes burned with ice-cold flames as he glared at Niall, his sullen mood clearly making a reappearance. "Rowan and I are—I mean, *were* foster brothers. We grew up in the same household in Honolulu. We might not have shared flesh and blood, but we shared everything else. I would never have killed him. I loved him."

Swiveling on his heels, Bodhi turned away, bowing his head. His body shook, and Gus felt for him. The loss of a sibling must be one of the worst things in the world. Gus was an only child, so he didn't know what that kind of sorrow would feel like. But he had an inkling the pain was terrible and soul-shattering.

Niall and Hughes exchanged glances again. Gus had no doubt they would revisit this issue soon too.

Then Hughes turned his attention to Quentin Cross. "And you, Mr. Cross, were…?"

Quentin, in his female persona, nodded, his long red hair waving about. "I was making sure the stage was ready for the midnight performance. You see, we're doing a musical of…." His voice faded as he gulped, his long red lashes fluttering. "*Were* doing a musical. It was supposed to be shown at midnight. We had done the rehearsals during the day, so now all we needed was to get the place ready for the show. Ethan here had promised to assist me once he'd finished his duties at the barn. Much of the stage area was already completed. Only a few last touches were necessary. A bit of flowers and clothing arrangements, that sort of thing."

Gus didn't know if it was the feminine role Quentin played or a natural gift, but he had a beautiful, melodious voice. Were he a singer, he would undoubtedly be a success. If Quentin performed in drag shows, he could have easily used his real voice instead of a recording.

"This stage is indoors?" Hughes asked for specifics.

"Its structure is very much like that of a barn," Quentin explained, pointing his sharp-nailed finger past the office and up the path toward the barn. "It's indoors, yes, but the wide double doors can be opened, and the front half of the roof can be pulled aside with a crank so it becomes an outdoor stage."

"And were the doors open when you started working there?" Hughes asked.

"No, not yet." Quentin shook his head, pursing his luscious lips. For such a lanky man, he had extremely full and pouty lips, Gus thought, watching the man closely. "I wasn't going to do that until I had the stage prepped and ready to go. You see, the theme of the musical wasn't common knowledge, as it was meant to be a surprise." His shoulders sagged, and he appeared crestfallen. "I came outside to open the doors when I heard the commotion in front of the office. Apparently Alex, Bodhi, and Jacob had found… Rowan."

Like the others, Quentin looked positively ill saying the words, his face pale but going green, and he held on to his stomach like he felt it churning.

It seemed all the prime suspects had been close to Rowan and loved him or considered him a friend faerie, not someone who should be killed. Gus usually had a good sense when people were lying to him. In this instance, though, he had no clue as to which of these unusual, but kind and polite, men might have done the dastardly deed.

Evidently the investigation had only just begun.

And in the heart of the case stood Alex, a man Gus had once seen as a potential mate for life, despite Alex's shortcomings. Gus had a terrible feeling things would only get worse before they got any better.

Chapter 9

"WHAT DID you think of their statements?" Gus asked Niall and Hughes once they were back in the car and on the scenic mountain road back to Tacoma.

Niall sat in the backseat again, lounging sideways. "You mean did Virg or I think one or more or all of them are liars?" After Gus confirmed this with a nod, Niall shrugged. "Too soon to say. None of them seem to have firm alibis. Then again, none of them appear to have any clear-cut motives either. We need to know much more about the victim, his background, and his last known whereabouts."

Gus listened carefully. He'd often wondered why Niall had chosen to become a private investigator instead of a cop, like his father, Owain. Instead, Niall had a military background, and he had never gone the police route. Niall had the same kind of discipline and procedural habits as a lot of cops. And yet he wasn't one of them. To Gus, that was curious. But Niall rarely liked to talk about his life choices. He wasn't the kind of man who second-guessed a single decision he had ever made.

Hughes's cell phone beeped and, while driving, he flipped the lid open. Then he let out an unsurprised grunt. "The two blood samples— one from the necklace you received, the other from the body—they're a match."

Niall whistled low from the backseat. "It's really Rowan Tuff, then."

But Gus frowned, far from convinced. "How do we know that? I mean, just because a man matching the description of Rowan Tuff bought a similar necklace, delivered it to me bloodied, and then got beaten into a pulp, none of that means we have a positive identification."

Niall shifted in his seat and sounded skeptical. "You think we're being messed with? That the body isn't in fact Tuff's?"

"One of the prime suspects, Jacob Marlowe, identified the body, or what was left of it, by his clothes. Never mind any possible motives he might have. But just because we were told that the body belongs to Rowan Tuff and because the blood samples match, that's why we assume the body is Rowan's. That's weird roundabout thinking. What if the body isn't Rowan?"

Hughes sighed. "The kid's got a point there, Junior. We need a better ID of the body if we are to conclusively state that it's Rowan Tuff."

"Did Rowan live full-time at the sanctuary, or did he have a house or an apartment in the city?" Gus asked, pleased that his voice and opinion had been heard.

"We're looking into that," Hughes replied succinctly and then shut up.

Gus decided to do the same. The two-hour car trip soon had him nodding off.

They had almost reached Tacoma by the time Gus flinched awake to the buzzing of his cell phone in his jeans pocket. As he pressed the light on behind the screen to see who had texted him, he saw instead that his house alarm had been triggered.

"Oh my God," he called out, straightening up on his seat and simultaneously startling the other two men inside the car. "Niall, someone's in our house."

GUS HAD expected Hughes to carry a sidearm. But he was ill prepared to see Niall take out a gun from a back holster, previously hidden by his leather jacket. Gus couldn't but wonder how many other concealed weapons Niall had on him.

The shop front and back doors were locked tight, and the alarm there uninterrupted. But the side door on the second floor, the apartment floor, was unlocked. A silent alarm had been triggered, and a cop car sent on its way, but Hughes had called it off.

Hughes first, Niall second, and Gus holding the rear, they ascended the wooden stairs by the side of the building. Since it was late summer, the end of July, it was still light outside when they'd parked by the sidewalk. They had no cover of darkness to conceal their approach. The porch light above the landing and the door cast a mellow glow anyway.

As Hughes gently pushed the door farther ajar with his foot, Niall waved Gus to a crouch. "Stay down. Stay here. I'll come back for you." Niall's firm tone indicated he would entertain no arguments from Gus.

Thankfully Gus had already decided to hang back since he was the only one unarmed, so he merely nodded in reply.

Hughes and Niall vanished into the shadows of the house. Gus waited for their return with bated breath, half-crouched, half-sitting on the stairs, one butt cheek on a step, the other not. He fidgeted in place, unsure whether hearing shots, shouts, or nothing at all was a good sign or a bad one. Time seemed to slow to a snail's pace, and Gus started to speculate whether he should follow the men inside. He might not be able to help them in a gunfight, but he could guard their rear.

Just as Gus rose, Niall peeked out from the threshold. "Come on in, babe. Everything's clear." He shook his head, clearly dismayed. "You'll never believe who's broken in here—and who's still here. Take a wild guess, I dare you." Niall's pursed lips and knowingly quirked eyebrow told Gus the whole story before he even stepped inside.

Gus hurried inside past Niall. Hughes stood in the living room, his weapon holstered, so apparently there was no real threat. Gus understood why once he walked into the room.

Huddled into the far corner, a bottle of red wine tucked against his chest, sat none other than Autumnsong, crying. Occasionally he hiccupped. Judging from the mere inch of garnet liquid in the bottom of the bottle, he'd downed most of the wine already. Another empty bottle lay beside him.

Gus glanced over at his spring-green liquor cabinet. He wasn't much of a drinker, so not much had been in the cabinet to begin with. The doors with steel mesh windows hung open to show where Autumnsong had gotten in and taken what he needed.

Bewildered, Gus glanced at Hughes, then at Niall. Both men shrugged, saying nothing. Gus could relate. What the hell was Autumnsong doing here?

As usual, Autumnsong wore black—from his skintight jeans to his body-hugging tank top. His black feather boa sat discarded next to him, which was uncharacteristic. Makeup trailed down his cheeks as he blubbered, mostly silently. His shoulders shimmied as a new flood of tears fell from his eyes.

In short, the usually devious twink appeared more than crestfallen; he was utterly despondent.

Gus had never seen Autumnsong display any emotion other than disdain, so this was a novel experience. And an awkward one at that.

Seeing Autumnsong, such a strong, forceful young man, so miserable was hard on Gus—even though he wasn't sure if Autumnsong was a friend or a foe.

Gus knelt in front of Autumnsong. "Hey," he murmured softly, placing his hand gently on Autumnsong's knee, making him start. "You okay?"

The young Asian let out a watery bark of cold laughter. "Great." He downed a gulp of wine, a few errant droplets falling from the sides of his mouth. "Awesome. Fabulous." Then he began to weep again, tremors wracking his slender frame, and he buried his face in his hands.

Shocked at the sight, Gus glanced at Niall over his shoulder, pleading for help. Niall coughed to clear his throat and then crouched next to Gus. He extended his hand, as though he were planning on touching Autumnsong, but then he retracted it.

"Hey, Autumnsong," Niall said quietly, his manner reassuring. Gus was grateful as he was well aware Niall didn't trust Autumnsong as far as he could throw him. "Maybe you've had enough, don't you think?" He gripped the bottle Autumnsong was hugging but didn't try to pull it away.

Slowly Autumnsong lifted his head and looked up at Niall, his gaze beseeching. Niall patted Autumnsong's arm and smiled briefly. Finally, apparently after some soul searching, Autumnsong relinquished his hold on the bottle, and Niall was able to take it from his hands.

"I'm so sorry for breaking in," Autumnsong muttered between sobs, wiping his nose and eyes with the back of his hands and making an even bigger mess of his smudged makeup. "I was just so lost, you see. My Ro-Ro… I miss you so much."

Hughes shifted to stand behind Niall, leaned down, and whispered in his ear loud enough for Gus to hear, "I'm, uh, gonna head out, Junior. See you all tomorrow." He slipped out quietly, leaving Gus alone with Niall and the bereft Autumnsong.

Gus knew what he had to do. "Kin? We have a spare room here. Stay the night. Stay as long as you need to. You're safe here with us, okay?"

Niall's widened eyes and gaping mouth spoke volumes about his level of surprise, but Gus refused to allow Niall's reaction to deter him. Autumnsong's allegiances were unknown to them, but at the moment he had clearly hit rock bottom, and Gus wasn't the type to kick a man when he was down.

Autumnsong stared at Gus with bloodshot eyes wet with tears. "R-really…?"

Gus nodded firmly. "Absolutely. You're welcome to stay here. I know this may sound like a cliché, but things will look brighter tomorrow, after a good night's sleep." Gently he nudged at Autumnsong's arm, and the young man stumbled to his feet, swaying as though he hadn't slept in ages.

Silently Gus escorted Autumnsong to the guest bedroom. Without a word he helped the poor soul out of his tight clothes and tucked him under the blanket in his underwear. He didn't kiss Autumnsong on the forehead, though he was tempted. For the first time since they had known each other, Gus saw Autumnsong differently: as a frail human being. And whether he liked it or not, he empathized.

Gus closed the bedroom door with a soft snick, and only then did he let out the breath he'd been holding. He slumped against the wall, feeling as tired as Autumnsong undoubtedly did.

"You really are the best person I've ever known." Niall's whisper sounded loud in the quiet, snapping Gus out of his stupor. "No one else would have offered shelter to his… enemy might be pushing it, so… dubious acquaintance? That works. This was a kind thing you did, babe. I'm proud of you."

Gus let Niall pull him into a hug, their bodies flush against each other, and butterflies danced in his belly, quickly rising toward a fevered frenzy of arousal and lust.

"Hold that thought for a minute or two, okay?" Gus requested softly. "I want to check with Izzy that the day's gone well at the shop."

Niall released him with a smile and headed toward the foyer, most likely to reset the alarm code and to ensure the place was locked up tight.

Meanwhile, Gus called Izzy, who told him everything had been smooth sailing, that the cashbox and receipts were secure in the safe, and that he would be available for additional part-time work in the future. Relieved, Gus headed to the master bedroom in search of Niall.

GUS FOUND Niall slowly undressing. He always folded his clothes neatly on the chair by the window. He wasn't one for clutter. A habit ingrained in him from his military days, Gus surmised, and he appreciated the precision and cleanliness.

Niall apparently heard him come in because he asked, "That blowup at the sanctuary, babe… what was all that about?"

Gus swallowed. "I love nature. You… don't."

Niall gave him a quizzical look. "What's that supposed to mean? I don't mind nature. I've been known to go hiking in the Cascades from time to time. Good workout."

Gus's jaw dropped. "But… but at the sanctuary you said… you said you hated bugs, and you didn't want to trek uphill, and you didn't want to eat any blueberries."

Niall chuckled. "Yeah. But to be frank, babe, I said those things where someone had been gruesomely murdered. Understandable, don't you think? I was predisposed to dislike the whole place. As for blueberries, well, I'm more of a raspberry kind of guy. And bugs, who the heck likes bugs?"

Perhaps Gus had overreacted. He didn't know much about Niall's hobbies because he worked such long hours and rarely had time for hobbies outside of his workouts at the gym. Maybe he owed Niall an apology for being so judgmental. But Niall just laughed in a sexy tone, and Gus forgot what he'd been about to say.

Gus yanked his own shirt off, tossed it onto the other chair, popped the buttons on his fly open, and plopped down on the bed. By then Niall was in his underwear, so Gus gripped the waistband and pulled the gorgeous hunk on top of him. Gus spread his legs, and Niall settled between his thighs, resting his weight on his straightened arms, braced on either side of Gus's body. Their hardening cocks aligned even through the layers of fabric, and their hips shimmied in unified rhythm as Niall dipped his head down and they kissed.

Niall immediately assumed control of the kiss. He wiggled his tongue past Gus's lips and plunged it inside his mouth, tasting and licking Gus's own. Gus pushed his hips up to meet Niall's, needing more and wanting everything. The day had been exhausting, but lovemaking with Niall was never a hardship or a chore.

Unfortunately, the thought of the day's events brought a clear image of Alex unbidden to Gus's mind's eye. His kiss stuttered, and he had to turn his head away to force the picture of his ex out of his consciousness. Gus wanted to be encompassed by Niall, inside and out, and Alex's image did not help.

"Babe, you okay?" Niall asked, caressing Gus's cheek.

Gus loved Niall's kindness, consideration, and heart more than anything. So why was he thinking about Alex? They had parted ways so long ago it was practically another lifetime. There was no cause for these musings.

"I'm fine," Gus said, for the first time lying to Niall. He pulled Niall down for another kiss but it felt all wrong. Guilt ate him up inside, and he stopped again, sighing in desperation. Alex didn't matter; memories of him mattered even less.

Niall rubbed his nose on Gus's cheek. "It's been a long day. Let's take a shower and go to bed." Niall started to pull off Gus, who panicked and grabbed him, yanking him back down again. "Gus, what the hell?"

Gus closed his eyes and let go of his boyfriend. "I'm sorry, Niall. I didn't want to think about him, but he just popped in there."

Much to his surprise, Niall chuckled. "I figured Alex wouldn't slip your mind easily. I bet seeing him disturbed you. I saw it in your eyes."

Gus looked up at Niall. "I'd put him behind me. I don't spend time wondering what he might be up to, where he could be, or who he might be with. He's not a part of my life anymore. So why am I thinking about him? And here in our home, of all places?"

Niall shrugged. "He's a part of your past. If you hadn't met him, you wouldn't be the man you are today. You could be someone entirely different, and you and I might never have met at all."

Gus shuddered in sudden fear. "I'd hate that. I love you."

Niall kissed him tenderly. "I know that, babe. I don't doubt that." Then he slid his hand lower, over Gus's belly, and gripped Gus's cock, a slow and steady stroke making Gus shiver. "And I bet I can make you forget all about him."

Niall wasn't wrong. He delivered on his promise and sent Gus into orbit in a haze of sensual pleasure. Niall seemed to be everywhere at once. He threaded through Gus's hair with the fingers of one hand, while his other hand ghosted over Gus's back and then returned to fist Gus's cock. Niall's touches were enhanced by his scent and taste filling Gus's whole world, Niall's flavor in Gus's mouth and his aroused body odor in Gus's nostrils enflaming him into a firestorm of desire. Niall licked his way down the column of Gus's neck, suckling softly and marking him. Gus wound his arms around Niall and raked his nails over the broad, muscular back.

Niall was strong; he could handle many things Gus couldn't. Like carrying the unsettling memories of Gus's past lover, who no longer had a place in Gus's life. The image of Alex had been just a flicker, nothing more. A mirage that vanished in the heat of Niall's kisses.

Niall licked around Gus's nipple, tongued its shape, nipped it lightly with his teeth, then pulled it between his lips with gentle suction. Gus moaned and arched into him, wordlessly begging for more. Flicking his tongue here and there, Niall hungrily lapped at Gus's skin, his chest and then his abdomen, dipping lower with each new openmouthed smooch.

When Niall took Gus's cockhead in his mouth and sucked, Gus cried out—and slapped a hand fast over his mouth. Good Goddess, they had a houseguest.

"Oops. Think he woke up?" he asked, worried.

Niall laughed. "I'm pretty sure Autumnsong's seen and heard his share of sex stuff and noises. Forget about him. Concentrate on me."

To reinforce his demands, Niall sucked Gus's cock into his mouth, taking him deep down his throat and swallowing. Gus almost creamed himself then and there, with his dick buried to the root in Niall's heavenly wet heat. He could have come. But he refused to.

"Niall, please, let me suck you too."

Gus's plea was met with a grunt. Whether it spelled yes or no, Gus had no idea. Then Niall let go of Gus's prick and moved up Gus's body, taking his time to fondle and grope, kiss and touch. When he reached Gus's mouth and took him in a savage kiss, Niall aligned their bodies, and the rhythm took them.

Niall moved fast, and Gus did his best to match. He couldn't get enough traction while on his back, so he wrapped his legs around Niall and left the rocking up to him. Niall squeezed and held on to Gus tighter. He pumped his hips against Gus's, pushing their hard cocks and tightened balls into a frenzy, both of them rushing toward the climax they chased in unison.

"Oh my God," Gus whimpered, shuddering so hard he feared his bones might shake loose. The bed started thudding against the wall, not quite banging, but close.

Niall chuckled hoarsely—*evil bastard*—and wiggled his hands between their writhing bodies, took their cocks in hand, and started a fierce stroke up and down, sliding effortlessly on precome and sweat. The smell of sex spread around them like perfume.

"Fuck, babe, you feel so goddamn good," Niall murmured hotly before smashing his mouth over Gus's and taking his breath away, leaving him a quivering mess. "Love watching you 'cause you always come undone so beautifully."

Gus bucked into Niall, holding them together. Rainbow-colored lights flashed behind his eyelids, and there was a buzz inside his head like a swarm of bees. "Gonna come."

"Oh, yeah, baby," Niall crooned into his ear, nibbling on Gus's earlobe. "Come for me. Love to see you, feel you." His grip didn't lessen. If anything, the pumping got harsher and faster.

Their hips jerked in sync, both of them close. Gus cried out, his muscles grew taut, his body tensed, and his cock throbbed like crazy. Pleasure crested inside him, and he rode the wave to a series of sweet explosions of delight. Every cell in his body felt energized, galvanized for the sole purpose of driving Gus out of his mind and rocketing him into sensual space. He spilled his sweltering seed between them, stickiness smearing on their skin as they moved as one.

"Oh fuck, yeah," Niall muttered above Gus.

Apparently watching Gus climax was just the push he needed because he threw his head back, groaned loudly, and shot his load over Gus's stomach. Gus smelled the briny juices, like he'd done many times before, and loved the scent.

Niall collapsed on top of Gus, a dead weight. Gus shoved as best he could and got his lover's body rolled over onto the bed next to him. He kept his arms around Niall and kissed him lazily wherever he could reach. The ceiling kept spinning in his vision, so he wasn't in a hurry to stop his slow explorations of Niall's body.

"Should I move, babe?" Niall asked, his voice already muffled by a pillow and impending sleep.

Gus chuckled, relaxed and at ease. "Nah. Sleep easy, hon." He snuggled closer to his lover and allowed dreams to wash in over his consciousness.

Their problems hadn't faded but would wait for their awakening come next morning. Nothing for them to do at the moment but rest and recuperate. Tomorrow would arrive in its own time.

Chapter 10

"HOPE THIS is okay."

Standing by the percolating coffee machine, Gus started and turned around in a flash. Lately he reacted like a scaredy-cat a lot when he was alone at the apartment that he'd come to view as his and Niall's home. But they couldn't be together 24/7. Gus had a store to run, so Niall had left to run errands involving the case, probably at the precinct. To be honest, Gus had forgotten about their houseguest.

Autumnsong stood in the kitchen doorway without any makeup on, his hair all over the place, and wearing Niall's baggy, gray, and worn hoodie and sweatpants. For the first time since they had known each other, Gus saw Autumnsong as the youth he must have been before he hid himself underneath that sass—a kid dressed in adult clothes, practically lost in them or buried under their weight.

The young man spread his arms, a question in his quirked eyebrow. "All I could find."

Gus smiled kindly. "You look fine. I'm sure Niall won't mind."

Autumnsong rolled his eyes. "Yeah, right. 'Cause he's such an understanding kind of guy." He plopped down on one of the kitchen chairs like a bored teenager expecting to be waited on by his parents, hand and foot. "Got any decent mocaccino?"

Gus smiled past gritted teeth, promising himself not to get angry over a poorly behaved houseguest who had just lost his friend. "I think I can whip one up, sure." Thankful he'd gotten a new coffeemaker, he set about making another cup—while his own cappuccino got slowly colder. "I washed your clothes. They're beside your bed. How did you sleep?" Gus asked to be polite.

Autumnsong snorted, clearly back in his prickly, sarcastic mode. "Swell. Once you two had finished your horizontal mambo."

Gus went stone-cold rigid. Last night Autumnsong had been a wreck, resembling a human being; this morning, he was back to being a cynical dick. "Niall and I are a couple. We live together, and we're recently engaged.

We find each other stupidly hot, so we have sex whenever we want in the privacy of our own home together. You want cinnamon in your coffee?"

Quiet followed. Gus let Autumnsong stew in silence. If he was gonna stay with Niall and Gus, Autumnsong would have to tolerate their relationship, any and all parts of it. Including the late-night sex sessions.

"Whatever." Autumnsong scoffed. "Where's my mocaccino?"

With a steaming mug of coffee in hand, Gus turned to the young man. "Would it be a violation of your world-hating ways to show some manners? Like saying please or thanks?"

Autumnsong pursed his lips. "You want to play house and home with your ruggedly ugly buddy, that's your business. I want my coffee so I can get the hell out of here."

Gus frowned. "You want to leave? Last night I told you that you can stay here as long as you want or need. I meant it."

Autumnsong's world-weary mask cracked for a split second but was soon back on in full force. "Nah. I couldn't handle all this placid domesticity. Too close to a Stepford household, if you get my drift."

"Yes, I saw the movie." Gus sat down and shoved the mocaccino mug over the table to Autumnsong. "You want to be treated like an adult? Fine. Our offer still stands: you can stay here if you want. And judging from last night… I'd say you want to."

Autumnsong grimaced, hugging the coffee cup but not drinking. "Why? 'Cause I drank all your booze? I'll buy you more." Despite his words, he didn't make to leave. He sat in place and sipped his coffee as though he were enjoying a leisurely teatime.

Gus decided to face the issue head-on. "Was Rowan your boyfriend?"

The comment got Autumnsong's undivided attention—and amusement. "Was he my what? No, man. No. He was *not* my fucking boyfriend." Gus must have looked confused because Autumnsong sighed impatiently, a smirk playing on his full lips. "Rowan was my… my brother."

Gus damn near broke his jaw as it fell open in shock and surprise. "*Your brother?* But I thought… I was under the impression Rowan was *Bodhi's* brother."

Autumnsong rolled his eyes again. "So fucking what? A person can't have more than one brother? What kind of twisted logic is that? Bodhi, Rowan, and me, we grew up in the system, with the same foster family. We're brothers in everything except blood."

"Oh." Gus was at a loss for words. "I'm so sorry, Kin."

Autumnsong crossed his arms and shrugged—but his aimlessly wandering gaze and trembling jaw told Gus he wasn't in control of his emotions or as detached as he claimed to be. "Yeah, well. Life's shit and then you die. No surprise there."

"That's a bit too jaded for me," Gus said softly. "Were you two close?"

Autumnsong shrugged again but remained rigid, poorly masking his sorrow. "Rowan had his own circle of friends. I had little to do with them."

"A lot of Radical Faeries embrace the femininity in men, choosing drag." Gus would have figured those commonalities had either brought Autumnsong into the fold or that the community had contributed to the birth of his twink persona.

Autumnsong stared at Gus like he'd grown a second head. "So? Me wearing makeup, body-hugging clothes, and feathers puts me in the drag category? You that narrow-minded?"

Gus bristled, stiffening. He found it difficult to defend himself against Autumnsong's insults. Because he'd seen a picture of Autumnsong with his brother, probably taken at the sanctuary, had he assumed Autumnsong was one of them? Gus himself hated when he was labeled with prejudice or classified in a certain way simply because of his cute blond looks, his Wiccan faith, or his being gay. And now he was accused of doing the same?

Perhaps Autumnsong sensed Gus's emotional conflict because for a moment he looked remorseful. "Forget it. I know you're not like that."

The comment surprised Gus. Autumnsong choosing not to shoot Gus down in flames? Unprecedented. "I hope not." He took a sip of his own chilled coffee. Then again, coffee tasted the same hot or cold. "What was your brother like?"

Autumnsong stared at the table, most likely not even seeing it, and scraped a nail over the grain of the wood. "Rowan was always the kindest and sweetest of us brothers. He never complained, never argued, never talked back, never behaved badly. If I believed in angels, I'd say he was one."

The answer both pleased and puzzled Gus. Hearing Autumnsong talk of someone with such warmth was one thing; hearing the characterization made it harder for Gus to understand how or why Rowan had been killed. Rowan sounded like a person without an enemy in the world.

Gus empathized and said softly, "He sounds nice. I wish I'd gotten to know him better when I met him at the shop."

Autumnsong's head and gaze snapped up. "You what?" A dark fury twisted his lovely features. "You met Rowan? At your shop? When?"

Gus was honestly surprised Autumnsong hadn't known about Rowan's curious visit to The Four Corners. "I'm sorry. I thought you knew and that's why you came here of all places. I saw him the day before he died. He seemed shy and scared. We didn't really speak. He bought a deadly bane symbol necklace and left. That was it."

Autumnsong's hands fisted on the table. His brown, almond-shaped eyes burned with a black fire of retribution. *If looks could kill....* Gus swallowed. Then Autumnsong jumped to his feet and started pacing, his usually smooth brow deeply furrowed. It was clear he was seething. He almost had steam coming out of his ears. Gus couldn't imagine why his reply had antagonized Autumnsong so deeply.

When he stopped, Gus knew to expect nothing but bad things. "Rowan… he seemed scared?"

"Yes." Gus nodded, deciding to be completely honest with Autumnsong. Just because his guest wasn't the most forthright person in the world that didn't mean Gus had to be same. "He was acting stealthily and kept giving me surreptitious glances. Niall thought he might have been a stalker. Wouldn't have been my first. But he seemed so afraid I concluded he wasn't a creepy guy. He seemed, I don't know, kind of lost? Like he had something to say but he didn't know how to do that."

Autumnsong stopped unexpectedly and let out a deep sigh, slumping. "This is all my fault. I talked with him about you. About your involvement in certain murder cases." Shocked, Gus started to speak, but Autumnsong shushed him with a furious gesture. "I needed him to know what kind of relationship you and I had."

Gus suppressed a cringe. He had no idea whatsoever of what kind of relationship he and Autumnsong actually had. Friends would have been an exaggeration, but the same could be said about enemies. What had Niall called him? A dubious acquaintance? That sounded along the right lines. Well… they might be leaning a bit more toward a possible alliance now, Gus dared to hope.

"So Rowan came to the shop to check me out?" Gus concluded.

Much to Gus's surprise, Autumnsong smiled, a sweet, bashful gesture unlike any Gus had ever seen on him. "Rowan was the smallest of us brothers, but he was also the most protective, and that made him the strongest. His heart…. We relied on his goodness to steer us on the right path. He was our moral compass." He closed his eyes, and tears welled, spilled onto his cheeks. "God, I miss him so much."

Gus did something he wouldn't have thought himself capable of three months ago. He came over to Autumnsong and hugged him. At first Autumnsong didn't react, remaining unresponsive and rigid. Slowly his muscles lost their tautness, and he melted into the embrace, his arms shaking and encircling Gus's waist. Gus felt his T-shirt grow wet from Autumnsong's sorrow, but he didn't let go. Autumnsong's trembling, willowy body pressed against Gus's, and Gus realized how young and fragile he still was, in spite of his bravado and occasional bullshit.

"This may sound like a cliché," Gus whispered. "But you've got friends here, so feel free to fall apart. We'll help you get through this. And Niall and Detective Hughes will find Rowan's killer." He patted Autumnsong's back gently and caressed his hair, simply making soothing little gestures to make their new friend feel comforted and supported.

"Rowan was a flower child," Autumnsong murmured, his voice choked and thin. "He didn't have an enemy in the world. Everyone loved him."

A horrible thought occurred to Gus. He actually feared saying the words out loud. But he had to, for the sake of the truth, justice, and Autumnsong's continued health and well-being. At least so the thought was out there for consideration as a possible motive for murder.

"Listen, I don't wanna make things worse, but…." Gus worried about the repercussions of his words, but he managed to push them out past his lips. "But could the killer have been after… *you*? To send you a gruesome message? I mean, you… you probably have enemies, considering everything you know and are involved with." *Like Satanism.* Gus left that unsaid.

A loaded silence hung heavy between them, despite the close quarters. Autumnsong's breathing changed: hitched and then grew labored. His grip around Gus's waist tightened. Then in a cold, hard tone

Gus had hoped Autumnsong had left behind, with them at least, he said quietly, "Let go of me."

It was contradictory since it was Autumnsong who still held on to Gus. Nonetheless Gus released Autumnsong, who immediately stepped back, his expression stone-cold. But it took only a moment of observation for Gus to realize that Autumnsong's murderous look wasn't aimed at him. Clearly someone—or several someones—had sprung to his mind, people capable of such a heinous act as attacking their enemies through their families, friends, and loved ones. Gus couldn't even imagine that level of brutality and cruelty. It was unconscionable.

"I need to go out," Autumnsong said suddenly. "I'll be back. Will you keep me in the loop on whatever you find in your investigation? Can I trust you?"

Gus frowned. It was his ethical duty to remind Autumnsong that vengeance served no purpose—as opposed to justice, which balanced scores—and to prevent him from committing crimes. "Yes, you can trust me. But please, don't do anything… you can't take back."

Autumnsong gave him a wry smile. "Like kill someone? That's something you don't have to worry about. My enemies, those who took Rowan away from me, they won't be granted the sweet oblivion of death. That I can assure you."

Leaving the echo of his grim promise still ringing in Gus's ears, Autumnsong turned and left the room, most likely to dress and get to his dark work. Gus felt conflicted. Should he try to stop Autumnsong from leaving? He had a sneaking suspicion Autumnsong wouldn't allow him to interfere with his plans, whatever they might be. But he felt he had to at least try.

Walking to the guest bedroom, Gus found Autumnsong nearly dressed, his black attire like the garb of an assassin hell-bent on carrying out his threat.

He glanced up when Gus walked in. "Come to stop me, goody-two-shoes?"

"I will tell you everything we learn during the investigation," Gus said emphatically, "*if* you promise not to do anything illegal or unethical with this… vendetta of yours. The culprits will be brought to justice, and they'll go to prison for the rest of their lives." He refused to surrender and stared Autumnsong down. "Promise me, Kin."

Autumnsong regarded Gus with a cool expression, revealing nothing of what went on inside his head. For a moment neither one moved an inch. Two steadfast men took in each other's resolve.

Finally Autumnsong inclined his head minutely. "Agreed. Silly do-gooder."

Then he strolled past Gus and left the house. Gus heard the front door open and then click shut. Apparently Autumnsong wasn't the type to leave with doors banging. Nice of him, Gus thought and returned to the kitchen and his abandoned cup of coffee.

As he sat down, Gus realized that despite Autumnsong's promise, he had no real way of ensuring the young man on a mission lived up to his vow. The investigation was now a race: Gus simply had to make sure that he, Niall, and Hughes got to the murderer first.

Not just for justice, but to save Autumnsong's soul.

Chapter 11

"WHAT NEW leads do you think we'll get by reinterviewing the suspects at this stage?" Niall asked Hughes as they drove toward the sanctuary again.

Niall asked because he had serious doubts about this procedure when they themselves had no new information with which to confront the suspects. The best course of action for cops and sleuths was always to only ask questions to which you already knew the answers. Nothing made suspects crumble faster than the facts and the truth.

"I'm mostly trying to ascertain the relationships these people have with each other," Hughes replied coolly. "I mean, this, um, cult engages in orgies and free sex. And that kind of stuff always leads to trouble in my book."

Niall grimaced. "They're not a cult. Gus would bust my balls if I ever said something like that. So let's try to keep an open mind, shall we?"

Hughes barked out a laugh. "Your boy's smart, I'll give him that. But this is a murder investigation, and I ain't gonna start chanting or dancing naked in a circle in order to find the killer."

Niall grinned wickedly. "Oh, I don't know. Don't knock it till you try it."

He waggled his eyebrows at the shocked expression on Hughes's face and then burst into guffaws. Hughes just grunted unhappily and then punched Niall on the arm, quite hard to boot. That didn't stop Niall from enjoying every second of his friend's discomfort.

Finally, once his mirth had subsided, Niall asked, "So what did you find out about the suspects? Such as Alex Kittridge?"

Hughes gave him a knowing glance. "You mean Goodwin's ex? That Kittridge?"

Well aware he deserved the merciless ribbing, Niall growled. "Is there more than one man involved in this case with such a douchebag name?"

Hughes chuckled as he drove the car up the narrow mountain road toward the Mount Paradise Sanctuary. "The good professor's got no criminal record, if that's the kind of dirt you were on the lookout for."

"What, nothing?" Niall sighed, disgruntled at the news. "Even Gus's friends have got records for political activism as proof they've stood up for something. Guess the professor considers that beneath him."

"Now you're just asking for a world of hurt, Junior." Hughes shook his head, kind of like Owain, Niall's father, did when he was disappointed or knew better. "Besides, what does any of it matter? Goodwin's with you now. Hell, you two are engaged, for fuck's sake."

Niall had to pause there for thought. Hughes was right. Gus was with Niall now, and judging from the way Gus had behaved the day before, there was no love lost between him and Kittridge. If anything, Gus had seemed uncomfortable meeting Kittridge again after so many years.

So rationally Niall knew his prejudices were baseless and his jealousy pointless. Yet he couldn't dispel the negativity. Niall loved Gus. Before meeting Kittridge, Niall had never had to consider the possibility he might lose Gus to another man. Sure, Niall had known full well that Gus wasn't a virgin, that he had a sexual past, ex-boyfriends. But had Niall ever had any desire to meet one of them in person? Fuck no.

And even if Gus hadn't been thrilled to see Kittridge, Kittridge had certainly seemed pleased to see Gus again.

"Is he really a professor?" Niall asked.

"As it happens, Alex Kittridge is a tenured professor with joint appointments, whatever the hell that means, at not one, but three separate institutions of higher learning. I gave him my permission to leave the sanctuary to teach his classes. His absence might raise questions about the case the SPD is unwilling to answer at this time."

Niall murmured an obscene word under his breath. Damn. He'd hoped for bad news, like no place wanting Kittridge on their staff. No such luck. "He's got lots of classes, then, huh? How fancy. At what schools?"

Hughes puffed out an impatient breath, so obviously whatever news he had, it wasn't going to be good. "The University of Washington, Whitman College, and… the University of Puget Sound."

Niall fisted his hands when he understood Hughes's reticence and minor hesitation. The University of Puget Sound was in Tacoma, a mere four miles, or ten minutes, away from Gus's shop and apartment. *Son of a bitch.*

"That position in itself doesn't mean Kittridge might want Goodwin back, you know?" Hughes sounded perfectly logical. One thing didn't necessarily lead to the other. But… it was oddly suspicious and mightily convenient.

"No, it doesn't." Niall heard how his tone had dropped low, become dangerous and cold. He didn't seriously believe Gus would either succumb to Kittridge's charms or betray Niall's trust. But the knowledge that the two men shared an intimate history made Niall extremely nervous and quite irritable.

Perhaps wisely, Hughes moved on with the subject. "The other suspects have citations from the courts for misdemeanors, public protests, political activism, and the like, exactly like you said. All were pled out before they got to court. None of our suspects have outstanding warrants, unpaid debts, or anything else that stands out as criminal. They don't condone violence, they don't mess around with guns, and most of them are vegetarians, which means there's more meat for the rest of us."

Niall snickered. "That's generously progressive of you."

"Shut up, Junior." Hughes grumbled under his breath the rest of the way to the sanctuary.

ONCE THEY'D parked and walked into the compound, they were immediately met by a uniformed officer clearly in distress. He was young and probably somewhat inexperienced, so his pale anxiety was understandable. He led them uphill to the sun altar, the murder site.

"That wasn't here when I reported for duty this morning, sir." His voice quivered ever so slightly as he pointed at the ground in front of the altar platform.

Standing out against the green lawn, charred grass and dirt spelled out *Faerie Fire, Faggot Fire*.

"What the fuck?" Hughes was old-fashioned; he typically used curse words like *shit, Jesus H. Christ, damn*, or *goddammit. Fuck* was a rare occurrence, and Hughes using it never failed to make Niall cringe.

The young officer looked away from the soiled earth. "It wasn't here when I arrived in the morning, sir. I did a perimeter check when I thought I heard a noise, but it was just a gopher. When I came back, and I couldn't have been gone for more than a minute or two, I found the grass on fire. I stomped on it, and then I saw it was actually writing. I took pictures with my cell phone. The odor's dissipated now, sir, but it smelled like lighter fluid."

Hughes nodded. His sigh was muted. The reaction told Niall that Hughes was content with the young officer's actions and sharp observations. "You didn't happen to see anyone hanging around, did you, son?"

"No, sir. I'm sorry, sir." The young man frowned as he stared at the ground. Clearly he was less than pleased with his results. "I was too busy putting out the flames."

"You did fine, son." Hughes turned to Niall. "Does that phrase ring any bells with you, Valentine?"

Niall shook his head. There was so much he didn't know about new religious movements, despite living with Gus, who was a practicing Wiccan. "Nope. I'll call Gus."

As Niall pulled out his iPhone and tapped the screen, Hughes asked the young officer, "How many people are on the premises as we speak?"

The officer checked his notebook. "Only the persons who were advised not to leave—Jacob Marlowe, Bodhi Jha, Ethan Sadler, and Quentin Cross—plus a day guest named Frank Sadler, who is apparently Ethan's husband. Alex Kittridge was allowed to leave for work, and he's currently at his job in Tacoma." He nodded toward the path downhill. "The rest are all at the office, or at least they were the last time I checked. Once I found the burning writing, I ordered everyone into one single location, and the office seemed the best option. I didn't lock them in, though."

Niall didn't hear or listen to anymore since the line was ringing. He hoped Gus wasn't busy with a customer, or this effort at information gathering would be a bust. Hughes couldn't delay the questioning much longer.

"Hi, Niall" came Gus's chirpy voice. In the background soft sitar music played, and that confirmed Niall's guess: Gus was indeed working at the shop.

That was why Niall chose not to waste time with pleasantries. "Babe, do the words *Faerie Fire, Faggot Fire* mean anything to you? It's kind of urgent."

An alarmed gasp came from the other end of the line. Niall prayed Gus wouldn't start asking questions now when Niall had no answers to give. But then Gus said, "I'm sorry, Niall, but I have no idea what that means."

"Shit." Niall sighed. "Guess it was just a long shot."

"Does this have something to do with the Radical Faerie case?" Gus asked, but he didn't stop to give Niall an opportunity to reply, as he added, "Because if it does, you could always ask… Alex. He's your best source of information about the Radical Faeries, from a scholarly point of view, I mean. I myself am not an expert."

Niall would rather have peeled off his own fingernails with pliers than ask for the hot professor's help in anything. If Niall were dying and Kittridge the only human left on the planet, then he might—no, not even then.

But Niall quickly remembered why he couldn't do that. "He's not here in the sanctuary today. He's at work." Then he growled when he suddenly caught on to where this conversation was heading. And, *fuck*, he didn't like it. "I hate to say this but… you might have a better chance than me in speaking with… him." Man, he sounded jealous and pissed and ridiculous.

"What do you mean?" Gus sounded confused. "I'm working. I don't have time to go to Seattle and track Alex down at some—"

"He's working at the University of Puget Sound." Niall said nothing more. He merely listened to the minute change in Gus's breathing. Niall was convinced now that Gus hadn't known about that. This was good news. Gus meeting with Kittridge for an exchange of information when Niall wasn't there… that was all kinds of bad. But needs must.

"He is?" Gus asked. Niall made every effort to hear the slightest indicators of how his boyfriend felt. He was pleased to note Gus's mildly irritated tone. "That's just a few miles away."

"Yeah, I know, babe." Niall sighed, rubbing his forehead, which was throbbing in an unpleasant manner. Was it because of Kittridge? Probably. "I didn't know either. But he's there, so you should be able to ask him about that phrase on your lunch break. Maybe. Please?"

A moment of heavy silence fell on the line. Niall sensed Gus's hesitation. The feeling that the two of them hadn't parted ways amicably intensified. Then Gus said in a curt tone, "Fine. I'll call you if and when I have something. Bye. Oh, and Niall? Be careful. Love you."

The click that ended the call sounded ominous and foreboding. Niall didn't like any of it. Sending Gus to a man who had broken his heart didn't sit well with Niall, who wished he hadn't been a two-hour drive away. But he was stuck too far away to make a difference in the situation, so all he could do was grumble under his breath and commiserate the apparently inevitable rendezvous between former boyfriends.

Hughes tapped Niall on the shoulder. "You okay, kid?" When Niall nodded in reply, Hughes shrugged and pointed the path downhill. "Ready? Let's go."

THE OFFICE was cold despite the roaring fireplace, but the small, red-painted log cabin still *felt* cozy and warm, thanks to the earthy ambience. Sparsely furnished, the single-room cabin had a wooden desk and a leather office chair, two small armchairs, a coffee table, an archival cabinet, and one dresser. The clock on the wall ticked loudly. A radio played music from the 1960s, static making listening a rattling experience.

Marlowe, Bodhi, Quentin, and Ethan waited in the room, no one speaking. Marlowe occupied the office chair, Ethan and Quentin had each sunk into an armchair, and Bodhi paced impatiently on the floor covered with a simple green rug.

Behind Ethan's chair stood a man Niall didn't recognize. He had to be Ethan's husband, Frank Sadler. Much to Niall's surprise, Frank was nothing like what he had expected. There was no chance he was a Radical Faerie. His unmarred, symmetrical features caught Niall's attention. He was a prime example of a handsome man—who didn't seem to have a feminine bone in his body.

Though his age was indeterminate at first glance, his toned physique in an immaculate and expensive suit and tie suggested he was a man who made it his business to look his absolute best. His dirty-blond hair was parted on one side and shaped in a wavy, airy style, and his sapphire-blue eyes took everything in with sharp focus and undoubtedly extensive intelligence.

He glanced at his luxurious wristwatch, frowning as though time itself offended him by moving forward without his permission. Perhaps he had appointments to keep, Niall surmised.

Quentin Cross sat in the other armchair, but now he stood in a rush and hurried to Niall and Hughes, his expression nervous and his gestures jittery. "Detective, may I please speak with you in private? It's really very important." His imploring gaze shifted from Hughes to Niall and back again.

Pursing his lips at the interruption, Hughes gave a chin-lift, indicating they should move out to the porch. Once they had done so and the door closed behind them with a soft snick, Quentin let out an anxious breath, wringing his hands.

"Sorry to spring this on you at short notice," Quentin started, lowering his voice to a level such that no one could eavesdrop from inside, "but I have to clear the air and tell the truth. You see, my statement wasn't entirely, um, honest." He glanced over his shoulder at the office door, as if to make sure no one was there. "I don't know if you've yet had the chance to inspect the recording made in the love shack during the night of the murder. I don't know if Ethan shows up on it or not, but… I can assure you he was there, in the love shack, spying on the orgy."

Niall narrowed his eyes. "How do you know this?"

"Because…." Quentin looked mortified and ashamed, his face crumpling. He seemed on the verge of tears, blinking hard to fend off the flood. "Because I… I spied on *him*. On Ethan." He slumped, appearing crestfallen at the admission. "I couldn't say it inside, not with his husband in the room, but…. Look, I'm not proud of how I feel about Ethan but I… I can't help it. I knew it was wrong to watch him in a private moment, but…."

Quentin's jaw trembled, and he wiped tears from his puffy eyes. Niall had no trouble identifying the emotion he witnessed. The shame born from falling in love with someone who was unavailable. He empathized and appreciated the confession freely made.

Still, he retained some of his skepticism and doubt. After all, it was conceivable that Quentin knew Ethan had committed the murder and now, out of love for him, chose to protect Ethan with a lie. Anything was possible in love and war.

"Mr. Cross, are you willing to revise your earlier statement to that effect?" Hughes asked, though his tone implied he already knew what the answer would be.

Quentin nodded eagerly. "Yes, yes, of course. I'm so sorry, Detective, that I didn't tell the truth sooner, but I was… embarrassed."

Hughes pursed his lips but nodded. "I understand, sir." He gestured to the uniformed officer—what was his name again? Niall had no clue. "Please give your statement to Officer Holt here."

Quentin offered the young man a shaky, bashful smile. "Of course. But I, uh… please excuse me, I'd like a brief moment alone first. I must ask forgiveness from Chandra, the Moon God, and Ardhanarishvara, the joining of…. Oh, forget it. You wouldn't understand."

Niall bristled a little, though in all honesty, it was likely he wouldn't actually get it. Nonetheless, he made a note in his mental Rolodex to check out those words later. "Where will you be?"

"At the moon altar," Quentin replied, waving his hand generally westward. "It's at the other end of the compound from the, uh… sun altar. Up in the hills. Everyone knows the location, so you can ask anyone." He hesitated as though not knowing what to do, his long black lashes fluttering as he blinked. Then he gave a short smile and a quick bow and rushed off, his silk gown fluttering in his wake, the fake jewels glimmering in the sunlight.

"He's a bit of an odd one," Hughes commented as he watched Quentin's back recede uphill to the west.

"As opposed to…?" Niall snorted sarcastically. "Now what? Talk to Ethan again?"

"Yeah, I think so." Hughes didn't knock on the door but simply pushed it open and reentered. His gaze landed squarely on Ethan. "Mr. Sadler, we'd like a word with you in private." He didn't ask, but neither did he command. A simple but an effective tactic, in Niall's opinion.

But it was Frank Sadler who spoke. "Will my husband be needing his lawyer present?" His tone, though a lovely, melodious baritone, was cool and definitely antagonistic.

"Not at this time." Hughes remained composed as well, though Niall could tell he was far from pleased by Frank's approach. It seemed Frank had at least one significant thing in common with these Radical

Faeries: he disliked and distrusted the establishment, especially members of law enforcement.

Ethan gave his husband a quick nod of acquiescence. Then, with Marlowe in the lead, everyone vacated the room except for Niall, Hughes, and Ethan. The young man appeared unsure how to behave, fidgeting as though he couldn't decide between standing up or remaining seated. Hughes sat in the other armchair, deciding for Ethan. Niall leaned against the sturdy desk, his hands crossed over his chest, silently waiting for Hughes to do his thing.

"Mr. Sadler, we've gone over the recording made in the, uh, love shack on the night of the murder," Hughes said in a serious tone of voice. "I'm afraid you do *not* appear on camera. So there's no proof for your alibi."

Ethan flushed beet red, worrying his bottom lip. "Oh, I see. Well, um… would it help if I told you… everything they did? I remember… pretty much the whole… thing." It wasn't hard to see his embarrassment over what he'd witnessed. Niall suppressed a laugh.

Hughes shifted on his seat, looking mightily uncomfortable. He was a traditional sort of guy who believed sex belonged in private and in the bedroom. Still, he said, "Sure, if you can recall any details."

For the next ten minutes, Ethan gave Niall and Hughes a blow-by-blow description of the orgy in the love shack. Niall hadn't seen the film, but judging from Hughes's depressed look, it soon became clear that Ethan's recollection was spot on. He wouldn't have had time to view the film before the police confiscated it, and he wouldn't have had an opportunity to speak with the so-called players in the film before they left the grounds, so it was evident that Ethan wasn't the killer.

Hughes leaned back and sighed, stopping Ethan's tale midsentence. "That's enough, Mr. Sadler. We get the picture. Loud and clear. Thank you."

Ethan gave an awkward smile. "Was that, uh, sufficient? I could go deeper into the details of what the men—"

"No, no. That won't be necessary. Thank you, though." Hughes's emphatic tone made Niall grit his teeth so he wouldn't laugh out loud.

The windows in the office were open, and a pleasant breeze caressed Niall's skin.

A gunshot rang in the distance, echoing in the hills.

"What the hell?" For a big, robust man, Hughes was quick on his feet, up and out the door in seconds. Niall followed on his heels. They stopped outside the porch, scanning their surroundings. "Where did it come from?"

Jacob Marlowe stood by the unlit fire pit and pointed uphill to the west. "Over there!" he shouted.

Niall passed Hughes as he raced up the path. He also passed several solitary trees with shrines under them, a small pond with a brook running past it, hand-cranked water pumps and full red water barrels that functioned as fire stations, a large outhouse building, sun decks, picnic sites, and a variety of other altars.

When he reached the right place, he knew it immediately by virtue of a rapid-fire sequence of startling images:

The young police officer lay on the ground, blood trickling from a fresh gash to his head and smearing his hair like a macabre dye job. He had drawn his service weapon; it rested beside him, loosely clutched in his hand. Niall couldn't tell if the guy was dead or merely unconscious.

Beyond the downed policeman, a tiny pond, lush with green water plants and white floating lotuses, fronted a platform made of gray stone. Atop the platform rose a pedestal bearing a lunar goddess figure with a crescent moon over her brow. The lovely statue must have once appeared serene and benevolent, but now the shape on her forehead formed part of a crude, threefold, crescent-shaped biohazard symbol covering the statue's face. From the looks of it, the desecration had been done by means of a chemical burn, maybe using acid. Niall's theory was confirmed when his focus shifted to the stone platform at the statue's base, where some corrosive liquid had scorched the words *Faerie Flood, Faggot Flood*.

Finally Niall's gaze fell upon the pond itself—wherein floated, half-submerged, the unmoving body of Quentin Cross.

Chapter 12

GUS WAS walking down the hallway leading to Alex Kittridge's room at the University of Puget Sound when his cell phone beeped, indicating a text. It was close to lunchtime, so the place was crawling with students and faculty members leaving classrooms and lecture halls to hurry to the bathrooms or the cafeteria.

Gus had to lean against the wall to read the text from Niall. *Ask K about Faerie Flood & Faggot Flood.*

Frowning, Gus wondered where the new weird line had come up. He texted back: *?*

He didn't have to wait for more than a few seconds. *Quentin FUBAR. G2G.*

Gus's heart damn near stopped beating. Quentin Cross had been hurt or attacked? Was he beaten beyond recognition, or was he, like the first victim, dead?

Feeling queasy, Gus took a few steps sideways to plop down on a bench occupied by students with their eyes buried in their gadgets. Gus felt like he'd been punched in the gut, and his vision blurred. He wasn't sure if he should throw up, pass out, or do both. Briefly he considered the possibility that none of the people around would even notice if he keeled over.

First Rowan, now Quentin? The knowledge of their fates hung heavy over Gus—like a dark cloud. He had to shoulder some of the responsibility. Rowan had a curious connection to Gus, and Quentin's attack had occurred when Gus should have already found the killer and prevented further loss of life.

Memories of the past months flowed through his mind like a mocking parade of all his mistakes. The bombing at the circle of friends, too many now dead, buried, and gone, never to be seen again. Gus couldn't bear to lose anyone else. His family had diminished with each new murder case. He was tired of attending funerals, of saying good-bye, of never again being with those he cared for and loved.

His sorrow faded, and anger replaced it. A fire of justice burned inside him. Refueled with the desire for retribution, Gus stood and, with a determined stride, headed directly to Alex's door. He knocked out of politeness but then refused to wait for admittance.

Alex sat behind his dark wood desk, writing on a piece of paper, perhaps an essay. He appeared engrossed in his task. At the sanctuary Gus had been so surprised to see Alex there he hadn't noted how different Alex looked. He had lines at the corners of his eyes and mouth, his brown hair, though stylish, showed gray streaks around his temples, and his formerly strong, athletic body appeared a bit more rounded, his posture more than a bit slouched.

He's grown older. The observation made Gus hesitate. Yes, he remained skeptical, and wary about Alex's motives. But on the other hand… he sympathized. Growing older hit some men extra hard, and the natural progression either embittered or mellowed them out. Which applied to Alex?

When the door closed with a small slam, Alex raised his gaze in surprise. The second he recognized Gus, his eyes went wide. Then he smiled broadly and stood, removing his glasses and placing them on a stack of papers on his desk.

"Gus, goodness. I didn't know you'd be coming, or I would have—"

"Would have what, Alex?" Gus cut in, a host of negative emotions swirling in his brain. Perhaps he'd just grown tired of all the bullshit, the lies and secrets and mind games. He was done. "Told me that you teach at a school mere miles away from my house and business? Seems to me you should have done that years ago."

Alex's enthusiastic tone and expression faded, and anxiety rose in its place. "I see. Am I to understand you question my motives for not disclosing that fact to you? Why should I have informed you of any of my actions or decisions when we're no longer together? Does our past bond make you privy to all the details of my life—past, present, and future?"

The answer sounded completely rational, Gus had to admit. Exes had no obligation to share aspects of their lives. But… Alex was a special case. He'd been so brutally honest that it had a way of sounding a lot like lies. And keeping this kind of secret from Gus, the man Alex had once professed to love?

"Your words make sense—I'll grant you that." Gus was raised right after all, so he had to say it. "But you and I both know there's more to it than that. You, among other professors, taught me to look beneath what we can see, to scan beneath the surface in order to find answers and solutions. 'Cause there's always a hidden story, a deep motivation, a secret, a key that unlocks a mystery."

Alex sighed. "I was talking about myths and legends, the tales that survive generations, and the faiths people construct around themselves until they encompass entire societies and nations, a shared delusion. I wasn't talking about individuals but peoples as a whole."

"Yes, but they're not mutually exclusive," Gus countered. "What motivates a person can be the same thing that motivates a larger group. But we're not talking about groups or nations. I'm referring to *you*, and you're hedging. And that makes me fucking suspicious."

Gus jolted inwardly at his own words, barely recognizing his cynicism and skepticism. Suspicious of what? He had started out questioning Alex's motives for moving back to the area, but the larger issue here was Alex's possible involvement in the attacks at the sanctuary.

Did Gus really think Alex could be capable of murder? He could no longer say with any degree of certainty. Gus had trusted many people over the course of his life. More than one had shown their true colors and disappointed him. Thankfully, though, not many had crossed the final moral line and gone on a killing spree.

Alex regarded Gus for a moment, silent and blinking. Then he released a long exhale, slumped, and plopped down on his chair heavily, the leather creaking and the screws screeching metallically.

"You're right, Aug—I mean, Gus." Alex fiddled with his glasses, seeming nervous but also defeated, as though he carried the weight of past sins on his shoulders. "I took the job here some time after I returned to the US to… to see if you and I could… reconcile and patch up our relationship."

Gus closed his eyes, rubbed his forehead in frustration, and counted to twenty. "You're out of your mind, Alex, if you think our so-called relationship could be mended with a simple patch. Not in a million years. We were bleeding pretty damn hard in our hearts before we broke up. It was a matter of survival for both of us. In the end, we weren't good together or good for each other."

Alex smiled ruefully, his gaze still aimed at his glasses, though he probably looked right through them. "Yes, I know. I guess I was just… hoping, you know? As the years went by, I… I realized you'd been the best thing that ever happened to me. You'd loved me even though I'd been a prick. I walked out because… because I didn't know any better, because I was greedy and wanted both you and a stellar career. I was too arrogant to see the numerous things I did wrong. I wronged you, and I just… I regret that now. I walked out on you because I stupidly thought I could have my cake and eat it too, and that you'd still be waiting for me once I got back. When I did, two years later, and found you gone… I took some time to mull things over, so when I was offered this position, I thought the universe was trying to tell me something."

For a long and painful time, Gus had waited to hear Alex say those words, to show that he understood and cared about the agony he'd put Gus through. But now that Alex had finally seen the light—or as close to it as someone like Alex could, because he sure as hell didn't believe in messages from the universe—Gus found that it was *he* who no longer cared. Too much water had flowed under that bridge, and in the process it had washed away Gus's emotions and memories of their past together. Everything had faded into obscurity, never again to be revived.

"I'm glad to hear you say that, Alex, I really am." Gus sat on the chair opposite Alex's desk and serenely met his ex's gaze. "I didn't think you'd ever really get the way you'd treated me, taking me for granted, believing I would always blindly follow you and sacrifice my own goals in favor of yours."

Alex blinked, his forest-green eyes glistening with unshed tears. "Was I truly that bad? Had we no good times at all?"

Gus shook his head. "Sure, we did. But not enough. I was starstruck, and you were—"

"And I was stuck-up," Alex interjected with a self-deprecating chuckle.

Gus gave his ex-boyfriend a lopsided smile. "Maybe. Let's face it. Neither one of us was ready for a mature relationship. I was too young and naive, and you were too—"

"Jaded, disillusioned, and unwilling to compromise and commit." Alex twiddled with a pen over his desk, his gaze glossy and turned inward. "I suppose I was flattered by your attention, attracted to your youthful exuberance and enthusiasm, your fresh perspectives, and—"

"Unquestioning adoration," Gus finished for Alex.

For many years now, he'd been able to take a step back and judge his past relationships with dispassionate eyes. Gus suspected Alex had liked being the center of attention, the rising star in his field, the golden boy everyone wanted in their institutions of higher learning. There had been no room in Alex's life for anything other than a trophy boy toy. After a while Gus had wanted more, things that Alex had been unable and unwilling to give.

"Yes, that too." Alex's smile cracked, and he looked down.

"Alex, none of that matters anymore," Gus said emphatically in an attempt to end this pointless rehashing of things long since turned to dust. Their relationship was dead and buried. "I have one last question, and I want the truth. Did you come here to live and work close to me to apologize, or to get back together?"

Alex shrugged, his gaze conflicted, his expression tense and strained. "Ideally… both. But I'm not dumb enough to still believe both are either likely or even possible. Not anymore. Not after all these years." He leaned back in his chair and regarded Gus with a mystifying look. "I was the first love of your adult life, I think. So if I tried to seduce you now… I might even succeed. For a time. No happily-ever-after for you and me."

Gus spoke through gritted teeth. "You're right about that. You are incapable of giving me the kind of relationship I want and deserve. Besides… I'm with someone."

Sighing, Alex feigned a bored expression, one that Gus remembered well but not fondly. It was one of his deflection tactics. "Let me guess. That gumshoe at the sanctuary. The one who kept giving me the stink eye. I wasn't completely oblivious even under those horrendous circumstances."

Gus relaxed into his seat. Alex was showing his cards. Jealousy and envy were traits Gus wouldn't have thought Alex capable of, him being so self-centered most of the time. Could Alex really think that getting together with Gus would fix whatever Alex believed was wrong with his life? It was a foolish notion, pure fantasy.

Either way, it didn't matter to Gus. Not anymore.

"His name is Niall Valentine. We live together, and we're engaged."

Gus observed Alex's sneer crumbling with no small amount of satisfaction. His throat worked convulsively, a few beads of sweat popped up on his forehead, and he bit down on his lower lip, hard enough to be noticeable. Gus wasn't a mean person. But Alex had hurt him. Then again… it did seem kind of pointless to hang on to an old grudge when Gus had moved on. Alex was in the past; Niall was in the present and more than likely in the future as well.

"You're, uh… happy together?" Alex asked, clearing his throat, seeming intent on keeping up appearances.

"Yes, we're happy." Gus spoke the truth because at this point it was the only course of action that made sense. "He puts me first, and I do my best to put him first. Sometimes we argue, like every couple. But we stick by each other, and we dedicate time to keeping our relationship going strong. I love him a little more every day." Gus sighed. "That's not to say I didn't love you, Alex, but… it was puppy love. We both had other things on our minds. We didn't try to maintain a relationship. We just occasionally slept in the same bed."

"Colleagues with benefits, eh?" Alex commented, his voice sarcastic before he shook his head, seemingly angry with himself. "When I saw you again at the sanctuary, for a moment I… I thought you'd tracked me down somehow and come to see me." Alex scoffed at himself. "That's so stupid, I know. Wishful thinking. I am aware that any hope of you and I ending up together is long gone. But I… I suppose I still cling to a—"

"Alex, stop." Gus frowned, starting to get irritated at how they kept going around and around in circles, both of them trying to convince the other of their points of view. "That's not going to happen. Not now, not ever. We had our time, a chance. But it's gone." Gus straightened up and shifted the conversation back on track. "Besides, we have more pressing matters to discuss."

Alex's brow furrowed. Gus couldn't tell if he was perplexed or miffed. "Oh?"

Gus nodded, mostly to himself to reassure that he was headed in the right direction. "I need you to tell me what you know about the Radical Faeries. Specifically the phrases *Faerie Fire, Faggot Fire* and *Faerie Flood, Faggot Flood*. Do they mean anything to you?"

Alex's frown deepened as he leaned forward, elbows on his desk, the twiddling of his pen in his fingers increasing in pace. "Is this related to the murder investigation?"

"Alex, please, just answer the question." Gus didn't plead with his tone even though he used that particular word. If anything, his tone was harsh and commanding.

Alex let out a peeved breath but nodded his acquiescence nonetheless. "It rings a bell, sure. Wait a minute." He rummaged through his notebooks, paper stacks, and file folders. Finally he pulled out a binder and flipped it open. "Ah, here it is. The RF have a comic called *Nomeansyes*. It's available online. In one strip there's a paragraph that states *'Faggot fire, faggot flood, faggot land, faggot blood. So mote it be by faggot hands. Usurpers web unraveled.'* That particular strip refers to truths that might be hard to confront or that instill fear. It refers to calling out those who claim to be revolutionary but at heart are nothing of the kind. According to the strip, this process of accepting people into the fold based on blind faith leads to the dilution of radical movements, as moderate thinkers and inactive activists are introduced."

"You mean people like fakers or posers and such?" Gus asked for confirmation.

Alex inclined his head. "I am a researcher. I accept nothing at face value. I concede to the probability that everything can have multiple meanings and interpretations. Simply because the artist in question viewed the strip as such, that doesn't mean someone else interpreted it the same way. You were one of my best students, Gus, so I'm sure you understand that."

There was a difference between knowing and understanding, that much Gus knew all too well. So sure, he was aware that one person's interpretation could vastly diverge from another's, even the idea's creator's initial vision. But knowing that didn't help with the matter at hand. Gus needed definitive answers, not vague theories.

"That's all well and good, Alex, but tells me nothing about what we're dealing with or what kind of person we're facing." Gus tried to avoid getting annoyed with Alex's evasiveness, but it was hard.

"The phrase is a clue?" Alex asked with obvious curiosity. "A message left by the… the murderer?"

Alex had always been savvy, able to see beyond what wasn't being said. This once, though, Gus would have wished Alex hadn't been so quick-witted. Gus couldn't tell Alex anything. After all, he was still a suspect.

Or was he?

Gus had received the text from Niall about the attack on Quentin when Gus could be relatively certain Alex was fifty miles away, sitting in his office at the university. Gus would know since he'd stood outside the man's office door right then.

Unless Alex had hired someone to do his dirty work, it was unlikely he was the person behind these murders.

Unimaginable relief washed over Gus. Seeing his ex-boyfriend as a potential killer had strained his faith in mankind and in his own choice of men to trust and open his heart to. Now Gus was reasonably confident of Alex's innocence.

At least when it came to Quentin. Rowan was another matter entirely.

"In the original poem, faeries aren't mentioned at all?" Gus asked, for confirmation.

"No." Alex shook his head, staring at the copy of the poem in his files. "The Radical Faeries are of the disposition that to own the queer terminology and identities is more honest than struggles to gain social acceptance."

"Owning one's identity is important for most, I think," Gus commented.

"Not true everywhere, I'm afraid," Alex remarked, sounding glum. The corners of his mouth turned down. "We live in an age where hate- and fearmongers spew their venom throughout society, brainwashing people into believing that violence alone is the answer to whatever ails them or is wrong in their lives or with the world. These converts find their identities through a social group and are thus practically without individual identities. They only think their thoughts are unique. But they are mere mindless drones."

Gus harrumphed. "Gays, lesbians, and all unconventional sexual groups have tried to assimilate into straight society throughout history. But those decisions and actions were born out of fear for their lives, fear of torture, violence, shame, humiliation, and devastation. Generations since then cannot pass judgment on—"

"That was not my meaning, Gus," Alex interjected. "My only point was that Radical Faeries derive value and significance from the *other*, and from the us-versus-them mentality that has existed and still exists among most, if not all, cultures, societies, and nations in the world. They take derogatory terms and make them their own. Queer, and proud of it. And then they redefine the terms once more in the spiritual sphere and become a movement."

Alex had a way of simplifying things in class, Gus recalled. But his words now sounded like a speech. Gus had to ask himself, exactly how close was Alex to these faeries?

"I don't remember you being in a hurry to don women's clothes," Gus stated, going for a casual tone and a whatever-rocks-your-boat attitude.

Surprisingly Alex laughed. "Since the days of Malinowski, anthropologists and other researchers pursuing social, cultural, and religious studies have employed fieldwork as the most essential and best available method when learning about the ways of the *other*. I haven't gone native, if that's what you're going for, and I said as much earlier. However, I do consider most of the faeries as friends, not just informants. I admit that I… I have tried some makeup and a variety of hairstyles. But not dresses, not full drag." Alex winked at Gus. "Yet, anyway. I'll keep you apprised."

Gus chuckled. "Thanks. Good to know." To be honest, Gus wouldn't have cared if Alex started walking around the streets of Tacoma or Seattle in a pimped-out gorilla costume. In his eyes everyone had their own style. More power to them.

Then Alex grew serious and observed Gus with a frown. "I am not so inexperienced or foolish that I'd be under the misguided illusion I'm not a suspect. I just wish… I hope you don't think of me as a murderer. I'm a scientist. I study human life in all its forms. I do not take life."

Gus suppressed a sound somewhere between a chuckle and a groan. I do not take life? It sounded super cheesy, like something you'd hear a civilized alien or robot saying in an equally cheesy science fiction movie.

Alex seemed to notice Gus's trouble answering. "Does your, um… fiancé think I'm the killer?" The tone of his voice had become gravelly, and his attempt at a polite smile turned into a grimace.

"Alex? Don't go there." Gus stood, and Alex fumbled onto his feet as well, both men rigid and guarded. "Listen, I've got to get going. I'll talk to you later." Gus headed for the door.

"Wait." Alex rounded the desk and came to stand at Gus's side. Gus had forgotten that Alex was in fact two inches shorter than him. An odd thing to notice at a time like this. "When you told me about the poem, you also asked for my help in determining what kind of person is likely to be the murderer. I hope you believe me when I say that as a scholar, my goal is to remain objective at all times. In that spirit… I do not think any of the men I've met at the sanctuary could be killers. Despite their antiestablishment mentalities, it's not in their character to harm others."

Gus frowned, giving Alex's words some thought. "So you think we're dealing with an outsider? Someone who is mad enough or who has cause to hate the faeries for some reason? Or perhaps a serial killer hunting neo-pagans?"

Alex nodded, appearing serious. "Gus, in all the time you've been running in the same neo-pagan circles as I have, do you ever recall meeting one who believed taking life was okay under any circumstances?"

Gus sighed. "No. Never. Except perhaps in extreme situations, like self-defense against a rapist or a murderer." He checked his phone. No new texts, voice mail, or missed calls. Niall had to be pretty busy right about now. "Alex? Call me if you come up with anything you think might be of use in order to catch the murderer. After all, you know more about the Radical Faeries than any of us."

Alex smiled shortly. "I will. I want this villain caught as much as you do, or probably even more." He looked uncomfortable, rubbing the back of his neck and blushing.

"What aren't you telling me, Alex?" Gus asked in his no-more-mister-nice-guy tone.

Alex bowed his head, hiding his expression. But in a small, cracking voice he finally whispered, "I, uh… I slept with Jacob."

Gus swallowed. He expected to feel bad for any number of reasons. But the only thing he felt was mild indigration that Alex hadn't revealed this little morsel of information to Hughes or Niall. No jealous twinges, no sparks of envy, no missed heartbeats of longing. Gus was over Alex.

"Why didn't you tell Detective Hughes?" Gus asked coolly.

Alex pressed the bridge of his nose, as though he had a headache. "I am supposed to be a professional, for fuck's sake. God knows I've been in this line of work for decades. And I still made such a rookie mistake. After I'd worked here for a while, eventually I did realize you and I probably weren't ever getting back together. The hope remained, but it was faint. I dated—no, I hooked up with a couple of guys here and there. But in the end I was in a somewhat... fragile mental space when I began my research into the RF. When I first met Marlowe he was... charming, beguiling, and intelligent. I was, to use a phrase I've never used, swept off my feet."

Gus's jaw dropped. Alex had been swept off his feet? The man who loved himself like a lover and who had deep-rooted commitment issues? Alex had... fallen in love? Five minutes ago Gus still wouldn't have believed it possible, and he wasn't sure he believed it now.

Or perhaps Alex had fallen in love with someone else because Gus had never been the right man for him. That thought brightened Gus's mood considerably. For a few years after he and Alex had parted ways, Gus had thought he'd done something wrong or failed somehow, and that had been the reason he and Alex had fallen apart. But if Gus had never been the right man for Alex? It was a comforting and reassuring idea that Gus allowed to bloom in his heart.

Our breakup wasn't my fault.

Gus shrugged, smiled politely, and gave his ex-boyfriend a pat on the shoulder. "Well, Alex... you're in love. Congratulations. Welcome to the human race. Look, I'm gonna tell Detective Hughes about that, and he's probably gonna have a few choice questions for you. But he's discreet, and so am I. No one needs to know—until you want people to know."

Alex had blushed beet red, and he cringed in obvious discomfort. "Why would you say that? I'm not in lov—"

"Uh-huh." Gus chuckled and grinned good-naturedly, waved good-bye, walked out the door, and closed it after him.

There, in the bustling hallway, Gus stopped. Alex might not have told him much of any use in the investigation. But on a personal note, Gus knew for certain he had put Alex behind him for good. It also looked very much like Alex, the sophisticated player, had finally been ensnared by true love's kiss, whether he was ready to admit it to himself or not.

And Gus had Niall.

So mostly a productive meeting. Gus vacated the building, whistling as he went.

Chapter 13

"I WAS a boy when I heard this." Jacob Marlowe sat at the desk in the office, slumped in obvious defeat and misery, tears streaming down his cheeks. "Do you know this one?"

On top of the dresser was a CD player that was at least a decade old, judging from its size. A lovely melody that reminded Niall of a traditional ballad wove through the air. Niall nodded. "Yeah. It's 'Scarborough Fair' by Simon and Garfunkel."

Jacob smiled ruefully. "Yes. Listen to this part." Niall focused on the lyrics where two men sang in counterpoint, the first about finding an acre of land and the second about a forested hillside. "This part right here, the words inspired me to purchase this land and build the sanctuary. My own little safe haven for men like me who defy conventional perceptions of masculinity." He buried his face in his hands and started to shake. "And now it's all going wrong. My friends are dying, and there's nothing I can do to keep them safe. My Goddess, what has happened to my dream?"

Niall's phone beeped. He read the text from Gus about Jacob and Alex doing the nasty in secret. Niall wasn't sure how he felt about that. Was he glad that Alex had kept a secret and thus tarnished his stellar reputation? Or did Niall feel bad for Alex, a good guy who got caught by another man's charms and was now a liar?

Much to his surprise, Niall felt neither.

He faced Jacob again. "Is it true you and Alex Kittridge have a sexual relationship?"

Jacob looked up, stunned. He wiped the wet streaks from his cheeks, frowning in clear dismay. "Is that really a priority right now? Unless you think one of us is the killer."

Niall narrowed his eyes in suspicion. "This is a murder investigation, and you are not in any position to determine what's important and what's not. So stop deflecting and answer me."

Jacob swallowed hard and nodded, a full-body tremble shaking him. "Yes, Alex and I slept together a couple of times. But we are not in a relationship. It was just… an affair. Short-lived and satisfying, but not the stuff of legends."

Niall cringed inwardly. Gus's text said that Alex was actually in love with Jacob. Niall guessed the feeling was unrequited. Sucked to be Alex, Niall thought, and to his surprise he empathized with the professor's plight.

"Where exactly were you when Quentin was attacked?" Niall asked.

Jacob scoffed, but the sound seemed to be directed mostly at himself. "Why do you even bother asking me that? You saw me. I was at the fire pit. Too far away from the moon altar to have made it back there before you and the detective spilled out of the office. And, Mr. Valentine, I'm fifty-nine years old. I don't have it in me to do cross-country sprints anymore."

Niall had to give Jacob that one. A man almost in his sixties probably wouldn't have made the distance in a timely fashion. Did that absolve Jacob from the inquiries? Maybe. Maybe not. Because not everyone in their sixties, or older, were decrepit couch potatoes.

"Did you see the others? Bodhi or Sadler?" Niall continued.

Jacob nodded, looking tired and worn. It couldn't all be his age. It had to have hit the man hard to see his dream of a peaceful community of like minds being torn to shreds by the actions of a brutal murderer.

"Yes, I saw both of them, talking in the outdoor garden. Bodhi has a tendency to hide and retreat to the garden or the greenhouse when he's upset. Working the land soothes his spirit. As for Sadler, I don't know. This is, what, the third or fourth time he's even set foot on the land? He is not what one might call open-minded. I think he only tolerates us because of Ethan, who flourishes here." Jacob wiped a hand across his face and straightened up. "In any case, I saw both of them in the garden a few minutes before we heard the gunshot. I would have seen if either of them had gone uphill or run downhill."

Niall grimaced, again inwardly. This was bad news indeed. Jacob's statement meant that those suspects who were on the premises all had alibis for the attack on Quentin and the young police officer.

Fuck.

NIALL LEFT the office and met up with Hughes coming down the path from the direction of the moon altar. A few tech guys in white overalls passed them by, each carrying a heavy metal box, undoubtedly full of tools and evidence. Niall told Hughes everything Jacob had told him, about Alex and about the alibis everyone seemed to have.

Then another curious connection sparked in his mind.

"There are some disturbing parallels between this case and that first one I investigated with Gus," Niall said, harrumphing to himself. "Fire, water, earth…. It's all coming back to me now, and I'm getting this awful sense of déjà vu."

Niall still remembered all too vividly the body submerged in the bathtub, the burned man in the shop, and the young woman buried alive. The details were etched into his brain permanently. He shuddered at the recollection. He'd known ever since he was a child that people could be twisted, perverted, wrong, and evil. The Domville brothers had proven that point beyond a shadow of a doubt. The danger then had been tangible.

Hughes nodded glumly. "I hear you, Junior. Could there be a connection between the two cases? Between the Domville brothers and whoever is murdering people out here now?"

"I don't know. Everything we learned back in the spring suggested the Domvilles worked exclusively alone." Niall frowned and glanced over his shoulder at the office they had vacated. "I think, in the light of our narrow suspect pool alibiing out, we need to look into the possibility that the killer may be an outsider lurking in the woods outside the sanctuary."

Hughes went very still and serious. "You mean… a serial killer? Like the Green River Killer? Someone purposely targeting these faeries?" He shook his head, grimacing. "That could make this a federal case, and it would complicate things enormously. We would have to consider the likelihood that the victims might have been killed at random, for no other reason than being faeries. In that case investigating the victims and their lives for any signs of threats, problems, or enemies would be totally useless. That would put us back to square one."

Niall nodded, sighing. "I realize that. But we're running out of suspects. Quentin didn't bash his own head in. And while he was being attacked, we were all in the office."

Hughes shook his head emphatically. "That's not exactly true. You and I were in the office with Ethan. Everyone else was outside."

"Yes, but according to Jacob, he was at the fire pit, and Bodhi and Sadler were in the garden, and Alex was at the university, fifty miles away so not even in the neighborhood. Alibis, remember?" Again Niall looked over his shoulder. Through the window in the office door, he could see the broken figure of Jacob Marlowe sitting in his chair, weeping. "When the shot was fired and we all stumbled out, Ethan was with us, and none of the others could be the killer."

"Yeah, but that doesn't absolve them from Rowan's death," Hughes reminded Niall. "And remember what the lab boys said? The acid burn on the statue had been done at least three-to-five hours earlier. If the statue was defaced well in advance of the attack, then the window of opportunity required for Quentin's murder is much smaller."

"Yes, but the trip up- and downhill is long. You'd have to be pretty fit to make it there and back again in such a short time." Niall sighed. "I mean, I'm in pretty good shape, and even I got winded just walking up to the moon altar, let alone if I'd had to make a run for it."

Hughes grumbled under his breath. He clearly wasn't happy with the implications of the latest events. "Yeah, yeah, I suppose you're right. We've got to look at this from another angle." He was interrupted when his cell phone beeped with a text message. "The forensics just came through," Hughes said, reading the text as he went forward. "Rowan Tuff's blood was saturated with diamorphine."

Niall frowned. "That's heroin, isn't it?"

Hughes nodded. "Yeah, medical heroin. It's a toxin that affects pain receptors. With it in his system, it's possible Rowan felt no pain during his savage beating. I hope he wasn't still alive when he was finally incinerated. But if he was, the drug might have numbed some of the pain. If he was even conscious."

Niall whistled low. "That'd be a relief. Of a kind."

Hughes's eyebrows shot up. "Oh, wow. So the body definitely belongs to Rowan Tuff. The University of Washington's medical center had his blood sample on file from three years ago. He'd been a blood donor back then."

Niall didn't know what to say as he slowly absorbed the news. "So Gus was wrong. It wasn't a faked death. Rowan really is dead." He shook his head trying to clear his jumbled thoughts. "Any news on Quentin?"

"He's still at the hospital being checked, but it looks like he's gonna be okay." Hughes sounded relieved.

Niall felt the same. Quentin's heart had stopped when his lungs filled with water. But Niall's prompt action after dragging him out of the pool had expelled the water and CPR had restarted Quentin's heart. The ambulance had come in the nick of time. Quentin had dodged a bullet and was hopefully on his way to making a full recovery, if just to spite his would-be killer. If the young cop hadn't discharged his weapon, they never would have found Quentin in time. Speaking of which…

"How about the officer, what's his name?" Niall asked.

"Holt? He received a bad blow to the head. But he's in the ICU, out of danger." Sharing that piece of news actually brought a smile to Hughes's lips.

Niall understood that. Losing a comrade in arms, or in Hughes's case, a brother in blue, would have turned this murder investigation into an insane, out-of-control witch hunt. The media would have turned the whole thing into a shitstorm, the repercussion wreaking havoc in the neo-pagan community. It would have become a battle of faiths, fought with smear campaigns, and those situations never ended well.

"Craig Holt and Quentin Cross are strong men. They will fight." Hughes sounded certain of that fact, and Niall saw no reason to contradict his assessment.

"They're in the hospital, on the mend," Niall said. "The problem we have is that, according to Gus's message, there are two more lines to the poem. One refers to land, the last to blood."

"So… two more possible deaths?" Hughes grunted, clearly displeased. "This sanctuary is open on all sides. Apart from a few wooden fences to mark the edges of the land, there are no real walls to safeguard the residents here. There are no perimeter sensors, no tripwires, no security cameras, no guards, no doors or locks. We should consider evacuating every one of the suspects back to the city. If the killer is an outsider lurking in the vicinity, looking for an opportunity to take his next victim, we have no way of seeing him coming or stopping him. We're shit out of luck."

"Should we call for backup or, better yet, the feds?" Niall suggested, as worried about the safety of those left on the grounds as Hughes. "Or we could just get in the car, grab the suspects, and head back to Seattle. Let the local sheriffs and rangers deal with whoever's hiding in the bushes."

Hughes gave Niall the stink eye. "I doubt the local boys have the kind of knowledge or expertise it takes to catch a professional murderer or an organized serial killer. They know the territory, but that's all. I won't leave them in the lurch. Besides, if we evacuate these folks, and if the killer really is focused solely on faeries, then he'll probably follow us and still be our problem."

"We can protect these people better in the city," Niall reminded Hughes.

Hughes paused, seemingly giving the suggestion a great deal of thought. "Safe houses would work, yeah." His concerned gaze swept across the verdant landscape. "The real question is, will these people trust us, representatives of the police and the government, to escort them off the grounds to a locked safe house and keep them under protection indefinitely?"

Niall hadn't considered that aspect, and he sighed. "Bodhi will be a problem. He won't come willingly. Perhaps not even if Jacob begs him to cooperate. Bodhi doesn't trust us. Probably for good reason."

Hughes growled in anger. "Yeah, but unfortunately we don't have time for politeness or to placate Bodhi's delicate sensibilities. You're right. We've got to get everyone out of here, and fast."

"I will speak with Bodhi."

Niall and Hughes both started when Jacob spoke. He had snuck up on them unnoticed. Jacob looked miserable, his eyes puffy and red, his nose equally crimson, and his voice hoarse and thick.

"He will listen to me." Jacob nodded, mostly to himself, and walked off, hunched and defeated. Niall wondered if Jacob, seeing the end of his dream, had lost the will to live. The human mind was vulnerable, and the human heart was fragile. Nothing broke you like the loss of purpose and meaning in your life.

"Why would anyone want to harm these people?" Hughes murmured, his quiet voice bewildered.

Niall hid a smile. Hughes had started to see Jacob and the others as the good folk they seemed to be. His question had validity. Why these attacks on harmless folk who worshiped the earth, swore in the name of ethical living, and occasionally dressed up? Niall tried to put himself in the murderer's head and detect a motive that would make sense. Hating people who never did any harm and who stood for cleaner living, respect for the earth, and loving themselves and each other as sexual beings? Seemed counterproductive and pointless.

Could the killer be of a different kind of faith? A real hellfire-and-brimstone type who believed he was acting in the name of his own vengeful, worship-no-other god. That increased the suspect pool to cover half the nation, Niall concluded pessimistically.

While Niall was busy mulling over those meaning-of-life issues, Ethan and Frank Sadler walked up to them, hand in hand.

"Gentlemen, I would very much like to take my husband home now, please, if that's okay with you," Frank said sternly, clearly unwilling to hear counterarguments.

Ethan leaned into his husband, his innocent eyes wide and worried. He emanated fear and sadness, and Niall didn't want to add to that.

"I'd prefer you come with us to a safe house in Seattle," Hughes said gravely. "We'd appreciate your cooperation. There's a killer on the loose, and you could all be in danger of—"

"Absolutely not," Frank snapped. "I can't trust Ethan will be safe in such a place, with everyone gathered in one location with a huge bullseye on their backs. No, I'll take him home where he'll be—"

"Frank, please." Ethan held on to Frank's arm, his pleading gaze aimed at his husband. "I'd feel safer with them. They're trying to catch the killer, after all. Please?"

Frank frowned. Then he blinked and unwound. "Anything for you, my beau." His face grew stiff and sinister again when he turned his attention back to Hughes. "Very well. We'll come with you. But I warn you, Detective. If anything happens to my Ethan, I will have your badge."

Sadler clearly wasn't concerned for anyone else's life or safety, Niall observed. His sole focus seemed to be Ethan. Niall guessed that made Frank an extremely attentive and devoted husband, and he was glad the young man who appeared so defenseless had someone who had his back at all times.

Before Hughes could reply, Jacob and Bodhi joined them. Bodhi glared at them, sullen and snarling, but Jacob had his arm over Bodhi's shoulder, which seemed to calm him a bit.

"We're ready to go with you as well, Detective," Jacob said, smiling shortly.

Next to him, Bodhi crossed his arms and gave Niall and Hughes a scathing look. But in the end he must have agreed because he said nothing to contradict Jacob's words. Niall saw that as a blessing in disguise.

In under five minutes, they were all packed in one car and on their way to Seattle.

Chapter 14

"I HATE to say this, honey, but… damn, you look like week old vomit," Gus said with a grimace, his nose scrunched. "And smell like it too. Bad day at the office, dear?"

As Gus expected, Niall cringed, squared his shoulders, with unpleasant pops sounding from his joints, and grunted. "Don't even start with me, babe. It's been a horrendous day, and we've got nothing to show for it. Fuck. I'm so tired, I just wanna lay down and die."

Niall shrugged off his coat but left it on the floor and staggered into the living room, falling on his face on the couch. There he continued to grumble under his breath but was completely unintelligible.

Gus suppressed a grin as he picked up Niall's coat and hung it on the peg on the wall. He understood. Not everyone's daily failures or mishaps affected the lives of other people. Those who did carried a terrible weight on their shoulders.

"Wanna talk about it?" Gus asked as he strolled to the kitchen overlooking the living room and reheated dinner. Niall mumbled something into the couch cushions. Gus smiled. "Want some dinner? I made you some lasagna. Smell those aromas?" Gus made a theatrical production of inhaling. "Italian beef, onions, mushrooms, mozzarella cheese—"

"You had me at dinner," Niall muttered ravenously as he levered himself up from the couch, a huge grateful grin on his lips. He was a sucker for Italian food.

Gus chuckled. "Okay, papa bear. Sit down and have a beer." He placed a bottle of beer in front of his partner, the beer so fresh and cold the glass sweat.

The long-suffering sigh Niall emitted as he sat down came from somewhere so deep inside him that Gus surmised it must have actually hurt. "Once you've eaten, I was thinking of a hot bath and a nice rubdown in bed. How does that sound?"

After taking a big swig of his beer, Niall hid a small belch behind his hand and then nodded, his gaze already a bit blissful. "Sounds perfect, Gus. I swear, I don't know what I'd do without you."

Gus smirked as he pulled the food out of the still-warm oven and laid the plate before his fiancé. "I'm glad you're here too, sweetie. I'd hate to think of you going home from work to an empty, cold house with no one there waiting for you."

Niall swiped several forkfuls of lasagna into his mouth and washed it down with a few gulps of beer. "Yeah, I'd hate that too. I'm lucky to have you." He cast a warm, loving glance at Gus, who beamed at the sentiment and the praise. After a while he said, "I was kind of surprised to learn about your ex and Marlowe. I hate to say this, but Jacob told me point-blank that he saw the affair as nothing more than that. An affair."

Gus frowned, though he couldn't quite pinpoint why. "Alex is in love with Jacob. Not that he's ever going to admit that."

Niall shrugged. "That's his problem. What was it you called it? Karma? Yeah, karma's a bitch. He's finally being treated the way he's treated everyone he's ever been with. That kind of, oh, pattern, I guess? Yeah, a repeating pattern, cycles of repetition, karma and all that. That's what you believe, babe, isn't it? Setting the balance?"

Gus's frown deepened. He'd always seen his faith as a positive one. He'd never before had to consider that karmic blowback would cause pain and suffering to someone he knew and had known intimately. Was he really feeling sorry on Alex's behalf?

"There are only two laws of nature," Gus said. "Balance and change. At first they seem mutually exclusive. But they're not. Nothing is static or immutable forever, and everything changes. And changes. no matter how small or great, tend to stabilize, thus returning the equilibrium."

Niall offered a lopsided grin. "While that's really nice, what does that have to do with anything?"

Gus sighed ruefully. "Alex could be selfish as a—no, partner isn't the right word. Part-time lover, maybe? Anyway, unrequited love sucks and can twist a man, making him worse. I don't want that for Alex. He could have treated me better, yes, but then again, I could have done the same and been… I don't know, more to him."

Niall wiped his mouth with a napkin and leaned back, his eyes narrowing in suspicion. "Sounds like you still have feelings for him."

Gus shook his head, not even a part of him getting angry, because Niall wasn't making an accusation. "We started off hot, then cooled off, and by the time we went our separate ways, we were pretty icy. But… he's not an enemy. He's just an ex I harbor no ill will toward. Maybe one day we could even try to be friends." He sighed, the breath just whooshing out of him. Then he added, "But we could be nothing more than that. That ship has sailed."

Niall appeared pensive. "So, what you're saying is that you have the kind of feelings for him that you'd have toward any ex-boyfriend or ex-friend 'cause you're not a total dick?" His eyes danced with mirth, so his meaning became instantly clear.

Gus laughed. "Wow, got it in one, smarty pants."

Niall smiled but then grew serious. "If you want what's best for Alex, then I suppose you're not too happy about Jacob thinking their fling wasn't all that memorable or lasting."

Gus waved a frustrated hand about, pursing his lips. "Oh, who cares at this point? That is their business, not ours. Alex is a big boy. He can take care of himself. I want no part in his weird melodrama. And certainly not in the middle of a murder investigation."

Shrugging, Niall said nothing. He focused on eating and drinking, and to Gus that was fine. Rehashing a relationship from the past did neither of them any good.

"How's the case going?" Gus asked, mostly out of politeness.

Now that he'd figured out that Alex wasn't a likely suspect, he was less invested in the debacle than he'd expected. Was he attempting to distance himself from the negative emotions bound to follow? Had he simply seen too many dead bodies in his relatively short life span since he'd gotten to know Niall? No, Gus could and would never blame Niall for bringing these horrible things into his life. Gus had a lot to be thankful for because he had no reason to doubt Niall's commitment to him. Niall would die for Gus.

Of course, Niall did have a hunk friend hanging around for no apparent reason….

Gus forcibly shrugged the petty jealousy off his shoulders. It was unbecoming anyway.

"Oh, the case is going great," Niall grunted sarcastically. "One by one, Hughes and I, we've managed to reduce the suspect pool down to exactly zero. Now it's starting to look more and more likely that the killer is an outsider who's targeting faeries."

Gus gasped. "You mean… a serial killer?" Funny, but that had been his thought earlier.

"Maybe." Niall sounded skeptical, but his frown spoke of doubts. He was clearly of two minds about the whole thing. "I don't know for sure. But from what we've been able to deduce and prove, our suspects have alibis either for one murder or both, making it unlikely any of them could have done both murders. Unless they were in two places at once." His amused gaze hit Gus dead on. "Any magic in your bag of tricks that could explain that or make it feasible?"

Gus gave Niall an admonishing glare, though he couldn't keep the smile off his lips. "Magic is all around us, in every mundane miracle we dismiss, in every kiss from a loved one we believe we can repeat whenever we want." He chuckled. "But do I know of a teleportation spell that could make a killer move instantly in time and space, like doing jumping jacks? No, honey, I don't. You'll have to write to Hogwarts for that."

Niall laughed loudly, the lines of tension and the taut rigidity in his body vanishing as he relaxed. Gus was glad to see his fiancé unwind and allow himself a few moments of happiness and laughter amid a hard world full of brutality and death.

It was high time to shift gears, Gus decided, and take this death race in for a pit stop. "Okay. Enough shop talk. If you're done with dinner, it's bath time."

Niall quirked a lopsided grin. "You offering to wash my back, baby?"

Gus leered. "Honey, I'll wash any part you want, and with extra care and diligence."

TOWELING NIALL dry later, Gus took his sweet time. He rubbed along the length of Niall's back, down to his buttocks, and between his legs to caress Niall's balls most attentively.

Niall chuckled a bit breathlessly. "I think I'm dry enough. So how's about you and me make some rain?"

Gus laughed while rolling his eyes. "Gosh, that was cheesy. But I liked it." He nodded toward the bed. "On your stomach, mister. Now."

Shaking his head with what looked like disbelief, Niall scrambled naked onto the bed and settled comfortably on his belly. Once he stopped stirring and lay still, visibly relaxing, he let out a lingering sigh. "Can't wait to feel your hands on me."

Gus blushed at the praise and the arousal rising and smiled bashfully. Somehow those words meant the world when they came from the man he admired and cherished. "Don't move," he ordered softly and rushed to turn down the lights and fetch what he needed for a backrub.

He placed two clean towels and a tube of body oil on the bed, ignited two aromatic candles, and put on low ambient music by Jonn Serrie that evoked images of planets, stars, nebulas, galaxies, and universes. The scent of fresh linens added to the darker odor of black orchid in the oil, and Gus inhaled, finding the right mood.

Gus wanted to give his lover pleasure, but not in a sexual way, so he ensured his pants stayed on as he settled over the backs of Niall's thighs. He wetted his hands, warmed the lotion on them, and then pressed them over Niall's lower back. The muscles there jumped under the contact, feeling hard and strained, bunched with stress. With leisurely circles and modest pressure, Gus went to work.

With his palms Gus searched for the large muscles and gave them his full attention. He kept the pressure even and firm, without squeezing or nipping or staying in one place too long. Niall didn't have a hairy back, and neither did he have scars, except for one—a long thin line that stretched from the bottom of his right shoulder blade almost to the small of his back.

Niall had gotten it in a knife fight back in the Army, but he never talked about it. Gus didn't pry, but he often traced the silky white shape with his lips or tongue. This time he followed the line with his fingertips. Niall murmured something, sounding sleepy already. That was fine by Gus, who felt Niall needed sleep and rest more than sex and orgasms.

Gus spread his fingers and left their wake in the massage oil as he covered Niall's skin with his touch, gently pressing with his palms and the heels of his hands, alleviating Niall's stress. His skin was soft, warm, and malleable after the shower, and he'd gotten some summer sun too, though that was a miracle considering this was the Pacific Northwest.

Gus waited until Niall went totally pliant under his ministrations as he slid his hands wherever they wanted to go. With curved, fluid motions

Gus alternated between the softest touch and something a bit stronger. Niall purred, his hips moving restlessly, and Gus guessed his lover wasn't oblivious to the sensual aspect of what they were doing. Niall's cheeks pinked as he laid his head sideways on the pillow, and then his lips parted, soft and plump and moist. Gus wanted to lean in and kiss him, but this massage wasn't supposed to be about sex.

"Breathe, love," Gus whispered, encouraging his partner to chillax.

"Mmm…" was Niall's articulate reply, muffled by the pillow.

With long, steady strokes, Gus glided his hands over Niall's back. He couldn't help but ponder how much he relied on Niall's strength, physical and mental, as his partner in life. Niall's power and his ability to do some things Gus wasn't ready for or capable of resonated with Gus, exciting him in a way no other lover before had.

Gus's cock hardened and pushed impatiently against his zipper. How could it not? Niall was hot, and he wanted Gus. It was a heady feeling to be coveted so.

The rich after-scent of black plum, adding to the black orchid, wafted to his nose from the lotion. Gus fanned his fingers and searched for the harder parts of Niall's back: the girdle of his rib cage and the tiny bumps of his spine. With his movements, first up the sides and then down the middle, his motions created a crude heart shape. Gus smiled as he saw the design left in the lotion by his hands.

Adding some pressure, he kneaded the larger muscles, squeezing slowly. Niall's glutes, plump and muscular from work and exercise, were smooth and just a bit fuzzy under Gus's hands, the sensation at once familiar and erotic.

Then Gus raked his nails down Niall's back, from his nape to the crevice between his asscheeks. The result would have been the same if Gus had blown on Niall's skin: goose bumps arose everywhere, and Niall shivered, moaning low under his breath.

"Babe?" Niall murmured from the depths of the puffy pillow.

"Yeah?" Gus asked, suspending his hands.

"Fuck me. Please?" Niall rarely asked to bottom. He usually liked to top or frot or swap blowjobs, so Gus was mildly surprised. Then again, with the day he'd had? Perhaps it wasn't such an astonishing request after all.

"Yes." Gus rose up onto his haunches and popped open the top button of his jeans. He lathered the body oil onto his eager dick and then dripped several dollops in the tight space between Niall's buttocks. With well-oiled fingers he worked Niall's hole, gently and lovingly, not rushing, wanting Niall properly prepared so their sex would be equally good for both of them.

"C'mon, babe," Niall urged, pushing his ass up in the air, begging for a good humping. "Don't make me wait. I'm a fallin' asleep 'ere." His words slurred, but his body gyrated, seeking that elusive connection, moving almost entirely on automatic.

Gus didn't make his lover suffer. They'd discarded condom use a while back because they were exclusive and engaged, and they'd gotten tested. So it was safe for him to push his unsheathed cock inside Niall's willing body the same way Niall had been unsheathed inside him. Gus's cockhead breached the fluttering rings of muscle. The tight squeeze on his head felt like fire, suffocating him. But Niall breathed deep, and his channel gave way for Gus to enter slowly but surely till he was in to the hilt.

"How do you want it, love?" Gus asked, breathless himself, with sweat popping out of his pores and his muscles quivering from the urge to move. But he waited for the all clear.

Niall shook. "Hard and fast, Gus. Be rough."

Gus swallowed. That request was also uncommon for Niall. It seemed the murder case had gotten to him worse than Gus had anticipated, creeping under his skin.

"Okay," he acquiesced quietly. "But I won't hurt you, understand?"

Niall nodded but said nothing, so Gus assumed he had accepted that pain wouldn't be on the menu today. It pretty much never was with them, apart from an occasional butt slap, a couple of nail scrapes, and a bite mark or two. Gus wasn't so innocent or naive that he didn't get the appeal of that kind of sex. But he sensed Niall sought a connection and a release more than actual pain.

He gripped Niall's hips, withdrew slowly, and then pushed back in hard. Niall grunted but shoved his ass back. Gus started a deep pounding rhythm, plunging in and out of his lover's hot, pliant body. He lowered himself down over Niall's back, blanketing him. Then he hooked his arms under Niall's shoulders, took a firm grip, and spread his legs, trapping Niall between his thighs. This allowed him to go deeper, faster, and rougher, exactly how Niall wanted it.

For a while, they didn't speak, just panted and moaned. Niall clutched the sheets, his knuckles white while his skin elsewhere was ruddy and sweaty. His dark hair curled at the nape with sweat, and Gus kissed him there—and then sunk his teeth in the junction between his neck and shoulder. Niall jolted, and he twisted his neck to plant a sloppy kiss on Gus's lips.

"God, Gus. Gonna come," Niall whispered hoarsely, a desperate need burning in his eyes like a wild inferno.

Nodding, Gus pressed his forehead between Niall's shoulder blades, picked up the pace, and rammed his cock into Niall's channel, again and again. "Yeah, love. Gonna make you come so hard you'll see stars, and your cock will pour over us like a rainstorm. Gonna make you scream."

Gasping, Niall seemed utterly rapt at Gus's words. Dirty pillow talk wasn't often part of their bag of tricks in bed.

Gus slid his hand past Niall's hips and under his jerking body and took his shaft in hand, stroking the throbbing piece of meat with a rough hold. Every time he reached the cockhead, he swiped a thumb over the leaking slit, causing Niall to grunt and jump. He was so close, and that was all Gus needed.

Gus's body convulsed as instinct took over, and he spilled his seed in Niall's channel, crying out as the giant orgasmic wave washed over him. Not a single coherent thought was left in his mind. He felt faint as Niall pulled Gus's constricted fingers off his cock, and only then did Gus realize he'd had a death grip on his poor lover's tender member. Muttering apologies became pointless, however, when he felt the sticky hot wetness of Niall's spunk covering his hand. Sighing happily, Gus slowly eased himself out of his lover's roughly used channel.

Niall rolled on his back, a sated and well-fucked look behind his half-mast eyelids. "Thanks, Gus." Niall's drowsy gaze and slow smile told Gus he'd done well and given his lover some much-needed relaxation.

Gus smiled, finally able to draw a breath, think more than "oh yeah," and form words. "You're welcome. Don't get up. I'll clean you up. Now hush."

Niall didn't need to be told twice. His eyelashes fluttered for a second, and then he was off to dreamland, his shallow breathing a testament to how easily he'd fallen asleep, thanks to Gus's magic fingers and even more magical cock.

Gus got up gingerly and fetched a hot, wet towel from the bathroom. With it, he swabbed Niall's hole, and then he glided upward. He swiped gently over the delectable mess Niall had made on Gus's hands and his own belly, the sticky substance cooling off fast, until Niall was clean. Then he tenderly tugged on Niall's balls as he cleansed them, and Niall groaned a little in his sleep.

Niall's cockhead still had a few errant droplets of come around his slit. The area was sensitive, and the terry towel was coarse, so Gus licked his lips and softly sucked on the tip of Niall's dick. He licked around the mushroom-shaped head and probed the slit with his tongue. After his meticulous efforts, not a single smear remained.

Niall moaned, still asleep, and a smile tugged at his lips. Gus chuckled and whispered, "Sleep, love. Just missed a few drops, is all." Then he laid Niall's limp, thick cock on the groove of his hip, and then covered him with a blanket.

Gus retreated to the bathroom, closed the door, washed the dirty towel in the sink, and placed it on the radiator. He'd wash it later anyway, but he didn't want to throw a wet cloth in with the rest of the laundry. That was how mildew formed, and the smell was damn hard to get rid of.

As he washed off in the tub with a few soap suds and a mild rinsing, Gus smiled wide at the happy memory he and Niall had just made together. This case had come awfully close to the skin. Not quite as much as their last troubles, which had taken the lives of friends and family. Still, Niall's glum mood clearly showed how he felt about the faeries, people he hadn't known a week ago but whom he now wanted to protect.

To Gus, Niall was a hero. He vowed to appreciate and soothe his man more in the future, with or without sex.

Chapter 15

GUS WALKED out of the bathroom, drying his hair with a towel and whistling along with a catchy pop tune playing on the kitchen radio. Gus was in too high spirits to worry about Niall having already left—without Gus—to rendezvous with Hughes at the hospital to see if Quentin's condition had improved. Because it was still early morning and he'd barely shed the cobwebs of sleep, Gus almost bumped into Autumnsong standing by the coffeemaker, bold as you please.

"Jesus Christ, Kin, you scared the shit out of me." Gus panted for a moment but was unable to keep up the anger. The hot shower had melted his bones and mellowed his mind. "How'd you even get in?"

"You gave me a key, remember?" Autumnsong quirked an eyebrow, scoffed, and shook his head, appearing more bored than amused. He was also far more collected than he'd been on his previous visit. He'd added dyed purple and pink striations to his spiky, otherwise black hair. His typical heavy eye makeup and glistening lip gloss were firmly in place once more, giving him a pretty luscious look. He also wore several metal earrings in both ears, colorful ribbon bracelets on each wrist, and a variety of steel rings with occult symbols on them. The black feather boa around his neck, ever present and recognizable, completed his signature outfit.

"Oh yeah, right." Gus said nothing more. He retreated back to the quiet solitude of the bathroom, disrobed, and put on clean underwear, jeans, and a T-shirt, brushed his hair, and only then returned to the kitchen. Autumnsong stood where Gus had left him, leaning against the counter and sipping coffee, arms tucked against his chest.

"Did you leave me any?" Gus asked, grumbling under his breath and scowling at his surprise guest.

Autumnsong nodded. "Yeah. Help yourself." He moved aside, perhaps an inch.

Gus rolled his eyes. How nice of Autumnsong to invite Gus to have a helping of his own coffee. Nonetheless, he poured himself a cup and took a few swigs before saying anything that might start an argument.

The coffee tasted different than usual, though. "Did you do something to—"

"Gave it my own flavor and flare," Autumnsong cut in, his tone cool and disinterested.

Gus was pleasantly surprised. "It's really good. Thank you." When his uninvited guest didn't comment, Gus asked, "How are you?" Autumnsong gave him a pointed look, and Gus had the decency to blush mildly. "I just meant that you were pretty shaken when we saw you last."

Autumnsong shrugged. "I'm fine. Forget you ever saw that… that debasement."

Gus frowned, displeased. "No, I don't think I'll be doing that. It was good to see you as a human being, even if it was just once and in such a low moment for you."

Autumnsong snorted. "God, you're such a bleeding heart. Grow up."

Gus chuckled. "Funny. I'm older than you, you know."

"Like I could forget, Grandpa." Autumnsong placed his empty cup on the counter and sat down at the table. For the first time that morning, Gus got a good look at him. Autumnsong was restless: fidgeting, tearing his cuticles, drawing patterns on the surface of the wooden table with his nails.

"Kin, has something happened?" Gus asked with concern.

Autumnsong grimaced. "Please, stop calling me that. It's not my name anymore."

Suppressing a sigh, Gus sat down opposite his guest. "Okay. I'm sorry if I offended. It wasn't my intention."

Autumnsong blew out an impatient breath. "No kidding. You're such a sap sometimes. When you act so ridiculously sentimental, I forget you've solved actual murders."

Gus shrugged, refusing to rise to the bait. "Are you going to tell me what's wrong, or do I have to keep guessing?"

"You know the difference between a life lesson and a valuable lesson?" Autumnsong asked, confusing Gus further. Gus was forced to shake his head. "A valuable lesson is less likely to get you killed."

Gus smiled shortly. "Deep."

Autumnsong gave him a lopsided smirk. "Careful, Goodwin. You're in serious danger of becoming as cynical as me."

"Heaven forbid." Gus drew a theatrical inhalation and pressed his palm over his heart.

Autumnsong seemed amused, and honestly so, not his usual pretense or camouflage. Then he said quietly, "Since we last met, I've had a life lesson. Or, to be precise, I've had it rammed down my throat whether I liked it or not. Is what I hear true? Has there been another murder?"

Gus saw no reason to keep information from Autumnsong, who had the uncanny ability to find out the truth anyway. "No. An attempted murder. Quentin Cross was almost drowned. Niall's CPR saved his life. The paramedics might have had something to do with that too. It was a close call. Without a gunshot by Craig Holt, the police officer on the scene, Niall and Hughes might not have made it to Quentin in time. Quentin and Holt are both in the hospital. Quentin is in a kind of deep sleep, but at least he's not in a coma, thank the Goddess. Holt received a blow to the head. But according to Hughes, they're both going to be fine."

To Gus's surprise, Autumnsong's eyes had narrowed dangerously as he stared at him in complete silence, and his expression was a tense mask of cold rage. Gus could practically hear the cogs turning inside his brain. He wished the young man would speak out and reveal whatever it was he knew. Their lives could depend on that piece of information.

"Tell me," Autumnsong whispered softly, in a voice so filled with fury that Gus shivered upon hearing it, "Why do you, your man, and that detective assume that the same person committed both the murder and the attempted murder? The methods differed, did they not? A burning and then a drowning."

Gus frowned in bewilderment, cocking his head. "There were lines from the same poem found at both crime scenes. That suggests—"

"Stop. Tell me about the suspects. Whether they have alibis or not."

Gus realized Autumnsong was in full tactical mode, and nothing would change that. So he decided to be as clear and detailed as he could. "Okay. First, Jacob Marlowe, the owner and founder of Mount Paradise Sanctuary. When Rowan was murdered, Marlowe was meditating at the Gaia altar, which is on the other end of the compound, farthest away from the murder site. There were no eyewitnesses. When Quentin was attacked, Marlowe was tending the flames at the fire pit in the center of the area, in plain sight."

"He wouldn't have had time to attack Quentin," Autumnsong concluded.

Gus nodded. "Right. Second, Alex Kittridge, a professor of new religious movements who is studying the faeries and also acting as a caretaker. When Rowan was murdered, Alex was reading in the office building. He was alone, so no eyewitnesses. When Quentin was attacked, Alex was at the University of Puget Sound—talking with me."

Autumnsong quirked an eyebrow, managing to convey a sneer even with such a small gesture. "That seems to rule him out," he remarked lazily.

Gus bristled and gritted his teeth but again refused to be annoyed on purpose. "Third, Bodhi Jha, another caretaker at the sanctuary. When Rowan was murdered, Bodhi was doing chores at the greenhouse. Again there are no eyewitnesses. Of the suspects, he was closest to the murder site. When Quentin was attacked, Bodhi was speaking with Frank Sadler in the outdoor garden, and they were both seen."

Autumnsong looked away, his mask still in place. "You expect me to declare Bodhi's innocence from the rooftops because he's my foster brother?"

Gus shook his head. "No. You loved Rowan. I think you would stand against the killer regardless of who he turns out to be. Even if the murderer turned out to be Bodhi."

Autumnsong's long eyelashes fluttered as they veiled his gaze from Gus's inquisitive observation. Then he smiled a little, but it was rueful, so he must have come to terms with the possibility. "You're right about that. Go on."

Gus acquiesced because he sensed they were pressed for time. "Fourth, Ethan Sadler, a faerie who resides at the sanctuary during the summer. When Rowan was murdered, Ethan was supposed to be changing sheets in the barn, but he was spying on an orgy at the love shack. Quentin saw him there, having followed him there on purpose because he has a crush on Ethan, even though he was supposed to be arranging the stage for a theatrical performance. When Quentin himself was attacked, Ethan was in the office—being interrogated by Niall and

Hughes. Fifth, sort of, Frank Sadler, Ethan's husband. He's not seen as a suspect in Rowan's murder, as I think he was in Seattle at the time, and when Quentin was attacked, Frank was seen speaking with Bodhi in the garden."

"I see." Autumnsong's eyes flashed, but Gus had no idea what that meant. Interpreting the young man was an impossible task. "Now do you see the point to my initial question?"

Gus blinked, trying to sort his thoughts into some semblance of sanity and reason. "You asked me why we assume both crimes were committed by the same person, and I told you about the poem lines. *Faerie Fire, Faggot Fire* and *Faerie Flood, Faggot Flood*. Two lines of one poem that appeared at two crime scenes? It's not a leap to imagine—"

"Think outside the box," Autumnsong interjected with a warning tone. "Just because you can easily imagine it doesn't mean there's no other explanation."

Gus wondered what other deductions there were to be made, but he did his best to avoid disappointing his helpful guest. "Uh, the two lines of the poem… do kind of suggest…." Gus was having a hard time shifting to a different avenue of thought. He struggled with finding alternative possibilities. Then an idea struck him. "Although the first line was written *after* the murder, but the second line was already there *before* the murder attempt…."

Autumnsong rolled his eyes. "Finally. I swear, I thought I was going to have to bitch-slap you to get you to *think*."

Gus wracked his brain, trying to figure out what the timing of the poetic graffiti implied about the murders. He was convinced now that Autumnsong was not simply being difficult and dramatic. Autumnsong knew something, but he obviously had no intention of making things easy for Gus and sharing it. For some reason, he wanted Gus to work it out himself. When one notion finally occurred to him, it was sinister.

Gus gasped in shock. "Could… could there be… *two* murderers… working together? Oh. My. God." With fumbling fingers, he fished out his iPhone and started texting rapidly. Unless he warned Niall immediately of the potential danger, Gus might just suffer a nervous breakdown.

"Where are the suspects now?" Autumnsong asked, cutting in as he stood quickly.

"A police safe house in Seattle," Gus answered after finishing the text to Niall and Hughes. Autumnsong was gearing up for action, and that told Gus he needed to ready himself as well. "Why?"

Autumnsong headed directly for the front door, picked up his boots from the floor, and put them on. As he did, he said only, "We need to get there. Right the fuck now."

Gus didn't wait for explanations but put on his shoes and coat. If Autumnsong foresaw trouble, then trouble they would no doubt get.

NIALL HATED hospitals. Or maybe he hated doctors and nurses. He couldn't decide which was worse: the bleak, clinically cold buildings, or the indifferent, coldhearted people walking their dreary halls.

It wasn't like he was afraid of disease or getting ill. Hospitals carried sickness, yes, but more than that, they were pits of despair, pain, sorrow, loss, and death, worn like a crown of thorns or the weight of the world. If hope and healing wandered these halls too, Niall had yet to encounter them. They must have skittered here and there, ethereal like will-o'-the-wisps, intangible and uncatchable.

But they needed to be here. Hughes had gotten a call that Quentin was awake, so they immediately rushed over to ask him some questions. At the moment, Quentin was their only hope of learning more about the murderer. Or anything at all, to be exact, for they had precious little info to go on.

Unfortunately, when they reached reception, the nurse behind the desk informed them that Quentin had fallen asleep again. Despite her responsibility to aid the police in an investigation, her duty to her patients came first. Plus, after Hughes acted like his typical grumpy self, issuing demands, they'd been ordered back down to the first floor and the front waiting area. There Hughes stewed, and Niall tried not to laugh out loud.

They still sat there waiting after an hour when Niall received an urgent text from Gus. He read it and huffed out a surprised breath. "Jesus H. Christ." Hughes straightened up instantly and stared at him with an expectant look. "Gus thinks there could be two killers."

"What?" Hughes said with such a deep booming voice that people near them turned to see what the noise was about. "Why the hell—"

"The poem lines," Niall cut in, speaking fast while trying to catch on faster. "One was done after the murder, the other before. Gus thinks there's a possibility there are two murderers who work in unison. One did the deed, the other did the poem."

"Fuck, fuck, fuck," Hughes cursed out loud, earning some dirty looks. "You know what that means, don't you, Junior? Each and every alibi the original suspects had just went up in flames."

Niall had already comprehended that part of the new theory. Unfortunately, Hughes's interruption had cut off Niall's train of thought, and something was nagging at him, like rats eating through his carcass to expose bone. The epiphany eluded him. It hung on the tip of his tongue but refused to shed light on itself. *Dammit.* He'd been on the verge of discovery.

Suddenly Hughes jumped to his feet and rushed toward the reception desk. Niall started but followed on his heels, puzzled as to what had caught the detective's attention.

Then he recognized the young police officer, Craig Holt, who was standing awkwardly by the reception desk, a white bandage around his head and looking as pale as a sheet. A feverish glow in his eyes was a testament to the effects of the blow he'd received, both the physical and the mental.

When he noticed Hughes, Holt straightened and saluted. Niall was surprised. He didn't think anyone did that anymore, that outside of parades it was old-fashioned. Niall was pleased to observe the reaction, however, as it hinted at the respect the grumpy detective had garnered among his colleagues.

"Officer Holt," Hughes greeted the man with a softening in his features that told Niall he'd begun to view the young man as something of a protégé. "What are you doing out of bed? Shouldn't you be taking it easy on sick leave?" His fatherly admonishing tone amused Niall, but he wisely kept that to himself.

Holt nodded several times, standing so straight it had to hurt his spine. "Yes, sir, yes. I know I should but… I had to come and see for myself how Mr. Cross is doing. I heard he didn't die in the attack. Thank God." Stark relief eased his tense features, but he still appeared nauseated.

"You okay there, son?" Hughes asked, placing his big, work-roughened hand over the young officer's shoulder. That was unprecedented, Niall mused, as he'd never seen Hughes instigate physical contact, and certainly not with his subordinates.

Holt gave him a wan smile. His paleness and the black circles around his eyes attested to the pain he had endured. "I'm getting there, sir, thank you. Sir, if I may?" Once Hughes had nodded his consent, Holt said in a serious tone, "This case has become somewhat, uh… personal for me. I'd like to offer any help I can in apprehending the guilty parties, sir. I'll promise to take it easy."

Hughes smiled, seemingly pleased with Holt's initiative. "Very well, son. Go to the safe house, but, like you said, take it easy and return to the hospital at the first sign of trouble. Help the other officers keep an eye on the suspects since for all we know they could be intended targets. If anyone tries to enter there without a word from me, you and the other officers will arrest them. I appreciate your assistance, Holt, but do remember to watch out for yourself. You're not out of the woods yet. Head injuries can worsen in an instant."

Holt smiled with obvious gratitude. "Thank you, sir. I promise I'll do my best." Niall guessed the guy was like him, someone who hated sitting around in a hospital, feeling useless. That impressed Niall, and he decided he liked Craig Holt.

"Do you remember what happened?" Hughes asked, now back in detective mode.

Nodding wearily, Holt said, "Bits and pieces, sir. Mr. Cross and I walked to the moon altar. He was startled when we got there, and he pointed at the goddess statue. Its face was disfigured—with acid, I think. The symbol seemed familiar to me, but I can't recall…. Anyway, I heard footsteps behind me, but I didn't get the chance to turn around. The perp hit me on the back of my head, and I went down. I'd managed to pull out my gun from my side holster, and I'm pretty sure I fired a shot. But then… I must have passed out. I'm sorry, sir. That's all I remember."

Holt looked so downtrodden and miserable Niall felt the urge to hug him and console his wounded spirit.

"You did good, son," Hughes commented magnanimously. "Now rest awhile before going to the safe house. Just remember not to shoot us when we arrive." His gallows humor made both Niall and Holt chuckle.

Then Hughes added, "As for Quentin, he's not awake yet, so we're still waiting. And the symbol on the statue, the original crescent-moon shape, was tarnished with acid to resemble the commonly recognizable biohazard symbol."

Holt frowned and cocked his head. "Biohazard?"

"That seems to tie in with Rowan Tuff being drugged with diamorphine," Niall said.

"Medical heroin?" Holt repeated in confusion. Then he snapped his fingers, an act that was quickly followed by a cringe of pain. "Oh, that reminds me, sir, I checked into the background of the suspects." He fished out his notebook from his uniform shirt pocket and read from it. "I discovered something that could be related. Ethan's husband, Frank Sadler, is the chief medical officer of Malasum Pharmaceuticals. The corporation's basically big pharma, created in postwar Germany by one Otto S. Baer, a well-respected medical doctor. Frank Sadler himself is a pharmacological geneticist and toxicologist by training, and his past work dealt mainly with plant toxins."

Niall and Hughes exchanged a worried glance. How come this information had slipped under the radar? This was significant.

Niall did a quick web search on his iPhone for Frank Sadler, Malasum Pharma, Otto S. Baer, and pharmacology. He got hundreds of results, mostly articles in medical journals written by various scientists, more than a few referencing Malasum or Baer's original work in the field of clinical pharmacology. Frank Sadler had similar hits, so before he'd become a full-time businessman, he had been a capable scientist.

The weirdest things, however, were the search results when Niall looked up Baer and Sadler with the medical factor left out. Baer's name appeared in an old newspaper article in connection with one Friedrich Sadler, who apparently was Frank's grandfather. Both Otto Baer and Friedrich Sadler had died in the late 1940s, after the war but not long after the company was founded.

The obscure prewar article had nothing to do with the company, though. Instead, vague talk of theosophy and esotericism hinted at the existence of a secret cult that had thrived under occult-worshiping Nazi rule, with the figurehead being either Baer or Sadler.

Niall was utterly confused by then. The weirder and more abstruse the hits became on the search engine, the more perplexed and anxious Niall grew.

"What'd you find?" Hughes asked, startling Niall out of his odd musings.

Absentmindedly Niall noted that Holt had left while he'd been busy scavenging in the deepest and oddest levels of the Internet. "I haven't a clue. The founder of Malasum Pharma, Otto S. Baer, seems to have been a friend of Friedrich Sadler, who was Frank's grandfather. Both of them died in the late 1940s. And now the current Sadler, Frank, is working for a corporation created by Otto Baer."

"So?" Hughes asked, apparently as bewildered as Niall. "Nepotism has ruled corporate high rungs since the existence of mankind, and friends hire friends all the damn time, no matter how unjust or unethical that is."

"Baer and Sadler belonged to a secret cult existing during the Nazi rule of Germany," Niall replied, continuing to search for new nuggets of information. He was certain if he persisted in the excavation of buried secrets, something of importance would be uncovered.

But he didn't get the chance. The nurse behind the reception desk called out to Hughes, and once the men approached, she informed them that Quentin Cross was once again awake. Glad to hear of the positive development, Niall and Hughes rushed up to the third floor to the private room where Quentin was staying.

Out of drag and having barely survived a murder attempt, Quentin appeared so utterly different that for a moment Niall thought they'd gotten the wrong room. The beanpole of a man looked sad and sick, his fake tan and glitter gone, replaced by a pale complexion. Without his flaming red wig, Quentin had short graying hair that stuck to his clammy skin. The white hospital gown, lack of makeup, and dark circles around his eyes made him appear more dead than alive. In Niall's opinion, he would have been a better a fit in the morgue.

A bland smile and half-lidded eyes greeted them. "Oh. You're here. Mr. Valentine? I was told you saved me. Thank you." His voice was raspy and barely audible.

Niall offered him a short smile. "I'm just glad it worked. How are you, Mr. Cross?"

Quentin let out a brief chuckle that cracked. "All things considered I think you can call me Quentin. As for my well-being, I'll be grateful once I get out of here."

Niall snorted. "I can imagine. Don't tax yourself, okay? This is where you need to be at the moment." He exchanged looks with Hughes. "Listen, could we ask you a few questions? If you feel up to it, that is."

Quentin shrugged but then winced with evident pain. "I guess. I mean, my memory's a bit… hazy. Things aren't clear. I'll try, though. Ask away."

"Can you tell us what you do remember?" Hughes asked, taking out his notebook and pen and scribbling down Quentin's words, as unofficial as it was.

Quentin sighed. His gaze rose to the ceiling as though he were watching a movie being played there, the movie being his recent life-changing event. "We were walking uphill, the officer and I. When we came to the moon altar, I saw… the Goddess's statue had been defiled with scorched lines. I didn't really get a good look. I was pushed to the ground. I fell into the pond face first, and… and I think a foot on my upper back kept me down. Beyond that, I'm sorry, it's a blur."

"You didn't see the attacker's face or body or notice anything distinctive about him at all?" Niall asked, understanding they had lost a potential eyewitness and a good description of the attacker after all. "When you heard the officer being hit and firing his gun, surely you would have had time to—"

Definitely dumbfounded, Quentin stared at Niall with eyes as round as saucers and his mouth hanging open. "Gunshot? What gunshot? I didn't hear any shots. I was pushed down and then almost drowned. That's all she wrote."

At the exact same moment Niall and Hughes looked at each other and realized they'd been duped.

Chapter 16

THE SAFE house was located along Dexter Avenue North, in the northeastern corner of an apartment building. The place was constructed of light-red-colored cement blocks with patios and balconies, plus white-and-gray steel or concrete roofs, doors, and hallways. From the top floor, there were undoubtedly great views of the Space Needle and Lake Union to be had. At first glance, from afar anyway, the place seemed nice, convenient, and secure.

However, Gus and Autumnsong found that the main gate to the courtyard and the front door to the building were open for anyone to walk in from the street, one elevator didn't work, and the other was as slow as molasses in winter, and the hallways smelled of spoiled rubbish and animal urine.

Gus couldn't for the life of him fathom why the Seattle Police Department considered this a safe house. Perhaps the only reason that made sense was the fact that the West Precinct was only a few blocks away to the south. Still, Gus had his doubts about the whole deal.

"Did you notice?" Autumnsong asked as they stepped out of the elevator.

Gus scrunched his nose. "The pee's kinda hard to miss."

"No, not that. That the elevator was on the top floor. Where the safe house is."

Alarmed, Gus glanced down the quiet hall in both directions, but nothing stood out, and no one appeared in sight. "You think someone's already here?"

Autumnsong shrugged and headed toward the correct door. He knocked politely and stood in full view of the peephole. "We'll see," he commented in a level but fatalistic tone.

"Identify yourself" came a muffled command from the other side of the door.

Gus shifted next to Autumnsong and smiled, bringing up his driver's license in front of the peephole. "Hi. I'm Gus Goodwin. Detective Hughes might have mentioned me coming over?"

A brief silence followed. Then another voice asked, "Who's the other one?"

"A consultant," Gus lied quickly, smiling sweetly and hoping the cops inside took his word for truth. He hated lying to them but describing Autumnsong accurately, as the mysterious Satanist, they'd probably end up shooting him for argument's sake alone.

After a short silence, the lock clicked, and the door opened a crack. A stocky man with a rough stubble, a sulky expression, and a gun in hand stood as gatekeeper, preventing all entry. He gave Gus and Autumnsong a long, suspicious once-over before nodding grudgingly and opening the door wider to allow them to pass. Gus murmured his thanks and slipped into the room, followed soon by a placid-looking Autumnsong.

As soon as they were safely inside, the door slammed shut, and the goon-like cop said, "Up against the wall, guys. You've been vouched for by Detective Hughes, but I gotta frisk you."

As Gus assumed the pose he'd seen on TV cop shows, he gave Autumnsong a quick warning glare. He prayed the young rebel wouldn't start playing or teasing when the cop searched their persons. Gus feared Autumnsong would suggest a strip search or an anal-cavity sweep just to see the big man get flustered or angry.

By either divine intervention or serendipitous happenstance, Autumnsong neither said nor did anything to upset their warden. Gus released the breath he'd been holding.

Then he was able to take stock of his surroundings.

On the left of where they'd entered was an open kitchen with slab-granite countertops, steel appliances, and faux wood cabinets, and on the right was a small reading nook with a tall floor lamp. Directly ahead was the living room, with modern gray-white furniture—couch, chairs—the only exception being the glass coffee table. Beige walls, curtains, and rugs seemed drab, dull, and old-fashioned to Gus, but at least they were all clean. Doors on each side of the room led to bedrooms and bathrooms out of sight, and glass double doors led onto a balcony with a stunning view of Lake Union and the park.

There were two other police officers present in addition to their greeter. Both were in the living room with the suspects. The couch, chairs, and even the floor in the corner were occupied. One of the cops was a man in his late forties, with graying hair around his temples and in his trim beard. He had a small scar on his chin. The other one Gus recognized as the young officer from the sanctuary. Gus greeted the guy with a tiny nod, and Craig Holt responded in kind.

As for everyone else, it was hard to tell who might have been hiding the truth because they all displayed the same worry on their faces and radiated waves of anxiety.

Jacob Marlowe sat in one corner of the couch, his expression crumpled and his pose hunched. He had the look of a man who had lost everything he believed in, and he barely registered Gus's arrival.

Bodhi Jha sat in the lotus position in the corner of the room. Despite his serene pose, he kept a hawk's eye on everyone else, looking suspicious and antagonistic, as though expecting the world to cave in and leave him to come out on top. Ethan Sadler sat in the middle of the couch, hunched over, his frightened gaze shifting nervously between the people in the room. He visibly jolted when Gus came in, and he swallowed hard, as if mentally preparing himself for ill news, maybe about Quentin.

Frank Sadler sat next to him at the other end of the couch, with his arm around Ethan's shoulders. He sat stiffly, and his stony and hostile expression warned off anyone who might have approached. Clearly he took his role as husband and protector seriously.

Last but not least was Alex Kittridge, who sat awkwardly in an armchair, drumming his fingers nervously on the armrest and fidgeting in obvious discomfort.

Immediately upon seeing Gus arrive, Alex jumped to his feet and closed the distance between them. "Gus, oh, thank God you're here. What on earth is happening? Is it Quentin? What's wrong? Is he…?" He couldn't finish—just stood in place, pale and restless.

Gus shook his head. "No, Quentin's not dead. He's going to be okay."

More than one person let out a long relieved breath at the words. A sob escaped Ethan, while Jacob let his head fall back against the back of the couch. Alex managed a tight, shaky smile too and pressed a hand over his deflating chest, a bit theatrically in Gus's opinion.

At that moment Gus's phone beeped with a text. He pulled it out of his jeans pocket to read the message. But he didn't get beyond opening the screen to see that the text had come from Niall before Autumnsong stepped forward and grabbed his attention.

Autumnsong's determined, unwavering gaze landed squarely on Officer Craig Holt.

"Holt, is it?" he sneered. "Really? You and she always were far too predictable for your own good."

Gus frowned in confusion as he stared at the odd scene unfolding in front of him, the text forgotten. "Kin, what's going on?"

Craig pulled out a gun and pointed it at the two other cops whose hands had flown to their holstered weapons but who didn't have the time to pull them out. "Don't move," Craig said in a low, cool voice. The cops obeyed, though both shifted slightly to get nearer the other innocent people in the room, probably with the intent to protect even if it cost their lives.

Gus swallowed, throat tight with fear. The threat of death had become real, tangible, and imminent.

"HANDS WHERE I can see them, everyone," Craig commanded starkly. "Unless you want to die right here and now. Your choice."

Gus raised his hands toward the ceiling, as did the others. Except for Autumnsong, who crossed his arms over his chest, his expression bland and disinterested. Gus's blood ran cold. This wasn't the time to antagonize people, especially not someone who had a gun to their heads.

Craig shook his head in frustration. "Kin, you shouldn't have come. She has plans for you. Now I might have to kill you anyway."

Autumnsong shrugged, indifferent to the weapon aimed at him and the others. "When have you ever known me to give a shit about what she's got in store for me? She can rot in hell for all I care." Then he locked gazes with Craig, and Gus shivered at the burning hatred in his eyes even though he wasn't the target of that animosity. "Put down the gun now, and I'll spare your life."

Gus started putting the pieces together. There was only one reason for Autumnsong's display of wrath and vengefulness that Gus could see. "Craig? Why did you kill Rowan?" he asked.

Craig blinked at the interruption, having been engaged in some kind of battle of wills with Autumnsong, and growled. "You have no part in this, Goodwin, so stay out of—"

"He's not one for taking orders," Autumnsong cut in, his voice lazy. "And neither am I. You might as well tell him the truth."

Craig scoffed. "I've got a gun. You think he's going to believe me when I say I didn't murder Rowan?"

Gus was ahead of the bad guy and his game for the first time. "Maybe you did, maybe you didn't. But that doesn't mean you didn't want Rowan dead for some reason. And I'm betting it has something to do with Kin, Bodhi, and Rowan, and the three of them being brothers. The reason's in their past, right?"

A rustling of clothes alerted everyone's attention to the corner, where Bodhi had stood up and taken a step closer to Craig, murder in his eyes. "You killed Rowan? I knew something was wrong when I saw you come in, dressed in that ridiculous costume. But I thought you'd come here to help us. Because of her. But… you burned our brother?"

Gus finally started to comprehend the relationships of the people involved in this case. Not only were Autumnsong, Bodhi, and Rowan brothers—but Craig Holt was one as well? How could they have missed this? In his heart, though, Gus knew how: it was tough to see darkness in someone you knew. Hughes saw Craig as a colleague and a protégé, Niall as a brave ally who'd been heroically wounded in the course of the case, and Gus as a potential future friend. Not to mention the fact that Bodhi had not reacted visibly to Craig's presence at the sanctuary, probably with the learned caution of anyone who grew up in the system and never revealed their past to anyone if they could avoid it, let alone out someone else with the same background.

They'd all been blind and wrong. Craig was the enemy—even if he had told them the truth and hadn't, in fact, murdered Rowan. Gus had an inkling that Craig had wanted Rowan dead. But why?

"I didn't do it," Craig told Bodhi emphatically, his tone hard as steel. "I didn't drug and burn Rowan." So Craig knew about Rowan being drugged before he'd been set on fire, Gus mused. That meant he knew far more than he was telling about the murder and the murderer.

Bodhi, however, didn't seem inclined to believe a word out of Craig's mouth, and he continued to slowly advance toward him.

Now that Bodhi had garnered everyone's attention, including Craig's, Gus had a small window of opportunity to check the text he'd received from Niall. Surreptitiously he examined the lit screen hidden behind his thigh.

Holt lied, the text read; a little too late, Gus thought morosely. *Quentin didn't hear a gunshot. Holt tried to kill Quentin. Then he faked his own attack. We're going to the safe house to stop him. Please text me that you aren't there already.* Gus winced at the reproach but continued reading since he couldn't turn back time. *Frank Sadler's a fake too. His real name is Franz Sättler, a pharmacologist. He poisoned Rowan with a dose of diamorphine and—*

Gus didn't read further. Now he understood everything. Thanks to his education in new religious movements, he recognized the name Franz Sättler. And now he knew how the murder and the attempted murder had been committed and why. Well, at least one of them.

"You're related to Franz Sättler, the founder and creator of Adonism?" Gus asked then, startling everyone, including Frank, whose eyes widened in surprise and then grew wild as he must have felt cornered now that his secret was out.

Now no one seemed to know where to look and on whom to focus. The air was thick with tension, crackling with it like lightning rods gathering up the forces of a tempest.

"I… I don't know what you're talking about," Frank muttered, his behavior jittery and his tone strained. Even if he had nerves of steel, the jig was up, and time was running out. Gus had to keep them all talking and to give Niall and Hughes time to intercept the culprits.

"Yes, you do," Gus declared with a firm but soft voice, needing to buy time but not to antagonize these villains into doing something drastic and deadly. "Sättler created Adonism, which is a modern neo-pagan faith that—"

"*Ancient* pagan religion," Frank interjected, grimacing and snarling. Then his face fell, and he blinked hard. He'd just basically confessed, and Gus knew that, thanks to Niall, he was on the right track after all.

Gus didn't relent, though he maintained a diplomatic tone. "According to Adonism, our world was preceded by a dark world of monsters, which was destroyed. A new human world of goodness was then created by Adonis, a benevolent protector of humans."

"As it was written in the holy scriptures of the Bit Nur, the House of Light," Frank said with an exalted expression, blissful eyes, and a slowly spreading smile. Clearly he was a true believer. A fanatic. And that made him infinitely more dangerous than a common criminal.

Ethan had appeared bewildered by what was happening, but now he paled in fear and inched farther from his husband.

Frank saw this and smiled reassuringly. "No, Ethan, don't be afraid. For you are my Adonis, the most beautiful being in all of humanity. I chose you to be worshiped through adoration and sexual pleasure. I married you to see to it that every wish of yours would be granted and that the whole world would be laid at your feet. I could never harm you."

Shocked, Ethan seemed about ready to collapse from nervous exhaustion. He breathed shallowly, his lips quivered, and his eyes glistened with unshed tears. "Frank... stop. Y-you're scaring me.... I don't understand."

"Fear not, my love," Frank said softly, cupping Ethan's cheek and caressing it tenderly. "I stopped Molchos from getting you."

Ethan shook his head, clearly unable to comprehend a word that was said. Gus, on the other hand, was well versed in the topic at hand.

"Molchos is a malevolent deity who created the world of monsters that preceded us humans, and he's constantly trying to destroy the world of men," Gus said as he started to see all too clearly that Frank Sadler had gone mad—and Craig had fed his insanity.

Adonists did not believe in the perfection of humans, even though Adonis created them based on his ideal. Frank had twisted the original concepts of the faith to match his own views of what constituted manliness. He was right about one thing, though: Adonistic rituals were conducted through intercourse, so Frank worshiping Adonis by having sex with Ethan made sense.

But Gus wasn't done. "Frank? Who is Molchos? Is his name... Quentin?"

"Do not mention that foul name in my presence." Frank growled, baring and gnashing his teeth. "That vile loathsome creature. He was a monster, barely even a human. There was nothing masculine or powerful or beautiful about him. Did you see that fake red hair and those slinky red dresses and those red lips spilling their venom? I had to make sure he died."

"Oh my God," Ethan murmured in terror, a trembling hand over his mouth and tears streaming down his cheeks. "It was you. You tried to drown Quentin."

"No, he didn't," Gus cut in, turning his attention back to Craig, who hadn't lowered his gun even an inch. It was time for the coup de grace, to expose the guilty, so Gus said, "*Craig* did." When Craig didn't react with words or deeds, Gus turned again to Frank and Ethan to strike the final blow with truth. "But Frank *is* a murderer. He drugged and burned Rowan. You see, Frank and Craig are in on it together. They switched each other's murders."

A shocked silence fell on the room like a death shroud.

Chapter 17

"WHAT?" BODHI whispered in rage, his angry eyes switching between Craig and Frank, evidently not knowing whose throat to bite into first.

Gus kept his cool facade together by the grace of the Goddess. "Frank has his reasons to hate Quentin. Adonism, his faith, combined with his rigid and narrow views of what it means to be a man, led Frank to despise queer, feminine, and transgender men, with Ethan being the only exception because of his beauty. I venture a guess that in his eyes, Quentin isn't enough of a man."

Jacob Marlowe stood, his hands fisted at his sides, his features contorted in profound anguish. "How can you believe that, Frank? You think most men have the balls to slap on a dress, put on makeup, and walk outside among people with their heads held high? Brave to be themselves in the face of so much prejudice, hate, and violence? Quentin is more of a man than you could ever be, you murdering bastard."

Gus felt a chill. Defying convention and challenging the norm was all well and good, but pointing out that kind of bravery when faced with a gunman…. Jacob's timing for preaching from the soapbox sucked.

Frank's face contorted in revulsion, and he sneered. "He's disgusting. That's not how a man behaves or how he presents himself in public. That ridiculous buffoon doesn't have an ounce of masculinity in him. He's not a man, he's a wimp." Then he turned his hateful face to Gus. "Why did you have to get involved? Why couldn't you just leave things alone?"

Gus couldn't believe he had to defend himself from a twisted murderer's accusations. "Quentin doesn't deserve to die, and neither did Rowan. I couldn't let more innocent people die."

"Of course you could," Frank cut in with a scoff. "Humanity has committed unethical and amoral acts since the dawn of mankind in order to wipe out, kill, and destroy what's different or imperfect. Throughout history these people were called heroes, conquerors, liberators, rulers, kings. I saw human weakness of the flesh, I witnessed imperfection within a man who dressed up like a woman and pretended to be a woman. Naturally I sought to destroy such an abomination. I should be lauded and rewarded for doing my part in the betterment of humanity."

Frank's monologuing had derailed the conversation, Gus realized, when he saw Jacob gasp and open his mouth for an argumentative retort, and others in the room responded the same.

Gus quickly moved in. "Frank hated Quentin, but he was smart and realized his motive might be uncovered and he'd become a suspect. So when Craig approached him with a foolproof plan to take care of each other's respective problems, Frank jumped at the chance."

"You should have become a novelist," Craig said, chuckling. "Tall tales and flights of fancy."

Gus ignored the comment. "Exchanging murders was how the two poem lines came to be added separately from the actual crimes. The first line was added *after* Rowan's murder by Craig and the second *before* the near-fatal attack on Quentin by Frank. There were two people involved. One committed the crime, the other defaced the altars with scorch marks and acid. None of it was done by magic but by partners in crime working seamlessly together at different times."

"Extraordinary…," Jacob murmured in awe.

Gus continued with his narration. "It was clever of Craig to throw us off the track and distract us and obfuscate the case by allowing Frank's occult inclinations and the Nazi history angle to come to light. That concealed his true actions as the puppet master pulling Frank's strings— and would have done so long enough for him to disappear. If it hadn't been for Autumnsong, we all would have been fooled."

People around him were looking at one another, most everyone in astonishment, shock, and bewilderment. The cops, however, remained wary, Frank looked like he had a fire poker stuck up his ass, and Craig appeared merely amused. Autumnsong kept a cool facade at all times, though.

"Frank's motive for Quentin's death was clear. So what was Craig's ulterior motive?" Gus waited a second to see if anyone had any guesses, or if either Autumnsong or Bodhi would finally volunteer information of their own accord. But no one spoke a word, so Gus soldiered on. "I'm unfortunately in the dark as much as you when it comes to Craig's motives for wishing Rowan dead, so I can only hypothesize. One, Rowan knew a secret, and Craig wanted it buried. Two, Rowan was blackmailing Craig, who decided to solve two problems at once."

"Rowan was a good person," Bodhi cut in, grimacing as he snarled at Craig. "There's no way he would have done something so heinous or underhanded."

"Okay." Gus nodded, but in truth he was already running out of plausible theories. So he went with what he'd recently learned about murders. "Three, Rowan and Craig weren't true brothers by blood, so they were having an affair?"

"No." Autumnsong sounded adamant but as composed as ever. Bodhi eagerly nodded in agreement, which spoke volumes about how the two brothers saw Rowan. But had he actually been as angelic as he was being portrayed?

Gus suppressed an impatient sigh. "Fine. Four, Craig had a financial motive, perhaps to gain something valuable or priceless from Rowan's will? Did he stand to inherit?"

Craig started to laugh in earnest, his whole body shimmying from his mirth. "Oh my, aren't you grasping at straws. You really have no idea what's going on here, do you?" He looked at Autumnsong with playful reproach. "Too bad your new best friend's decided to be so tight-lipped, Goodwin, or you might already have solved this puzzle."

Gus had to bite his tongue so he wouldn't accidentally voice his agreement. It was true that Autumnsong held a lot back, and more than likely he knew exactly why Craig had orchestrated Rowan's murder. Why didn't he speak out?

"Five, six, seven, eight, etcetera," Gus went on, just barely able to conceal his growing frustration. "Revenge, guilt, hate, politics, religion, money, greed, envy, love, jealousy, plain evil—I could go on all day reciting possible motives. Would you consider confessing, maybe, to save time, patience, and sanity?"

Craig smiled and winked. "Why? Where's the fun in that? I like this. I want to play."

For the first time Gus was forced to contemplate the possibility that Craig was crazy or sociopathic. That would make figuring out any potential motive a job solely for prison therapists or asylum psychologists. Plus, madness meant Craig would be highly unpredictable and could go on a killing spree just for fun.

"Why don't you ask *me* that question?" Frank cut in suddenly, with a scornful sneer. "I was, after all, his accomplice and partner in crime. He's the one who warned me that Quentin was in fact Molchos in disguise. He said my Adonist instincts had clued me in on that abomination's true hidden nature and then confirmed my suspicions."

Gus had been so focused on Craig Holt that he'd quite forgotten Frank Sadler.

Craig, however, hadn't—which he proved by shooting Frank in the chest.

COVERED IN blood spatter, Ethan screamed. To Gus's surprise, Bodhi vaulted over the coffee table to shield Ethan with his body, while Jacob spread his arms and leaned over Ethan too. Apparently they guarded their own, or simply anyone in need of protection.

The two cops yanked out their weapons amid the confusion, pointed them squarely at Craig, and shouted, "Put down your gun!" They yelled at the top of their lungs and on top of each other until it was all just indistinct noise.

Much to Gus's chagrin, however, Alex sidestepped to stand half-behind Gus's back. Chivalry was indeed dead, Gus thought acerbically, but in the end he did understand. Instinctive reactions were hard habits to break. A second later, however, Alex seemed to notice his faux pas and stepped to stand next to Gus again, even a tad in front of him, squaring his shoulders to stand tall and proud.

Gus wondered if he could buy more time for Niall and Hughes to get there. "Who is she?" he asked, directing his words to Craig, who blinked briefly at the interruption. Perhaps he'd planned on killing everyone to be done with it. But Gus refused to go down without a fight.

Craig gave him a bewildered look. "What?"

"You, Bodhi, and Autumnsong have all talked about *her*. Who is she? Does she have something to do with the reason why Rowan had to die?" Gus had no reason not to ask.

Gus observed out of the corner of his eye that Autumnsong and Bodhi exchanged wary glances with each other and with Craig. Clearly the topic was significant in the extreme when all three men continued to behave as enemies and yet still kept a shared secret.

"Everyone has said that Rowan was a good person," Gus went on, despite the definite chill in the air. He was no longer certain if Autumnsong was still on his team or on a team of his own. "That he was the best of men, kind and giving and amiable."

Craig grimaced, for the first time appearing truly conflicted. "Goddammit, Goodwin, you don't understand what's at stake here. She…." He shook his head, worrying his bottom lip, and seemed unable to finish the sentence.

Gus prodded gently. "You didn't kill Rowan yourself, but he's dead because of you. If he really was so good, don't you think you owe him? To do right by him and his memory?"

Craig frowned, appearing hesitant, his lips parting as if to speak but then closing again. "Rowan was… sweet." Craig bit his lip hard now, probably to stop himself from trembling, or at least that was what Gus assumed based on how Craig's eyes glistened. "But he should have known better. He had a role to play, same as the rest of us. He shouldn't have betrayed her, or he'd still be—"

Autumnsong moved forward suddenly, closer to Craig. Swift as a snake, he swiped his hand over Craig's arm and then pulled back to stand tall and unwavering in the same spot he'd occupied before. Gus couldn't believe how fast Autumnsong had moved, like he'd glided through the air on a breeze or teleported with magical powers.

Craig sported a stunned expression. "You…."

His whisper echoed in the room briefly; then it died. His eyes widened in shock, but he didn't move, standing astride, hands still gripping the gun, shaking.

It wasn't until Autumnsong stepped forward again and calmly yanked the gun from Craig's hands that Gus realized Craig in fact *couldn't* move, even if he'd wanted to.

"What'd you do to him?" Gus asked, shaky and shocked at how quickly everything had happened.

Autumnsong glanced at him over his shoulder, a supercilious glint in his eyes, and a cocky grin gracing his full lips. "A muscular paralytic agent I concocted," he replied and lifted his hand for Gus to see.

One of his steel rings had a tiny needle embedded in it. Gus didn't even want to contemplate what harmful substance Autumnsong had coated the sharp object with.

"Will he die?" he asked, concerned that Craig might escape justice by being poisoned to death. Besides, Gus had values. He believed in the sanctity of life. And… dead bad guys learned no lessons.

But worst of all, Gus had his suspicions that Autumnsong had conveniently shut Craig up just in the nick of time. Whoever—or whatever—this mysterious *she* was, Autumnsong had in effect made sure Craig wasn't available for answers anytime soon.

"No." Autumnsong stared at Craig coolly. "The muscle and joint stiffness will last an hour or two. Plenty of time for the cops to deal with him."

He handed the gun over to the cops, and then he touched Craig's hand, a fleeting brush that must have tickled. Autumnsong had a merciless quality Gus had seen signs of before, but never to this extent. It creeped him out.

Autumnsong whispered in Craig's ear, "I warned you what would happen. You should have listened." Gus heard it because he stood so close.

Since Craig was for all intents and purposes incapacitated, and Gus was sure his ally wouldn't try to murder Craig in front of all these witnesses, Gus turned his attention to Frank Sadler. Immediately upon seeing him, Gus realized it was too late to help him in any way. He was dead and beyond resuscitation.

Ethan was crying his eyes out, with Jacob hugging him awkwardly. Bodhi stood there staring at the sight with something like shocked amazement, and pain contorted his expression. If Gus hadn't known better, he might have believed Bodhi to be paralyzed as well.

The threat of further deaths was contained. Gus let out a relieved breath.

Gus's brain, however, refused to let him stand idly by and do nothing. He still had no answers as to why Craig had wanted Rowan dead in the first place, or why he'd arranged such an elaborate scheme to get the job done. In his cover role as a police officer, Craig could have set up a less convoluted plot and framed some low-level criminal as a patsy.

And who was this woman Craig had referred to? Gus had a feeling she was indirectly responsible for Rowan's death. Her order had made Craig act. And her order had made Autumnsong interfere. Why? None of it made any sense.

Autumnsong, and probably Bodhi, knew the truth. Would they tell now—or ever?

Gus neared Autumnsong from behind and whispered in his ear, "We need to talk."

Autumnsong regarded him over his shoulder. "Later. Not here."

And that was the end of that conversation. For the time being.

When Niall and Hughes finally busted in through the apartment door five minutes later, everyone and everything had already settled down. The case was officially closed.

Chapter 18

"CASE IS unofficially still open," Gus said to Autumnsong as they sat at the kitchen table of Gus and Niall's place back in Tacoma, drinking sweet coffee, five long hours later. The summer sun had set, and night was closing in. "You promised me answers."

"Did I?" Autumnsong shrugged casually, but his demeanor remained tense, so he wasn't indifferent to the topic.

"Don't be evasive, Kin," Gus remarked, trying to be polite instead of frustrated since it served no purpose. Obviously Autumnsong struggled with this matter, and if pushed, he might just clam up for good.

Niall sat in one of the five chairs, grunting as he did so, and took a deep swig of his fresh, hot coffee. "Calm down, babe. I'm sure he's gonna come clean. Right?" he added, staring at Autumnsong over the rim of his cup. Oddly, though, Gus could have sworn Niall's eyes sparked with amusement.

Autumnsong rolled his eyes and pursed his lips. "Does that smooth-talking tactic ever work?" Niall chuckled but said nothing, so Autumnsong sighed and leaned back in his chair. "What I'm about to tell you will not leave this room, is that understood?"

Gus exchanged glances with Niall, who nodded almost imperceptibly, and then he gave his own agreement with a curt nod.

Autumnsong stared down at his coffee mug, swishing the liquid about as he fidgeted with it. "Rowan, Bodhi, Craig, and I, we all grew up in foster care in Hawaii. For a time, we lived under the same roof, with a woman called.... Her name was Faith Lanai then. It wasn't her real name. Over time I've tried to discover her true origins, but... she shrouds her past exceedingly well. Thankfully, she taught the same skills to all her children."

Gus rubbed his forehead, feeling the heat rising with his fingertips, the start of a bad headache. After the day they'd all had, he wasn't surprised. Too many revelations and revolutions for one day.

"So, this Faith Lanai was your… foster mother?" Gus asked for clarification. He had a ton of questions waiting, but he had to begin somewhere.

Autumnsong barked out a cynical laugh. "She is no one's mother, I assure you. Her maternal instincts, if she ever had any, withered and died long before any of us met her."

"Who is she, then?" Niall asked, appearing neutral about the whole thing as he slowly sipped his coffee. It was as if he felt nothing much about any of it, which baffled Gus considerably.

"Who?" Autumnsong shrugged. "I have no clear answer for that."

"Start from what you know and proceed from there," Niall prompted quietly, as though he didn't wish to intrude.

Autumnsong sighed. He had dark circles and wrinkles around his eyes, he sat slumped in a hunch, and despite his colorful makeup and attire, he came off as ashen and lifeless. It was as if he had aged twenty years in the span of a day. This business with his foster mother must have touched him far more deeply than even he was willing to admit.

"I was nine when I ended up at her house," Autumnsong said in a hushed, dull voice. Perhaps reliving whatever ordeal he'd gone through wasn't the best idea, Gus thought, concerned. But Autumnsong pressed on. "By then she'd fostered about a dozen children. When I arrived, there were eight of us, me included. Rowan, Bodhi, Craig, and me, and four others. Craig was the oldest, then Bodhi and me, and finally Rowan, the youngest. We stuck together, brothers in everything but blood."

"Was Craig his real name back then?" Niall asked.

Autumnsong gave him an admonishing glare and harrumphed. "Seriously? You need to ask that?" Niall smiled and shook his head, so Autumnsong rolled his eyes and continued. "Faith wasn't violent with us. She didn't rule us with terror or threats. No, she… you could say she seduced us with a… shall we say, a dogma."

Gus leaned closer, his suspicions aroused. "You mean, like with a religion? Like a… a kind of brainwashing?"

Autumnsong offered a knowing, lopsided grin without humor. "See? You can be smart when you need to be, Goodwin. You're exactly right. It was a kind of cult, with Faith as the queen bee." He chuckled quietly as he reminisced, his eyes glossy.

"At first it didn't seem harmful in any way. Reverence of the earth and seasons, showing gratitude for daily bounties, soothing chants, wearing garlands of flowers, dancing skyclad on the sandy beaches, enchanting ideals—the sort you appreciate, Goodwin."

Gus blushed. He wasn't sure if he was being complimented or insulted. He treasured his Wiccan values and ideals, the beauty and naturalness of his down-to-earth faith. It hurt his heart to hear that someone had taken their life-affirming beliefs and practices and then turned them to the service of something darker. So he chose to remain quiet and wait for their guest to continue.

Autumnsong gave a demure bow. "Faith proceeded slowly, over long stretches of time and displaying great patience. But I soon began to notice things, odd little inconsistencies and weird anomalies of behavior. People coming and going under the cover of darkness, hushed conversations outside in the back garden, writings with weird symbols, weapons hidden around the house."

"What did you make of it?" Niall asked gently, peeling an orange and swiping a chunk into his mouth, a tangy citrus scent spreading into the air.

"I was a kid, what did I know?" Autumnsong pursed his lips briefly before resuming. "I'd survived on the streets with my wits and swiftness. She sent me to school to learn how to read and write. But back home she taught me much about the world and the people in it. She often said she was cruel to be kind, that she showed us the dark underbelly of society and the darkness in men to protect us, to ready us for what would come."

"So basically she stole your childhood and innocence," Gus muttered under his breath. He had never met this woman, but he hated her already.

Autumnsong quirked an eyebrow, appearing amused. "You're so sentimental. But you are right. For Faith, the end justifies the means. No matter what they may be."

"This… cult of hers—she recruited you into it?" Niall asked, his narrowing eyes the only sign he took the topic far more seriously than he'd been letting on. Gus observed the subtle change with something akin to pride.

Autumnsong looked away, his face stony and blank. Gus knew it to be a convincing mask to conceal his emotions. "I don't think it'll come as any big surprise for either of you when I tell you her cult was, and is, the Cabal."

Gus looked at Niall, whose face betrayed nothing. But Autumnsong had been right in his assessment. Neither Gus nor Niall was surprised. Autumnsong had already been shown to have a link with the Cabal a few months back during the Moonlight Haven Coven case.

Perplexed, Gus frowned. Despite Autumnsong having ties with the Cabal, today's events had demonstrated a rift in the relationship, a crack in the ranks. For some reason, unknown as of yet, their new friend had acted against the interests of the Cabal, as represented by Craig Holt and his plot to murder Rowan.

But that discord between Autumnsong and the Cabal had started well *before* Rowan was killed.

"I can see the wheels turning in your busy head," Autumnsong said to Gus, chuckling. "Never a dull moment in there, I bet. Anyway… as you two probably have also guessed, mine and Faith's paths have… diverged."

"How many members belong to the Cabal?" Niall asked suddenly, his eyes predatory now, focused intently on Autumnsong. "What are their goals? Why did Faith want Rowan dead?"

Autumnsong whistled low. "Oh my. All of a sudden I feel like I'm being interrogated by the Spanish Inquisition." He smiled, seemingly without a care. Niall obviously didn't scare him in the slightest. "One, I don't know how many members there are in the Cabal. Faith organizes things in separate cells, with a sole nexus point: Faith. Two, their goals have grown—no, devolved toward a criminal state of affairs I disapprove of, to use general terms."

"Could you be more specific?" Niall insisted, his tone suggesting no other choice existed.

"No. I can't tell you what I don't know. But… I'm working on it."

Some assurance, Gus thought sourly. "And Rowan?" he asked.

Autumnsong shielded his eyes by lowering his gaze. But his jaw set, and he ground his teeth in silence. Then, in a voice so terrifying Gus felt a chill, Autumnsong said, "Rowan was my responsibility. His death… was my fault."

"You didn't kill him," Gus denied the accusation out of the goodness of his heart.

"Maybe not in person," Autumnsong remarked with cold rage. "But he is dead because of me. You see, he came to me three months ago. He'd grown fond of his friends at the sanctuary, and he wanted out of his... other obligations."

Niall gave Gus a warning glance, in effect telling Gus to say nothing. Gus acquiesced with a confused nod. Then Niall said, "I'm not going to ask about these other obligations. I have a feeling I know what they are." Autumnsong looked up in a flash, eyes widening. Niall didn't react in any way but continued, saying, "This is the third time, as far as I've seen, when the Cabal has meddled in the affairs of other faiths. The first time was when we met, during the Talbot murder case, which involved a satanic cult. The second time was a few months back, when the Moonlight Haven Coven was attacked because of a book, which is now in the wind, thanks to you. And this is the third time. So, I've got to ask... what exactly does Faith Lanai have against other religions?"

Gus stared at his fiancé in awe. Niall had made the connections between separate cases with some skill Gus apparently lacked. He'd viewed all three cases as individual investigations into three distinct crimes. But Niall had seen beyond that into the heart of things.

Which was that the Cabal seemed to have its fingers in every pie.

Autumnsong, however, smiled. "Smart snoop. Took you long enough."

"I suspected a connection during the last case when you popped up into the scene again," Niall said impassively. "So stop stalling and answer the question."

"To be honest—" Autumnsong started to say.

"That'd be a refreshing change," Niall murmured complacently.

"That's not fair," Autumnsong refuted with a smile. "I've never lied to either of you. If I don't share everything with you... well, lies of omission are lesser sins. Anyway, back to Faith.... She's been amassing wealth and connections since long before I met her. What her ultimate purpose is, I have no idea. All I know is that I want no part in it."

Gus swallowed hard. "Rowan... he tried to follow you, to leave the cult?"

Autumnsong's features grew hard as a diamond. To be his enemy had to be like facing the wrath of the gods—a fool's errand. "I don't know why Faith sent Rowan to the Radical Faeries. But I know it was nothing good. Rowan reached me through our own contacts, and I found him there. That was over a year ago, last summer. His doubts grew over time, I guess. When I saw him last, his whole attitude toward Faith had changed, but he still refused to leave his friends, even though I warned him Faith would find him."

"Wait." Niall cut in sharply with an astonished, angry tone that sent cold vibes up and down Gus's spine. "Are you saying Faith had Rowan killed just because he wanted out of the cult and to be free of whatever the Cabal's endgame is?"

"That's monstrous," Gus exclaimed in a gasp, a new kind of dread settling at the pit of his stomach. He'd read enough about new religious movements and understood how many of them could be categorized as brainwashing cults with charismatic leaders who ruled with an iron fist in a silk glove. Though Gus had researched them at length in college, he'd never thought he'd actually come into contact with one in his personal life.

"I don't know that for sure," Autumnsong replied slowly, his tone vague and hesitant. "But… I wouldn't put it past her. Faith Lanai is beyond dangerous, an evil unlike anything you've ever encountered. And now… she has you two in her sights."

Suppressing a whimper, Gus looked at Niall. But Niall was watching their guest, his face as cold and rigid as Autumnsong's. Gus envied his fiancé's inner strength, how he could keep such a calm facade when confronted with such a terrible hidden threat. He did his best to collect his own thoughts and emotions and put up a brave face.

"How much do you know about her?" Niall asked then, his voice steely, unwavering, and determined. "You knew, for example, that Officer Craig Holt of the SPD worked for Faith, even though you'd never met him. How?"

Autumnsong smiled slyly. "Faith has a weakness that I've used to track down parts of her past and some of the cells in her organization. She uses surnames that refer to woods or forests, trees or the earth. Always. I know a few: Forêt, Gehöltz, Bosquecillo, Lundgren, Strom. Her Hawaiian surname, Lanai, means arbor."

"What does that have to do with Craig?" Niall asked, frowning.

Autumnsong smiled shortly. "The surname he used, Holt. It means wood or grove. Guess the apple doesn't fall far from the tree. Poor joke, I admit, but there you have it."

Gus let out a laugh in a whoosh. "That's it? A name? You could've been wrong. That could have been a simple coincidence. Life is a series of happenstances that mean nothing."

"Yes, but this was easy to check," Autumnsong replied. "I confirmed who it was as soon as I saw him. Ta-da! Theory corroborated."

"Why would Craig agree to commit murder for Faith?" Gus asked, cringing at his own words. Throughout history millions of people had killed for their faith. This was just another example of how easily humans could turn on each other. Even their own brothers.

Autumnsong locked gazes with Gus, his hazel eyes burning with a vengeful fire Gus was glad he wasn't the target of. "You'd have to know her. She can be very… persuasive. She has a way of turning things inside out till you don't know what's real, and the only thing you have is her truth. Craig… he's a fanatic follower. He'd do anything Faith ordered him to do. Anything. As we've clearly seen."

"What kind of evidence have you gathered against her?" Niall asked, curious. "I mean, logically I'm assuming you have some way of keeping the dogs off your door and that you have a plan of attack if and when push comes to shove. I don't know you through and through, but I know you have a backup plan buried somewhere in that noggin of yours."

"I do have a plan of action and evidence against her. And no, it's none of your business." Autumnsong stood, as if the conversation was over and he had nothing more to say.

Niall stood too, slower and in a more menacing manner. "We're not done. This crazy bitch is after us as well, so—"

"I can't help you any more sitting here," Autumnsong interjected, his eyes as steely as Niall's, steadfast and strong. Gus suspected this was where Faith had failed with Autumnsong too, trying to make the rebellious young man jump when he didn't wish to.

Niall appeared ready to argue, but Gus knew better. He rose from his seat, placed a hand on Niall's arm, and stopped him before he could get any further. Niall looked at him with a frown, obviously displeased.

"Kin is right," Gus pleaded his case. "He's told us as much as he can for now. If we want more, we have to let him find his own way to defeat Faith Lanai. Besides, we've got to get some rest, and tomorrow we'll go to the police station and see if Craig Holt, as he calls himself, might be willing to flip sides and tell us all he knows about Faith and the Cabal."

Autumnsong scoffed as he headed for the front door. "Unlikely. But by all means, do bash your heads against the wall if that makes you feel better. Later." With a determined stride, he walked out the door and vanished into the dusk. Gus feared for his safety but was aware Autumnsong could take care of himself.

The question was, could Gus and Niall? Against the resolute Faith Lanai with the Cabal at her beck and call?

Chapter 19

"LUGHNASADH IS day after tomorrow," Gus murmured as he lay in bed next to Niall—who hadn't said a word since Autumnsong had left. Niall seemed to have taken exception to Gus allowing Autumnsong to leave without telling them absolutely everything, and Gus felt depressed and alone and rejected.

Niall sat with his back against multiple plush pillows stacked against the headboard, squinting at the glowing screen of his iPad. At first he appeared oblivious, as though he hadn't heard Gus speak. When Gus repeated what he'd said, Niall's jaw tightened, and his knuckles turned white with how hard he squeezed his tablet, so he clearly had heard but chose to ignore Gus.

Gus suppressed a sigh, slid down to lie on his side turned away from Niall, flipped the switch to shut off his bedside lamp, and firmly closed his eyes. But sleep refused to come, taunting him with the fact that he was trying to sleep while angry and hurt. His heart ached, and his stomach knotted painfully.

"The best way for Kin to help us survive is for him to be free and out there, working in the shadows," Gus muttered, mostly to himself. He certainly didn't expect Niall to contribute to the conversation in any meaningful way. Therefore, he supposed he was really monologuing. "Kin told us that there's so much he doesn't know yet about Faith and the Cabal and what they're planning. He can't stay here to satisfy our curiosity, or we could…."

His voice cracked. Even though he gulped hard to clear his throat, he couldn't push the word out past his lips. *Die. We could all die.* Gus shuddered and pulled the covers tighter around himself in the hopes that the chills he'd just felt hadn't been Faith Lanai dancing over his grave.

Or Niall's grave. That would kill Gus as surely as a knife through the heart.

A strong, warm hand touched his shoulder, startling him. Then Niall's soft voice said, "I know, Gus. I'm sorry, babe. Guess I'm becoming a curmudgeon in my old age. It's just that… we usually talk with each other first before deciding on a course of action, you know? But with him—with Autumnsong—it's different. You and he get together, and things go awry."

Gus flipped around to face Niall, part pissed off, part confused. "What the hell is that supposed to mean?"

Niall went stiff again, and his soft smile faded. "Are you really asking me that? Okay. How about today, for example? You and he have a cozy little chat and then decide to go off willy-nilly, without backup, to check out a freaking theory and confront a murderer—no, scratch that, *two* murderers. You do this alone, without telling either me or Hughes first, let alone bringing us along to maybe, oh, I don't know, save both of you from getting fucking killed?" Niall shook his head, and his body shook, too, as additional proof of how mad he was. "You know what? Scratch the other thing too. I'm not fucking sorry."

Gus's cheeks burned at the reproach. He fumbled his way back to a sitting position to buy time so he wouldn't bite Niall's head off like he wanted to. "That is unfair. I didn't know about Craig Holt or Frank Sadler or that they were the—"

"That's right," Niall cut in, his voice tamping down the triumphant tone. "You didn't know. But you did it anyway because of him. Autumnsong had his theory, and off he went to prove it. And you followed like some obedient lapdog."

"I only wanted to help," Gus argued. Anguish unlike any he'd ever felt constricted his chest, making it hard for him to breathe, squeezing his heart till it bled, and pushing hot tears into his eyes, where they threatened to overflow. "It was a police safe house. There were three cops there. How were we supposed to know one of them was bad? And that one of the people we were *all* trying to protect would turn out to be such a psycho?"

"Oh, for fuck's sake, Gus." Niall slammed his iPad on his bedside table so hard it was a miracle it didn't break. "That's exactly my point. You didn't know. You should have waited for me and Hughes. You put yourself and others in harm's way by pulling a crazy stunt like—"

"If Kin and I hadn't gotten there when we did," Gus cut in, enraged, "then everyone would likely be dead. Craig Holt wouldn't have waited much longer. He'd just gotten there. Kin and I, we stopped him. We bought time for you and Hughes. It wasn't our fault you two didn't get there in time."

Niall glared at him, his mouth set in a thin, white line and his eyes firing up a storm. "You're missing my point, as usual."

Gus gasped. He'd thought he and Niall were good together, if not always in sync. Most of the time anyway. "What *is* your point?" Gus asked, growing weary of the argument.

Niall stared him down brutally. "My point is that when it comes to Autumnsong, your judgment is impaired. It's like you stop thinking. He tells you what to do, and you do it, forgetting or ignoring basic common sense and any instinct for self-preservation."

"No, that's not it," Gus denied. "No, this is about you making the false assumption that I chose, or would always choose, him over you."

Niall drew in a sharp breath. "You think I'm… jealous?"

Gus stared back with equal fervor. "If the shoe fits."

"You're delusional," Niall replied vehemently.

Gus opened his mouth to let out all the ugly words hanging off the tip of his tongue. But he couldn't. He refused to become a nasty person uttering snarky words to someone he loved.

So instead of speaking, he shoved the covers aside, got out of bed, and walked into the bathroom to cool off, closing the door behind him. Leaning against the cool wooden frame, he felt thin and worn. Life had mowed over him today in the form of agents of evil, and now he'd brought the same hatred that motivated them into his home, into his life, into his bed.

"No, I won't be that guy," Gus murmured to himself.

He pressed a palm over his chest where his heart pounded restlessly. A foul part of his psyche demanded he return to the bedroom to argue again until he won. The better fey of his nature pleaded with him to forgive and forget, and urged him to remember how he felt about Niall.

The better part of his soul understood why Niall was angry. Autumnsong had led them into a dangerous, life-threatening situation, and Gus could have died. All without Niall knowing about it. Naturally he was angry. He was hurt by Gus's dismissal and afraid of what might have happened.

Gus opened the door—and came face-to-face with Niall, who'd been about to knock. Niall blinked hard, opened and closed his mouth, and looked as uncomfortable as a man could get, rubbing the back of his neck.

"Gus, I…," Niall started to say. Gus was dying to speak his mind, but instead he chose to wait and hear his beloved out. Niall let out a long, pained breath. "Fuck, babe, I'm sorry. I didn't mean it. Any of it. And you're right. I wasn't really mad about—"

The mounting apologies were too much for Gus. "No, Niall. *I'm* sorry. I should have told you everything. I got caught up in Autumnsong's frenzy. I was blind. I didn't see the danger—or I ignored it. I was thinking about the danger everyone *else* was in and just… acted without a second thought. That was stupid of me."

"Yeah, it kinda was." Niall sighed. "But… it was brave too. And you were right about one thing. If you hadn't gone to the safe house, Craig would have killed everyone. Hughes and I, we were too far away. We wouldn't have gotten there in time. You bought us a window of opportunity to get there. even if we didn't make it there before Autumnsong… did his thing." Niall let out a sarcastic chuckle. "That guy, I swear he'll be the death of us all."

Gus didn't wait a moment longer. He threw his arms around Niall's neck and embraced him heartily. Niall wound his own arms around Gus's waist and back and pulled him closer. They stayed that way for a long while, neither one speaking. Niall even rocked them gently back and forth in a soothing manner.

"I hate fighting with you," Niall finally whispered in Gus's ear, his hot breath tickling Gus's skin and shifting his blond curls. "Never feels right."

"Me too," Gus murmured back, planting a soft kiss on Niall's cheek. "I can think of a dozen things we should be doing in bed instead of arguing."

"Only a dozen? *Pfft.* I can think of a hundred, at least," Niall replied, laughing quietly intc Gus's hair, breathing deeply and swaying them about.

"Yeah? How 'bout you put your money where your mouth is… stud," Gus teased.

Niall laughed. Then he cupped Gus's asscheeks, lifted him so Gus could wrap his legs around his waist, carried him to bed—and for the next two hours showed Gus exactly where his money *and* mouth were.

THE FOLLOWING morning Niall awakened with a beam of bright sunlight aimed directly at his eyes. Blinking owlishly, Niall peered next to him in bed and scanned around the room but saw no sign of Gus anywhere.

Then the lingering scent of strong coffee brewing awakened his senses. Beckoned by the alluring odor, Niall found his stumbling way to the kitchen, where a smiling Gus waited for him, holding a steaming mug of coffee. Niall growled a vague thank-you and then proceeded to pour the molten liquid down his throat. At last he started to feel like a human being again.

"Come on, sleepyhead," Gus said with a laugh. "Get your clothes on. It's time to go to the police station and see what Craig Holt has to say. Chop-chop."

And that was how a shower-fresh Niall ended up driving to Seattle twenty minutes later. Well, actually Gus did the driving, but Niall… supervised. But he didn't nag or passenger-seat drive, no sirree. He just observed.

When an hour later they parked close to the Seattle Police Department headquarters's modern and sleek white building, the commotion out front caught their attention immediately. In the shade of two lush trees, in front of the edifice's double doors, Detective Hughes stood arguing animatedly with two tall, stone-faced men in immaculate suits and ties.

Niall had been around the block too many times not to recognize government officials when he saw them. "Shit," he muttered as he crossed the street toward the quarrelsome threesome, with Gus in tow. He had a bad feeling in the pit of his stomach that he couldn't shake.

"…dooming our case against Holt," Hughes was saying with a growl as they approached. "This is our collar, goddammit."

"What's going on?" Niall asked loudly as he stepped closer, assuming a cool facade to keep his own emotions in check.

Hughes spoke through gritted teeth, glaring at the two government agents. "These two monkeys from the FBI are taking Craig Holt into immediate custody."

"What?" Niall couldn't believe what he was hearing. "Why?"

When neither of the men replied, Hughes answered for them. "Domestic terrorism."

Niall actually chuckled at the response. "That's insane. Holt's many things, but he's not a terrorist. He's a murderer, to be sure. Where the hell does terrorism enter into it?"

"Craig Holt's also a victim of brainwashing by a powerful cult leader," Gus interjected, so innocently that Niall wanted to hug him forever. "Plus, he's the only one alive who can give us answers about the person who made him conspire to murder Rowan Tuff. You have to let us talk to him."

Finally one of the feds said, shaking his head, "I'm afraid we can't allow that, sir."

Both Niall and Gus were ready to argue their point, but they didn't get the chance. The double doors opened, and out walked Craig Holt, accompanied by feds, one at each side, holding his arms. His wrists were bound by handcuffs as he was a prisoner. But his smug smile stayed in place.

"Sorry, guys, but I've got to go," Craig called out to them with an arrogant tone and a laugh, winking shamelessly. Autumnsong might have defeated him back at the safe house, but now he was on top of his game again, or at least that was what his conduct suggested. Niall puzzled over Holt's hidden agenda and how he planned on getting out of this mess. Probably by making a deal with the government in exchange for his testimony, even if said testimony was likely to be a work of pure fiction.

Hughes shook his head fiercely and grumbled obscenities under his breath. Niall knew their hands were tied, both the cops' and his own, and did the same, just quietly inside his head. The government did whatever the hell it wanted because one, they could and two, for them the ends justified the means. *Bastards.*

That was when Niall caught sight of Autumnsong out of the corner of his eye standing by the side of the building, half out of sight, his face rigid and displeased. His arms were crossed over his chest, and he stood astride, as though barely holding himself in check.

Niall understood. He felt the same impotent urge to rip Craig Holt a new one.

"See you later," Craig exclaimed as he was escorted toward an unmarked black car.

His laughter stopped short as he jolted. The feds at his sides were speckled with blood.

The shot that killed Craig was completely silent.

Niall froze. He felt like he was watching an action movie where an unknown assassin shot the bad guy in the chest, killing him in an instant. In a movie it felt like justice. In real life Niall stood still, immobilized by shock, his brain and senses unable to process what had just happened.

He was knocked down onto the pavement when a body slammed into him and brought him face first onto the ground. Asphalt scraped his cheek painfully. Because of the dust clouds kicked up by the frantic crowd, he couldn't see, and with everyone yelling and screaming, he couldn't hear.

"Man down!" he heard vaguely, as though listening through water distorting the voices and sounds. He couldn't tell who was shouting. "Over there! Hold your fire! Call the paramedics!" Beyond a few phrases, it all faded into indistinct background noise for Niall. He had no idea who was hollering to whom, let alone about what.

"Oh my God," the person above him whispered, over and over, in sheer panic.

It took Niall more than a few seconds to realize the person was Gus. He had shielded Niall from any other bullets flying around, not that Niall had heard any, not even the first.

"Gus? Stay down," Niall murmured, wrapping his arms around Gus and flipping them over so that he covered his boyfriend, keeping him from harm. He peered around and saw people running and cowering behind trees, doorways, and cars. It was mass panic.

When Niall twisted his neck to look in the other direction, he saw three agents crouching by the black FBI vehicle, taking cover behind the car, all holding weapons and periodically peeking above. One agent clutched his shoulder, fingers bloody, probably from a gunshot wound.

Next to them, on the ground, lay the unmoving and absolutely dead Craig Holt. A large gaping hole in his forehead, right between the eyes, was testament to that fact. Whoever had shot him knew exactly what they were doing. *A professional killer.*

Fuck. Niall cursed inside his head. Faith Lanai was indeed a force to be reckoned with. And now they had lost their sole source of information about her and the Cabal's ongoing activities.

Hughes half crawled, half skittered toward them. "You guys okay?" He had his weapon drawn, and he looked serious, but he didn't scan his surroundings like the other officers and FBI agents near them. That told Niall that a search for or a pursuit of the suspect was in progress. Hughes confirmed as much when he said, "We know where the shot likely came from, and no more shots have been fired in the past five minutes. So we're safe to retreat inside the station. On three, got it?"

While Niall was still stunned that five minutes had passed since the last shot, probably at one of the FBI agents, he had to ask, "Any civilians hurt or killed?"

Hughes shook his head in a rush. "Not to my knowledge. Now come on."

Niall and Gus pulled each other up and, following Hughes as fast as they could, they entered the station lobby. The brightly illuminated white interiors appeared sleek, functional, and clinical. The place was crowded already, with uniformed officers guiding teeming people to steer clear of the windows at the front. The noise was alarming, and everyone seemed rattled, with a few crying or simply staring blankly in shock.

Niall empathized. Hughes directed them straight to the back, toward the bullpen where the desks were, and sat them down in plastic chairs along a bustling corridor. He told them he'd be right back, and then he was off. Niall hugged Gus, who shivered in his embrace.

There was a surreal quality to the whole situation, Niall thought. He looked around, watching people scurrying by, talking really fast with that wild, anxious look in their eyes. They were scared and worried, and Niall couldn't believe this was his life. Flashbacks of his past in the Army broke through to the surface of his mind, and he was appalled to find himself again in this headspace, where terrible, violent, gory things happened, beyond his control.

To dispatch those visions back to a buried corner of his brain, Niall focused on Gus. Niall admitted to himself he'd been surprised when Gus had decked him so fast and efficiently. He was proud of his boyfriend. No, his fiancé.

"Thanks for what you did for me outside," Niall whispered into Gus's blond hair, since Gus's head lay on Niall's shoulder. "You were brave and strong and amazing. A hero."

Gus shook his head but didn't otherwise move. "No. I just... I would've died if...."

"I know, babe. Me too." Niall hugged Gus tighter, hoping to relieve some of the stress they both felt. Niall hoped Gus hadn't seen Craig's head get blown off. Then again, he'd missed it too. For the most part, anyway.

Then he remembered what he'd seen. Or more specifically, *whom* he'd seen.

"Did you see Autumnsong out there?" Niall asked.

Gus nodded. "Yes. Briefly. He was coming toward us when...." Gus paused, and Niall waited with bated breath. Had Gus seen Autumnsong get hit? *Please, God, no.* "He wasn't shot, I think. But... he was close. When Craig was... when he went down, I forgot about him. All I could think about was you. Sorry if I hurt you when I jumped you."

Niall actually chuckled at that. "Jesus fucking Christ, that should be the last thing on your mind, Gus. Besides, you've jumped me plenty of times in bed, and I'm still here."

Gus looked up at Niall then, his cheeks rosy and his eyes warm, if a bit glisteny with unshed tears. "I love you, Niall," he murmured, a shaky smile gracing his full lips.

At that moment Niall knew exactly what the first step on their future path would be, so he said, "Tomorrow's that harvest celebration of yours, isn't it? Lammas or something. Well, I want to marry you tomorrow. No more waiting. We're *so* done waiting."

The half-shocked, half-exalted look on Gus's face was priceless.

Chapter 20

"DID YOU know that Lughnasadh is considered an auspicious day for handfastings?" Juliette Hayes asked Niall, even though Gus was right next to them and knew very well.

They stood together in the large backyard at Juliette's house in West Tacoma, where a large patch of forest stood between her house and the Narrows. It took five to ten minutes to drive from Point Defiance Park, where Gus and Niall lived, to Juliette's house. Her place was big, located at the end of a road, hidden away from prying eyes under the trees. Her Moonlight Haven Coven gathered there each sabbat and esbat, and Gus loved it.

"No, I didn't know that," Niall admitted with a smile he shared with Gus, adding a hot and suggestive wink at the end. "I guess my instincts serve me well."

Gus rolled his eyes playfully. "Yes, they do, Master Yoda."

Niall apparently decided to ignore Gus because he addressed his next words to Juliette. "How do these handfastings typically go?"

"For Wiccans, there is no one single formula that fits all," Juliette replied, an amiable smile casting a warm glow around her. She was like a sister to Gus, or sometimes like a mother. A curvy, full-bodied woman, Juliette had short brown curls and affectionate brown eyes, and she wore an earth-hued, body-hugging dress that reached her bare feet.

"Thank you for arranging this ceremony for us on such short notice," Niall said, with a subtle bow of gratitude. His attentive manners made Gus's heart flip, and he fell further in love with him.

It also didn't hurt that Niall looked dashing and sexy in his jeans, dress shirt, silk tie, and vest, all white and pristine. Apart from the tie, he was dressed the same as Gus. They'd forgone tuxedos in favor of something they both felt comfortable in.

Briefly Gus stopped to consider how much his life had changed within a small amount of time. Last year around Lughnasadh, Gus had been single and searching for his soul mate. Now he had found Niall, who was perhaps a little rough around the edges, but they still suited each other to a tee. They had lived together for many months now and had settled into a comfortable routine.

With spectacular sex knitted into the fabric of their new lives as a couple.

In short, Gus couldn't have been happier.

"It was no problem at all," Juliette replied to Niall with a melodic laugh. "If Gus had decided to be married somewhere else, by some other high priestess, I would have been extremely upset. Extremely." She gave Gus a fake warning glare.

Gus chuckled. "Oh, come now, sweetie. You know there's no other woman for me but you, and could never be."

"I'll vouch for that," Niall commented from the side, causing both Gus and Juliette to laugh out loud. The light mood of the afternoon was set, and the sun was bright and the breeze soft.

"I'm glad we didn't spoil your coven's Lughnasadh celebration with our impromptu decision," Gus said then, grateful to Juliette for adjusting her plans. "Lughnasadh is the festival of first fruits and is usually honored on the full moon closest to the midpoint between summer solstice and autumnal equinox. Therefore, Juliette's coven will be having their party later in the night," Gus explained to Niall, who nodded as he listened.

"What does this party entail, if you don't mind a nonbeliever like me asking?" Niall directed his question to Juliette, who was the high priestess of her coven.

"Lughnasadh is the first harvest, August Eve, a time when the first fruits, barley, wheat, oats, and corn are harvested," Juliette replied, gesturing around them.

The edges of the backyard, where the open garden shifted into a forest, had been lined with makeshift tables. Empty spaces in between the dishes would later be filled with food and then consumed as a ritual sacrifice. The tablecloths were red, orange, and brown in color, fall flowers decorated the settings, and corn-dollies and grain cobs were placed here and there, far away from the unlit orange candles. In the east, where Juliette's house was, a cauldron surrounded by wheat stalks was placed close to the back patio, and in front of it lay a broom.

"Cool" was Niall's eloquent response as he calmly took in the view. "So this is another fertility ritual, then?"

Juliette gave Gus a wicked look, flicking her tongue at him. "Well… I confess I did try to convince my lovely young protégé Gus, here, to perform the Great Rite with his new husband as the coven celebrates the festival. Would you be interested in that, Mr. Valentine?"

The notion that he would be having sex with Gus in front of people he knew, even in the privacy of Juliette's house, sent both cold chills and hot flames through Niall's body. His cheeks flared as he muttered something unintelligible, rubbing the back of his heated neck. Gus and Juliette chuckled kindly at his awkwardness.

Niall decided to up the ante. "I might consider it—if Gus agrees." He aimed a sugary sweet smile at Gus, whose jaw dropped as his eyes widened in shock. It was Niall's turn to laugh.

Gus's eyes narrowed. "Careful, mister. Or I might just say yes."

Juliette grinned at their antics. "One day I'm sure I'll be able to convince you *both* to agree."

Surprisingly Niall found himself envisioning that exact possibility being realized in the not-so-distant future.

NEXT TO him, Gus was having similar thoughts, pondering if he might actually one day get Niall to fully attend their rituals, perhaps even skyclad. It'd be a short hop, skip, and a jump to the Great Rite from there, he mused with an inner laugh.

Voices started coming from inside the house, which meant their guests had arrived. Juliette hurried indoors to greet everyone, her dress flowing behind her.

This departure gave Gus and Niall an opportunity to be alone for a time.

Gus faced Niall, worrying his lower lip. "You sure you still want to—"

"To go through with this?" Niall cut in, sounding amused. "Hell yeah. You?"

Gus let out a relieved chuckle and nodded. "Yes. I do."

"That part comes later," Niall reminded him with a sly grin. When Gus laughed, Niall had another question to pose. "This Great Rite… when it's not just symbolic… when two people get it on for real… you ever done that?"

Gus sighed. "Is that important? You know I love you, right?"

Niall smiled and kissed Gus softly. "I do. I'm mainly just curious." His humor faded a bit. "If you have, it wasn't with… Alex, was it?"

Gus snorted loudly. "Hell, no! He wouldn't be caught dead performing a sex act for the masses, or even a coven of friends and family."

Niall scrunched his nose. "When you put it like that, I guess I wouldn't want to do that either, like… in front of my dad or something. I'm pretty sure that would result in some high-priced therapy sessions and lifelong impotency issues."

Gus laughed, loving that Niall could be himself even though they were discussing sex in public, purely theoretically of course. "Aww, poor baby. I'd bed-nurse you to health and vigor in no time, I swear."

Niall rubbed his nose against Gus's. "I'll hold you to that, babe."

Gus giggled. Then he grew serious. "I didn't invite Alex, even though we sort of made peace. I didn't think it'd be… appropriate."

Niall cocked his head. "You think he would have even wanted to come if you'd asked him? He didn't seem to me like the kind of person who'd accept being second best to anything—or anyone."

Gus nodded. "No. Alex wants to be the king of the hill. He wouldn't have come." Then he regarded Niall with a solemn vow to himself not to get weird. "Did you want to invite Logan?"

Niall shook his head. "He's out of town again. He's one of those people who don't like sticking around or sitting on their hands. What he and I had, it's long gone. He might have come as a best man if I'd asked but… I didn't. Plus, we don't have best men, now do we?"

Approaching voices, laughter, and music caught their attention then as the backyard began to fill with people. Firmly holding hands, Gus and Niall joined their friends and family.

But Gus had something important he needed to do before anything else.

"I'd like to introduce you to my parents, Niall," Gus said, gesturing to the two people who had just joined them. "This is my mother, Melody Goodwin, and this is my father, Benjamin Goodwin."

NIALL HAD been apprehensive and anxious about this meeting. He smiled courteously and shook the hands of his soon-to-be in-laws. "Hello. Nice to meet you both."

Melody smiled back, her sweet smile reminding Niall of Gus. So that was where Gus had inherited his innocent charms. Melody was a tall, thin woman with golden curly hair graced with silver streaks here and there. She wore businesswoman's attire, a knee-length, cream-colored dress and a white shirt with a cream-hued light jacket. Niall knew Melody was an academic researcher with a long list of credentials and publications to her name.

Benjamin, however, sported a polite but distant smile, and he shook Niall's hand quite briefly. He wore formal attire—a gray suit and a blue silk tie, both of which complemented his gray hair and blue eyes well. But judging from Benjamin's reticent, even chilly, behavior, Niall wasn't sure if the man would warm up to him, now or later. Niall wondered what the man's beef was with him.

Then Melody suddenly elbowed Benjamin in the side, and he let out a muffled grunt. "Please, Mr. Valentine, forgive my husband. He's still grumpy after the long drive from Portland."

Niall nodded politely. "Yes, of course, I understand. I know I speak for both Gus and myself when I say that we're both happy you could make it here on such short notice." He pressed his palm over his heart to show how heartfelt his gratitude was.

To his surprise it was Benjamin who said, "Thank you for inviting us. There's nowhere else we'd rather be." He smiled awkwardly but genuinely past Niall to Gus, whose smile transformed from small to wide and radiant in an instant. Benjamin stepped closer to Gus, fidgeting nervously. "I… I just wanted to say… I'm happy for you, son. Very happy. He seems like a… a good guy."

GUS COULDN'T believe how long he'd waited for this moment. To be honest, he had almost given up. But perhaps a son's desire to be close to his father never really went away. Tears brimmed in Gus's eyes, but he held them back, not wishing to appear weak in front of his father.

When Benjamin rubbed the back of his neck self-consciously, his blue eyes glistened with moisture too. His shy smile twitched, but in a choked voice, he said, "I'm sorry for all the time I wasted not being a part of your life, August. I'm a stubborn old fool—"

"You're not old, Dad," Gus cut in with a quirky smile and love in his heart.

Melody chuckled. Soon Benjamin joined her, if a bit more stiffly. "Yeah, yeah, point taken," he said. Then he grew serious, swallowing hard. "My old man…. Guess his lessons of what it means to be a man, and how a man behaves, stuck too hard." He stopped there, frowning, his eyes glassy, as if traversing an unpleasant memory lane.

Gus started in shock. He had always assumed his father was so rigid and bigoted in his views of the world because of his conservative Christian beliefs. For the first time, Gus had to accept the possibility that old sins cast incredibly long shadows. Sins of the father. Benjamin's father and Gus's grandfather, now long gone. Gus had never known him, and for the first time, he considered that a blessing in disguise.

His name had been Augustus. Gus had been named in honor of him. Perhaps it was no honor after all. When Gus had become a Wiccan, he'd chosen to view his full name of August as a divine premonition for his future spiritual path, a reference to his bond with nature.

If Augustus had been violent with Benjamin…. Righteous vitriol filled Gus. But it was fruitless. The man he loathed had been dead for thirty years, before Gus had even been born.

All Gus really knew about him was that he'd been a factory worker who'd suffered greatly during the recession in the early 1970s, when he'd lost his job. According to Benjamin, his father had resorted to drink and bar fights. Apparently this downward spiral and violent tendencies had extended to his home, to his wife and son. And that was unforgivable in Gus's book. There was no excuse for hitting one's spouse, let alone a defenseless child.

Benjamin touched Gus's shoulder, startling him out of his black musings. "Son, don't let that dark past poison your happiness today."

Melody embraced both men's shoulders, sobbing quietly but chuckling a bit too. Tears of joy, Gus concluded. "Listen to your father, Gus. The fact that we're all together on this fine day to celebrate your marriage to Niall proves that we've overcome your grandfather's shadow."

Had Gus's mother known about her father-in-law's violent past all along? What a terrible weight to carry. Nonetheless, as a family they had stepped out of darkness into the light together. That meant everything. Love had triumphed. Gus bussed his mother's cheek and embraced her tighter.

This revelation about Gus's father had hit a little too close to home, considering what had happened recently with Frank Sadler and his wish to murder Quentin Cross for not being enough of a man. Gus hadn't expected such a coincidence. This odd foreshadowing of events and peculiar synchronicity between a murderer's motivations and Gus's personal life silenced him in awe.

"You too, Niall," Melody called out, beckoning Niall into their clumsy group hug with a nod and a smile. Chuckling, Niall obeyed. Upon Niall's touch to the small of Gus's back, Gus was sure this was the happiest day of his life. If his father's touch wasn't as strong as it could have been, Gus was certain it was heartfelt and a long time coming.

Kind laughter and soft clapping finally broke the group hug. But Niall didn't remove his hand from Gus's back, pulling him closer to press against his side. Gus didn't mind one bit.

Then it was time to meet the other guests, to do the introductions, and to set up for the handfasting ceremony. Gus cast his eyes to the people around him, those he considered friends and family.

"I knew it! I freaking called it," screamed Joy Bennett at the top of her lungs, and she kissed Gus on both cheeks and then on the mouth. Her typically soft, shy voice was absent today.

Gus laughed. He hadn't known Joy a year ago but now saw her as one of his closest, dearest friends. She was also Juliette's new protégé and confidant, a beautiful brunette with soulful bedroom eyes, short hair, tanned skin, and an athletic, willowy body. At twenty-five years old, she epitomized the beauty and resilience of youth—which she'd almost missed out on due to nearly getting murdered.

"I'm so glad you came, Joy," Gus said, hugging her back. "I know your new job as an athletics instructor keeps you plenty busy these days."

She scoffed with a playful pout. "You must be joking. You know how much you mean to me. I wouldn't even be here at all if it weren't for you and Niall. Of course I wasn't about to miss your big day." Then she leaned in to whisper conspiratorially, "You and Niall going to do the Great Rite for us as a preview of your wedding night?"

Gus laughed so hard he had tears streaming from his eyes. "Jules put you up to this, didn't she? You two are a couple of dirty, dirty ladies. *And* predictable. No! We're not doing that, so you're just gonna have to use your imagination." He waggled his eyebrows at her, causing a fit of hysterical titters to burst out of her.

"Get your mind out of the gutter," a woman's voice called out, amusement in her tone.

"Say what? Hot sex between two hot guys belongs in the gutter now? That's so wrong. Besides, you watch gay porn with me all the freaking time," another woman said, also laughing.

Gus faced the two women with a wide smile. "Aeryn, Sydney, you came. Yay!" With a gleeful shout, he rushed to meet them, and then they were screaming and hugging and laughing together, undoubtedly deafening everyone else.

Both Aeryn Newton and Sydney Keen were in their midtwenties, strong and smart and at the top of their game career-wise. Aeryn was a defense attorney for a private law firm, while Sydney was a journalist, focusing on environmental issues and political corruption. Aeryn was a tall, slim brunette whose startling beauty came from both plastic surgery and strict athletic routines, while Sydney was a long-legged, ample-bosomed, redheaded woman whose loveliness came with an hourglass body shape from the bounty of nature herself.

Both women greeted Gus and Joy with embraces and swift chatter, like birds.

"You look contented," Aeryn said in a voice that was surprisingly deep and metallic for a woman. "We of course knew right from the start that you were going to end up marrying your private dick."

Sydney snorted. "Yeah, right. I seem to recall when you first met Valentine you were ripping him *and* his father to shreds with your sharp, sharp words. Isn't that right, Ballbuster?" She was referring to Aeryn's coven name.

Aeryn rolled her eyes. "And here I thought you were an awesome journalist. That's *old* news. Or am I wrong, Newshound?" Sydney fake-pouted at Aeryn, who just laughed back in response. Aeryn faced Gus again. "Thanks for inviting us. Since Jules arranged for a Lughnasadh party for tonight here anyway, we were overjoyed you settled on Jules's house too. It's afternoon, so we can celebrate you and Niall finally getting hitched—"

"We just met spring of this year," Gus cut in with a laugh.

"—and come sunset we can do the harvest ritual as planned," Aeryn went on as though there'd been no interruption. Then she gave Gus a slow, thorough once-over. "I like the casual look on you, sweetie."

The day was important to them but they both preferred the no-fuss, no-muss policy. Gus was glad their decision was approved by the attendees.

"Well, you guys know Niall and I've been living together for a couple of months now already, so we went with everyday casual instead of pricy primping," Gus remarked, smiling. "The suddenness of our plans kind of helped us in making that decision."

"I approve," Sydney said with a cool bow of her head, her red curls dancing. She too had come in a simple, floor-length dress that matched the color of her hair and had long sleeves. "I don't mind dressing up, but it's such a hassle sometimes. And I don't like hassles on festival nights, as I'm sure both of you agree."

Gus nodded. His usual style of dress was a T-shirt, long shorts, and flip-flops, tending to rock the California surfer look. Suit and a tie? No, sirree, never for him.

"Good afternoon," said a man walking up to them. He was in a formal gray suit and tie despite the day being quite warm.

Gus waved at him. "Hi, Rodney. Thanks for coming."

Rodney was an ex-scholar who had burned out and lost his tenured position. He was in his thirties but due to personal difficulties appeared closer to fifty. He called himself unremarkable, but Gus thought the man's brown eyes had a warm glow, his receding sand-colored hair was earthy, and his well-trimmed gray beard an unintentional fashion statement. Though shy and quiet, he had opened up within the coven.

Rodney gave Gus a bashful smile and a tiny bow. "Wouldn't have missed this for the world, August. I'm glad to see you and Niall are finally tying the knot." He then spoke to Aeryn and Sydney. "Don't you agree, ladies?"

Sydney scoffed, tossing her red curls like a wild horse throwing its mane about. "Just who're you calling a lady? Nobody here by that title."

Rodney's eyes widened. He opened his mouth to speak, but only a squeak emerged. A second later he realized he'd been duped when both Sydney and Aeryn drew him into a bear hug, laughing. In the women's embrace, Rodney relaxed and even cracked a smile. When they parted, he seemed lively and open again.

"Too bad Tom and Alec couldn't make it here today," Sydney said ruefully.

Gus frowned. He'd been out of the loop, apparently. "Oh? Where are they?"

"Tom took Alec to Hawaii for a relaxing vacation after all that shit that went down," Aeryn replied, then snickered. "I wouldn't be surprised if they come back snuggling and sated and happily engaged."

Gus's jaw practically dropped to the floor. "What? When the heck did that happen? Where have I been to have missed that?"

Sydney winked at him. "Oh, probably in bed with your Valentine."

Gus blushed but couldn't help smiling wide. Tom and Alec were together? That had to be the best news he'd heard in months. The twink nurse and the wounded ex-soldier had found each other after all. Gus was so thrilled for them he felt a buzz in his body.

Directing his words to his friends, Gus said, "Tell me absolutely everything…."

HAVING DRIFTED to the other end of the backyard, Niall observed his husband-to-be speaking with the two stunning women and the shy dowdy scholar, and smiled. After everything that had happened lately, nothing seemed to help Gus recuperate and return to his old self better than spending time with his friends.

"You two look happy," Owain commented next to Niall.

Owain was Niall's father, a former homicide cop, now in his early sixties, still vibrant and athletic. He was dating Juliette. Though they had a considerable age difference—Juliette was in her forties—they seemed fond of one another and spent a great deal of time together. Niall wouldn't have believed his father dating at his age but now realized he loved seeing Owain happy with a great woman.

Niall looked at his father and basked in his obvious pride. "We are. This is the right thing to do. We're both in that place in our lives when we're ready to stop, be a couple, and build our lives together."

"Yeah." Owain chuckled. "And there's all that love and sex too."

Niall grimaced. "Geesh, Dad. Stop." Yet he chuckled as well.

Juliette laughed melodiously beside them as she held Owain's hand. "What? You were born through immaculate conception, were you, Niall?" When Niall rolled his eyes, Juliette nodded toward Gus. "You'll make my protégé very happy. I know it." Then she gave him a wicked smile. "Maybe one day soon you'll think of becoming a Wiccan. After all, I've heard from Gus that you do enjoy his rituals in the nu—"

"Okay, moving on," Niall declared loudly, silencing Juliette, who burst into guffaws, Owain quickly chiming in. Niall growled but was not really annoyed by them having so much fun at his expense.

"What's all the ruckus?" Hughes asked in his grumpy manner as he walked toward them, nodding greetings to Juliette and to Owain, who'd been his partner on the force back in the day.

Juliette giggled. "We were just talking about ceremonies performed skyclad—"

"Which we won't be talking about anymore," Niall cut in, pursing his lips.

"Oh, Niall, don't be such a prude," Juliette admonished him mischievously, just before she bussed his cheek in a peace offering. "You know you love it."

"What the hell's skyclad?" Hughes asked, frowning in obvious confusion.

"Naked. Nude. In the buff. Without a stitch on." A tiny, delicate Latina stepped from behind Hughes's back and smiled radiantly. "Hi. I'm Regina Mendoza. I'm the King County medical examiner. You folks can call me Reggie. Nice to meet you all, and thank you for inviting me." She hugged Owain warmly. "Good to see you again, old man."

"He's not old when he's skyclad," Juliette cut in with a shameless wink that brought a deep flush of heat to Niall's cheeks. Thinking about his father's sex life…. No. Just no. Not that he wasn't happy for his dad, which he was.

Everyone laughed at Juliette's joke, even Gus, Sydney, Aeryn, and Rodney, who had all joined the group. Owain didn't blush, though, but instead behaved like a confident gentleman as he embraced Juliette's waist with a smile that seemed to be reserved just for the two of them, a look of intimacy shared.

"What's happening with the case?" Niall asked Hughes, and everyone got quiet, clearly wanting to hear the story straight from the horse's mouth.

Hughes grunted with displeasure. "Without either Frank Sadler or Craig Holt alive and talking, there is no case. The gunman, probably a professional contract killer, wasn't found. Where he took the shot was, however, but neither the police nor the FBI are hopeful about finding enough evidence to track down the guilty party. As for this Faith Lanai character, the FBI is looking into her and her cult, the Cabal. I don't expect they'll learn much. According to you, Autumnsong has been trying to find her for ages, and he was on the inside, so. ... Anyway, if the FBI do find out something pivotal, it's unlikely they'll share." Then he locked gazes with Gus, his eyes narrowing. "You heard anything from Autumnsong? He wasn't among the eyewitnesses, so we couldn't interview him."

Gus sighed. "Yes. He texted me this morning. Quote, *I'm fine. A.* Unquote. He sure can be succinct. And damn evasive when he wants to be." After he shook his head, he decided the topic of Autumnsong was an ill-fitting choice for his and Niall's special day. "Detective, have you heard anything about Jacob Marlowe?" Gus asked, concerned. He'd seen the man fall to pieces after his dream of a peaceful sanctuary had been destroyed by two heinous criminals.

Hughes quirked an eyebrow. "That story might have a happy ending after all. From all I've heard, the Mount Paradise Sanctuary has received busloads of Radical Faeries who've heard about the incident and wish to support Jacob Marlowe's efforts. Bodhi Jha and Ethan Sadler—sorry, Ethan Day (he's gone back to his bachelor name)—are participating in the reopening of the sanctuary, and apparently Quentin Cross will join them once he gets the all clear from his doctors."

Niall let out an astonished chuckle. "Wow. All's well that ends well? I admit, that's not what I expected. But... I'm pleasantly surprised."

Gus smiled, relieved at the positive news. "Yeah. Me too."

After a few more introductions and casual chats, Juliette said, "Now that everyone's arrived, how about we get on to the real reason we're all here? And that, of course, is Gus and Niall's handfasting."

All of a sudden, both Gus and Niall had butterflies dancing in their bellies.

Chapter 21

GUS WAS pleased to see everyone following Juliette's directions as she instructed their friends and family to form a circle around Gus, Niall, and Juliette, who would be performing the rite as she was a legally ordained Wiccan high priestess.

As people moved around to find a comfortable position in the circle, Gus savored the lush nature around him. He watched the verdant canopy of the woods sway gently in the summer breeze, listened to the birds singing in the trees, smelled the flowers Juliette had planted all around the back garden, and breathed in the many flavors of the earth. He was becoming in tune with nature, which meant the world to him as a Wiccan.

Niall held Gus's hand in his own that trembled and grew hot and a bit sweaty. Gus watched as Niall smiled at him, the gesture wavering and cracking. Niall was nervous, and Gus could relate. This wasn't how he'd pictured the summer ending.

Not that he was complaining. This was the happiest day of his life.

With everyone settled, Juliette spread her arms, and in a soft, soothing voice she said, "Dear friends, family, and loved ones. We have gathered here today on Lughnasadh Day to witness these two people, Gus and Niall, join hands and be bound by friendship, companionship, and love. This is a joyous occasion, and Gus and Niall wish to thank you all for joining them."

Around him, Gus saw only a sea of smiling faces. His heart jumped with joy, love, and gratitude. His eyes stung with fresh tears, even though he'd sworn to himself he wouldn't get all blubbery before the ceremony had even begun.

If he hadn't been holding a unity candle in his other hand, he would have wiped away the tears; as it was, a few errant droplets escaped to glide down his cheeks.

"Dear friends, aid me in casting a circle to sanctify the loving bond being created here today," Juliette asked formally, as part of the ceremony, but her tone remained casual and kind. "As you do so, visualize positive energies and growing love within our sacred space."

People were quick to follow instructions. They wielded their brooms and swept the perimeter, starting from the direction of the house, in the east, and walking the circle clockwise. Joy sprinkled saltwater in their wake as she was last to walk the circle.

Everyone seemed to be enjoying themselves. Reggie smiled wide, like an eager puppy, Sydney stuck out her tongue at Aeryn, who responded in kind, both acting like playful children, and even Rodney managed more than a single smile, which was quite a feat after the deep depression he'd suffered upon losing his job. Only Hughes did his shtick without cracking a smile.

Once everyone resumed their earlier positions, Juliette blessed and sanctified the rings. She rang a bell to signify the beginning of the ritual. Then she sprinkled salt on the rings, passed the rings through the flame of a red candle, sprinkled drops of water on them, and finally passed them through sage incense smoke.

Gus closed his eyes as Juliette invoked the guardians of the watchtowers to bless their rings, their handfasting, and their future together. He focused his mind on the profound love he felt in his heart for Niall and allowed positive emotions to fill him to the brim.

Most of all, he envisioned the rings they had selected for each other. A gold wedding band with a green emerald for Gus, and a silver ring with a moonstone for Niall.

"Gus and Niall ask the Lady and the Lord to pass their holy love and sacred light onto these rings and to their union," Juliette declared, her high priestess voice solemn and soft, a flicker of a smile gracing her full lips and twinkling in her eyes.

Juliette had always had a certain air of showmanship when it came to performing her role as high priestess of rituals. Her voice took on a potent quality, and her gestures grew into acts of formidable power. Jason Upton, a former member of the coven (now deceased) had on occasion called Juliette's "act" ostentatious. To him, the words had been a compliment. To Juliette, Gus, and others in the coven, an insult. Juliette might appear excessive at times, but it was simply a manifestation of her deep faith.

"The circle is infinite," Juliette proclaimed, casting warm glances at Gus, Niall, and the others, including all those present in her halo of influence and welcome. "It is magical, perfect, and everlasting. It is a ring without a beginning or an end. Like the circle, true love is infinite and magical. It blooms, flourishes, and allows for endless harvests of happiness. Love cannot be forced. It may be timeless or passing."

NIALL SWALLOWED hard as he locked gazes with Gus. They had talked about this earlier. Traditionally, the handfasting was a trial marriage that either lasted for a year and a day or "for as long as love lasted." To that end, a handfasting was more like a commitment ceremony, without any of the obligations that came with a legal marriage.

At first Niall had felt wounded when Gus had mentioned a time limit to their union, but he soon realized the value of handfasting, two people taking a chance to see if they were compatible before making any further legal commitments. Gus wasn't trying to offend Niall by suggesting their love had an expiration date. He was in essence giving Niall the power to determine what suited him, and them, the best for the long run.

"Today we celebrate the willing, consensual joining of two souls," Juliette continued, unaware of Niall's thoughts. "Two spirits who wish to share their lives and become one. Two hearts that beat as one in a single rhythm of love, devotion, and fidelity." She gestured to the unity candles held by Owain and Benjamin. "As your inner lights, Gus and Niall, were sparked by others, we ask that your parents light your flames."

With confidence, Owain stepped forward and took a white, tapered candle from Niall. On it was written Valentine. With more awkward, uncertain steps, Benjamin approached and took a similar candle out of Gus's hand. That candle read Goodwin. Together, the fathers lit the candles and then handed them back to their sons. Owain beamed, pride shining in his eyes, and he touched Niall's shoulder and nodded firmly. Niall smiled back, happy that his father believed in him and his relationship with Gus. Benjamin, however, offered a bashful smile. Gus's father might not really understand or approve of Gus's choices or lifestyle, but Niall knew Benjamin's presence at the celebration meant a lot to Gus, nonetheless, and he was happy for Gus. Then, out of the blue, Benjamin pulled his son into a quick and stiff hug. It didn't last long, but the gesture alone was a sign that their relationship might yet improve over time.

"Today Gus and Niall are joining together as one," Juliette continued with sunshine in her eyes and smile. "And so now they will light the candle of unity to show the universe that they are one light burning brightly in the darkness, invincible in their love."

A large white pillar candle, with both their names and a heart on its surface, stood on the tiny raised altar between the triangle formed by Juliette, Gus, and Niall. Together, holding hands, Gus and Niall lit the big unity candle with their smaller candles. A thin plume of smoke arose and scented the air sweetly, while a flickering flame cast a lively play of shadows on the intimate space between them.

TO GUS, fire always had a magical quality to it that he found mesmerizing. To know that the same fire now represented his relationship with Niall made it all the more miraculous and enchanting.

"In my humble role as high priestess," Juliette said with a widening, blissful smile and tears in her eyes. "I offer you blessings of the Watchtowers. Blessed be this union with the gifts of the East— new beginnings with each rising sun, breath of life, and contemplation of the heart, mind, body, and soul. Blessed be this union with the gifts of the South—warmth of hearth and home, light of life and love, and heat of passion and ardor. Blessed be this union with the gifts of the West—the rushing excitement of a raging river, the soft cleansing of a rainstorm, and the deep commitments of the ocean. Blessed be this union with the gifts of the North—a solid foundation to build on, fertility and abundance to enrich your lives, and a stable, safe homestead to call your own. May these simple blessings aid you on your journey together that begins today."

Gus felt dizzy with joy. He couldn't wait to be with Niall, in every sense, for their life together to truly start. He was certain they would be happy as a couple and grow old together.

Juliette held up the rings, one in each hand. "As these circles speak of eternity, so shall your love endure for a lifetime and beyond." Then she gave each man a ring. "Niall, please place the ring on Gus's finger," Juliette said. For the first time, her voice cracked as she clearly choked on emotions. Her brown eyes glistened with moisture. Once Niall had slipped the ring onto Gus's finger, both their hands shaking, Juliette asked, "Niall, do you promise Gus to be honorable and faithful, to share his laughter and joy in times of happiness, to stand by him and ease his burdens in times of difficulty, to dream and hope and create a life together, and to spend each day loving him more than the day before?"

Gus held his breath for so long his vision began to blur. He had no doubts in his heart that Niall loved him. A handfasting didn't have to be an official marriage. Of course, in their case it was since Juliette was an ordained minister. But they hadn't yet signed any marriage licenses. That was on the agenda for tomorrow.

Niall smiled wickedly at Gus, as though he knew what Gus was thinking. All he said was, "I do." A broken sob escaped Gus's throat, and his eyes grew misty as a veil of tears descended. Niall leaned in and whispered in his ear, "I love you, my Wicked Witch of the Northwest."

Before Gus could totally break down, Juliette swept in swiftly, possibly able to discern Gus's precarious condition, which she likely shared. "Gus, do you promise Niall to be honorable and faithful, to share his laughter and joy in times of happiness, to stand by him and ease his burdens in times of difficulty, to dream and hope and create a life together, and to spend each day loving him more than the day before?"

Gus nodded frantically, unsure if he still had a voice. "I-I do," he whooshed out on the force of his breath alone, a shaky sound that by some divine intervention resembled two words. He hugged Niall and murmured in his ear, "I love you too, Tigger. So freaking much."

Around them they heard giggling, clapping, a few sobs, and even a couple of muffled curses. Apparently the scene was emotional for more than just the two of them.

"Is there anything you wish to say to each other?" Juliette asked. "Now is the time."

Niall cleared his throat, so Gus quickly acquiesced to let his lover go first. He puzzled if he'd get a single word out when it was his time.

Niall, however, didn't seem to have a problem speaking. "Gus. You were a ray of pure sunshine when I saw nothing but rain."

Someone in the background muttered, "That's living in Seattle for you," and people chuckled.

Niall grinned, and went on. "You gave me your gift of laughter and joy when I felt alone and in pain."

Gus drew in a breath. Not just because Niall had come up with something that rhymed, but because he hadn't really known Niall had felt so down before they'd met. He waited silently to hear more.

Niall's smile wavered, and he blinked. He appeared less composed than he had when he'd started. "There may be a gazillion stars up in the sky. One shines far brighter than I could ever deny. I tell you that I love you. I'll stay with you forever. Believe me it's true, because I'll leave you never. I swear I would give anything to you—the moon, the stars, and the sunrise too."

Good golly. Gus's heart jumped up into his throat. Niall had really given his vows a lot of thought. Gus wondered if his own would ever measure up. Then he realized it wasn't a race or a competition, but an equal partnership.

"I LOVE you, Gus," Niall said as he finished his vows. He wasn't at all confident about how his words would be received. When Gus threw himself in Niall's arms, though, Niall let go of his anxieties and relaxed. He had felt mildly queasy as he spoke his words of promise, his stomach doing back flips. Yet now there was no place on earth he'd rather be. He looked at Gus and grew more in love with the man he'd never expected to meet or fall for. This was the right thing to do, of that he was sure.

Yeah, we'll work out fine.

Once Gus pulled away, he coughed to clear his throat. He looked nervous to Niall but, *oh*, so cute and darling. Niall suppressed a grin as he watched his lover regroup.

"Niall. I've come a long way. I've wished for many things. I've dreamed a thousand-and-one dreams, I've prayed a thousand-and-one prayers. I've whispered to the Goddess and to the God on many a lonely night. I've kept the faith. Now… I believe in *you*. I believe in our love, our future together, and our path we shall tread as one. The day you walked into my life, everything changed. *I* changed. I don't know how on earth I got so lucky as to meet you because you are… amazing. I fall more in love with you every day. Thank you for coming into my life and making this… *our* life. I give you my life, my heart, all of me, at the rising of the moon, at the height of the sun, at the dance of the stars."

Niall could barely contain all the feelings inside him from bursting through his chest. He felt ten feet tall, proud and grateful and in love. Gus's words were beautiful because they came from the heart and soul. His quaking voice only emphasized the depth and breadth of his emotions for Niall, who couldn't be more blissful if he tried.

He dipped down and kissed Gus on the lips. He had to, or he'd fall apart. And he didn't want to do that in public, even if those around were just friends and family who all understood and approved.

"Guys, we're not there yet," Juliette stage-whispered to them, and others chuckled. Slowly Gus and Niall broke apart, grinning goofily at each other. "The vows have been spoken. I ask you now to please join hands."

Gus shook all over as Niall took his hands. But at heart he was still, like the eye of the storm where all was serene and at peace. Like a tuning fork, something inside Gus resonated with something deep inside Niall. A harmonious rhythm of nature and love and lust and… forever.

Juliette raised the handfasting cord high above her head for all to see. Basically it was three different colored silk cords braided into one. Gus and Niall had chosen all three together. Green for Gus's favorite, blue for Niall's eyes (even though he insisted they were more gray than blue), and finally red to inspire passion, love, strength, and hearth of home.

Slowly but surely Juliette wrapped the cords around Gus and Niall's clasped wrists, the binding close to the skin but loose and comfortable as she tied the knot, forming an infinity symbol.

"As your hands are joined, so are your lives. This cord symbolizes the connection between you two. The ties of this handfasting are not born of the ribbons themselves but from the love, respect, vows, and hearts brought together here today. You are bound to each other with a tie not easy to break. Take this time of binding as an opportunity to learn what you need about one another, to grow in wisdom and love, to strengthen your vows and lives together, and to ensure that your love will last in this life and the world beyond. As one last bond, please kiss each other."

GUS AND Niall smiled at each other, both feeling light as air or feathers, and kissed to their heart's content. Gus tasted Niall's delicious flavor, and a need to be with his new husband fanned the flames of his desire. Niall sipped from the altar of Gus's lips, and his yearning to be intimate and alone with his husband made him quiver and quake.

Around them sounded raucous applause, sharp wolf whistles, and joyous laughter.

Then Juliette declared, "Ladies and gentlemen, please congratulate Mr. Niall Valentine and Mr. Gus Goodwin–Valentine."

Niall gasped, pulled back from the kiss, and stared at Gus, his eyes wide in shock. Gus winked and giggled, batting his eyelashes a bit bashfully. "I wanted it to be a surprise. Hope it's a good one…."

Laughing without meaning to, Niall embraced Gus so hard Gus's feet left the ground. Then he whirled them both around in a mad pirouette of loving. "Yes! Geesh! Yes, of course it's a good surprise, babe. Fucking amazing."

Niall then planted a hearty kiss on Gus's tittering lips, and nothing more was said for a good long while between them. Neither of them paid any attention to Juliette unwrapping the cord from around their wrists, all without breaking or untying the knot.

"And now, honored guests, please join me in clearing this sacred space," Juliette said chuckling. Her words didn't stop Niall and Gus's kiss, though. "As we close this circle, please send your loving energies and warm wishes to our newly handfast couple so that they may start their life together with your blessings."

Gus merrily forgot the outside world and let himself be swept off his feet by the kiss of his brand-new husband. He faintly heard Juliette walking around the circle, the others in tow, as she dismissed the quarters and the gods. Whooshing sounded from their brooms and their heartfelt chuckles rose to the air.

Niall ignored everything around him. All that mattered was Gus in his arms. A hunger born from a primitive instinct roared inside him, demanding he claim his soul mate. No, he wasn't about to carry out the Great Rite in front of everyone, but briefly he understood the impulse and the urge. Briefly. Nonetheless, Niall was certain this was the best day of his life.

GUS AND Niall stayed for Lughnasadh too. Their wedding night would keep. They did, however, jump over a broom because apparently that was a custom of handfastings. Niall had zero objections. He only wished he would have gotten to see Gus leaping the broom butt-naked.

Though Niall later denied it, he was curious about the festival. So they chatted, danced, and sung for many hours until the sun set. Niall was pleasantly surprised to learn that Lammas entailed eating freshly made corn bread (shaped in the form of a man) and apple pie and drinking wine as a sacrifice to the gods and spirits of harvest. In fact, there were a lot of dishes to dine on, he learned, and he stuffed his face with goodies until he wondered if Gus would have to carry him home or if he had to waddle there somehow on his own two inebriated feet.

The best part came when the sun was setting. Juliette, in her role as the high priestess, performed a corn dance. Barefoot but wearing little anklets with tiny bells on them, she twirled and leaped and stomped the grassy ground as though her feet were drums, each step creating a tinkling of bells. She wore a crown of red poppies and light brown grain cobs.

It wasn't until the next day that Niall learned he'd been so into the whole thing that he'd been promoted into the role of the Holly King, the harvest God around whom the Goddess (in this case Juliette) danced in a frenzy, showering him with her harvest offerings like wheat, mead, fruit, vegetables, bread, and wine. Apparently it had taken nothing short of a laughing Gus to rescue Niall from the Great Rite.

By the time Gus and Niall got back home to Tacoma, though, Niall's head had cleared of any haze. They climbed the side steps to the front door, where Niall stopped Gus, flipped him around with a pull on his arm, pressed him against the wall, and plastered his body against his.

"Mmm, you smell so fucking good, babe," Niall murmured, horny and a bit slurry.

Gus laughed as he avoided Niall's wet smooches. "Shut up, Tigger. You're so wasted you'll fall down if I let you go. Come on. We can make out inside."

"Why?" Niall whined, peppering Gus's neck with sloppy kisses. "Thought you loved the idea of public nudity and sex." Though he was intoxicated, Niall was starting to see the upsides of the Great Rite. Maybe one day…. "Wanna dance around your maypole, baby."

Gus giggled, rolling his eyes. His fresh-out-of-the-oven husband was making no sense if he was advocating the advantages of having sex on the stairs. "You've danced enough for today, hon. Come on. The bed's, like, twenty feet away."

"Shouldn't I, I don't know, carry you over the threshold?" Niall lisped awkwardly, his eyes squinting as he tried to see clearly what was in front of him. But everything was blurry. "Shit, what the fuck was in that mead?"

Gus laughed. "Alcohol, dumbass. And no, you probably shouldn't try to carry—"

But Niall had already hooked his arms under Gus's waist and knees, and hobbling on one foot, he muttered, "Wait a sec, babe, I'mma…."

Thankfully Gus managed to unlock and open the door before Niall assaulted him with his lips. Therefore, it wasn't a long drop when they came crashing down onto the floor in a heap of flailing limbs and muffled curses and chuckles.

As they lay there in the doorway, on the rumpled rug, with Niall finally passed out and snoring, Gus couldn't help but rejoice in how incredibly happy he was.

SUSAN LAINE, an award-winning, multipublished author of LGBTQ erotic romance and a Finnish native, was raised by the best mother in the world, who told her daughter time and again that she could be whatever she wanted to be. The spark for serious writing and publishing kindled when Susan discovered the gay erotic romance genre. One of her books, *Monsters Under the Bed*, won the 2014 Rainbow Award for Best Gay Paranormal Romance.

Anthropology is Susan's formal education, but she has set her long-term sights on becoming a full-time writer. Susan enjoys hanging out with her sister, two nieces, and friends in movie theaters, bookstores, and parks. Her favorite pastimes include pop music, action flicks, chocolate, and doing the dishes, while a few of her dislikes are sweating hot summer days, tobacco smoke, and purposeful prejudice.

Website: www.susan-laine-author.fi
E-mail: susan.laine@hotmail.com

SUSAN LAINE

SPARKS
& DROPS

The Wheel Mysteries: Book One

Magic is in the air when Gus Goodwin, a pagan shopkeeper and owner of the Four Corners' occult shop, meets a Niall Valentine, a mysterious PI investigating the disappearance of a local witch named Joy. What starts out as harmless flirting and information gathering soon turns into a partnership, with both men determined to solve the case.

Then bodies begin to pile up. Someone is using fire and water to kill witches associated with Joy, and it is up to Niall and Gus to find out what's going on. But when their friendship blossoms into something else, the unknown dangers looming ahead become even more frightening. If they can't solve the murders soon, they're going to get themselves killed.

www.dreamspinnerpress.com

SUSAN LAINE

DEVIL'S
OWN

Sequel to *Sparks & Drops*
The Wheel Mysteries: Book Two

A month and a half into their relationship, PI Niall Valentine and his occult shopkeeper boyfriend, Gus Goodwin, are hoping for a little time alone, but they're thrown into another murder mystery.

Niall's client, Angelina Talbot, is certain her new husband attempted to kill her, ambushing her in their bedroom, half-naked and covered in blood. Scared out of her mind, Angelina hit him with a lamp and ran away. Florian Talbot lies dead in the bedroom, his head smashed in with a lamp—but the door is locked from the inside. Is Angelina truly an unwitting murderer, or are more sinister forces at play?

With a family of eccentrics, borderline criminals, and Satanists, the real killer could be any number of people wandering the mansion that night under the cover of darkness. The entire Talbot clan thrives in secrecy. Still unfulfilled and utterly perplexed, Niall and Gus are tasked with shedding some much-needed light on the shadowy case.

www.dreamspinnerpress.com

THE WHEEL MYSTERIES

SUSAN LAINE

THE LOVERS.

FIREWORKS
& WILD CARDS

Sequel to *Devil's Own*
The Wheel Mysteries: Book Three

When Gus Goodwin's friend and mentor, Juliette Hayes, asks him to find out who's stealing small sums from the cashbox of her Moonlight Haven Coven, Gus agrees. What's the worst that could happen? They catch a small-time thief and, with any luck, retrieve a few bucks. Gus enlists the help of his boyfriend, PI Niall Valentine, and Niall's retired police officer father, Owain, to go undercover and solve the mystery.

On the night of the next full moon ritual, however, the coven is struck with a fatal blow.

Now Gus and Niall face more than a murder mystery. The coven is torn apart, and along comes an eccentric psychic and Tarot master—plus a familiar face both Gus and Niall had hoped was long gone. As fireworks ignite and wild cards are spread, Gus and Niall have their work cut out for them.

www.dreamspinnerpress.com

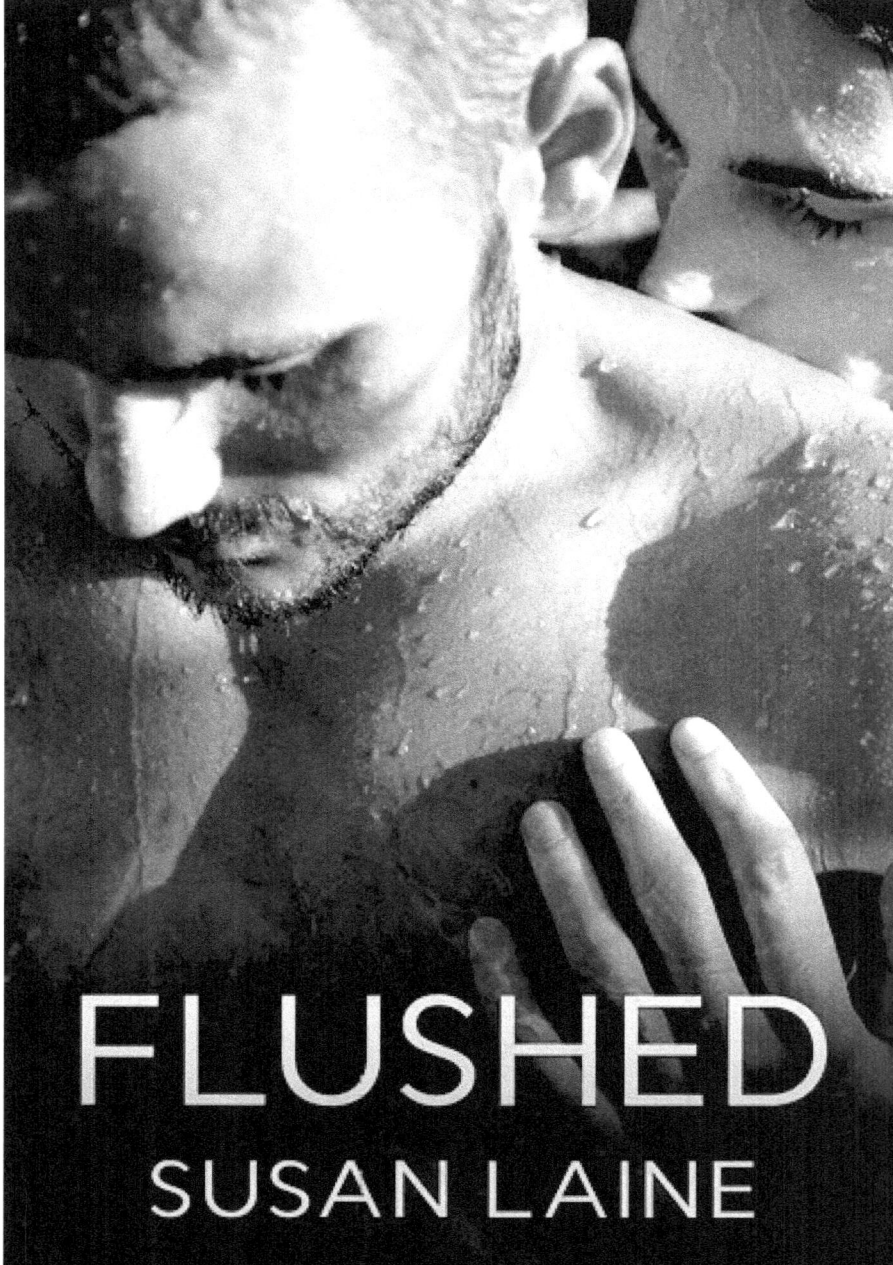

FLUSHED
SUSAN LAINE

To prove to his annoying older brother that he's a man, well-to-do sculptor Rupert Pemberton tries to repair his broken toilet. But he has no knack for practical tools and no know-how. After a flood of biblical proportions, he has no choice but to call for help.

A gorgeous hunk of a plumber named Paul Cooper shows up at Rupert's doorstep with a ready toolbox and a sexy smile. With Paul at his side, Rupert realizes he wants more than a quick fix. After a couple of cozy dates and a few bouts of steamy sex, Rupert wonders how he can keep Paul around for good.

www.dreamspinnerpress.com

HEROES AT HEART

Yellowbelly Hero

SUSAN LAINE

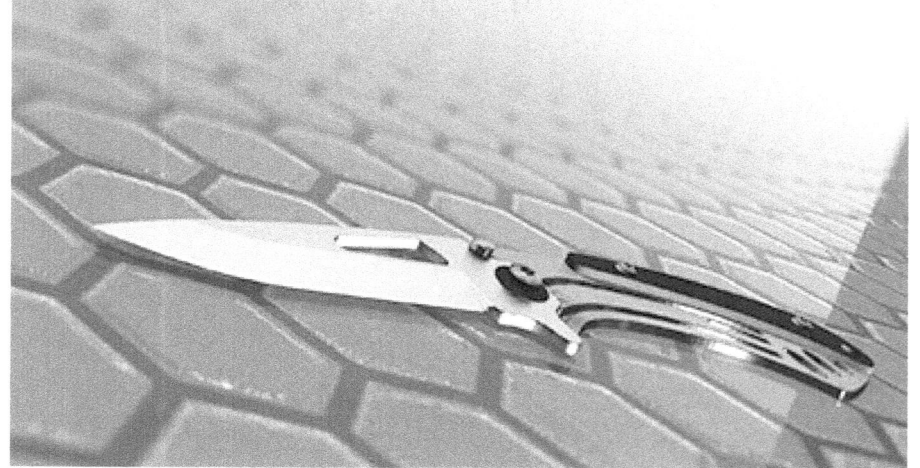

Heroes at Heart: Book One

Yancy Bell was bullied in high school for being a yellowbelly, not because of any cowardice, but because of his nervous bladder condition. It's Yancy's first year in college, and he's hoping to make a fresh start.

Three days before Christmas, the campus is empty. Having to pee on a midwinter night leads Yancy to meet Curt Donovan huddled in a dark shower stall. Curt's a troubled jock whose coming out went badly, so he plans to end it all.

But Yancy adamantly refuses to let Curt go through with his irrevocable plan. With just one dark night to talk Curt around, Yancy has to win the trust of a stranger who only sees one way out.

www.dreamspinnerpress.com

www.ingramcontent.com/pod-product-compliance
Lightning Source LLC
Chambersburg PA
CBHW060102260626
47160CB00005B/1767